LEGACY OF SORROWS

*To Margaret.
Best Wishes
Roberto*

3/11/14.

LEGACY OF SORROWS

The Witness
The Devil's Bridge

ROBERTO BUONACCORSI

THAMES RIVER PRESS

Legacy of Sorrows
The Witness – The Devil's Bridges

THAMES RIVER PRESS
An imprint of Wimbledon Publishing Company Limited (WPC)
Another imprint of WPC is Anthem Press (www.anthempress.com)
First published in the United Kingdom in 2014 by
THAMES RIVER PRESS
75–76 Blackfriars Road
London SE1 8HA

www.thamesriverpress.com

© Roberto Buonaccorsi 2014

All rights reserved. No part of this publication may be reproduced
in any form or by any means without written permission of the publisher.

The moral rights of the author have been asserted in accordance
with the Copyright, Designs and Patents Act 1988.

A CIP record for this book is available from the British Library.

ISBN 978-1-78308-241-4

This title is also available as an eBook

The Witness

Foreword

Because of my husband's Italian background, he finds it quite natural to write stories based on recent Italian history. This is one of them. His other book, *The Devil's Bridge*, is also based on a true story from that time.

I encouraged him to use his background and knowledge of those times to write these books which tell the story of events that should be written about lest we forget the horrors that war can visit on us.

Elizabeth Kim Buonaccorsi

Author's Note

This book is dedicated to the memory of the Italian civilians massacred in the mountain villages around Monte Sole by units of the 16th Waffen SS under the command of Major Walter Reder during the period of 29th September to 3rd October 1944.

Even though this book is a work of fiction, it is based on historical facts and it highlights the brutality and savagery committed by the SS in the Italian campaign during the Second World War.

The massacre of Marzabotto was the biggest massacre of civilians in the western European theatre of operations to take place during World War II.

One thousand eight hundred and sixty three Italian civilians were murdered during this operation, including forty-five children under the age of two.

To this day, the mountain villages still lie in ruins, uninhabited and overgrown with vegetation.

Prologue

I still find it impossible to tell people what it feels like to lose all the members of your family in one day. It's not that I don't want to talk about it; I really don't think that mere language can convey the intensity of these things. I lost my parents, my three brothers and my sister. I also lost my uncle and aunt, along with their son, my cousin. These were people that I loved and shared my life with on a daily basis. As if that was not enough, I witnessed my immediate family being murdered by the SS and my mother being raped before they killed her. I was also present when the women and children of Marzabotto, my home village, were herded into the local cemetery and mown down by machine gun.

After the massacres, I lied about my age and joined the Partisan resistance in Bologna until the war ended in 1945. I still find it difficult to make friends with people. I suppose it's a throwback to the horrors I witnessed when I saw the majority of my friends cut down in their prime.

Even though I am an old man now, I was not always so. I was once thirteen. That was when my childhood ended on the green slopes of Monte Sole.

When I close my eyes and day-dream, as all old men are prone to do, I can still see the flames reaching high into the blackness of the night sky. I can stand that. Flames are only flames. What I cannot stand are the screams of terror and the cries of the children pleading for mercy that still fill my mind, causing me to tremble as I did on that mountain so long ago.

Some of the killers were Italians; followers of fascism and Mussolini, people who spoke our language and shared a common culture, religion and heritage with us. Whatever entered their mind and spirit that night belonged to the pits of hell. How could they have done this to their own people, to men women and children who had never harmed them?

The other voices I heard that night were foreign, with harsh sounding clipped accents. I had never heard German spoken before and, after the killings ended, I was told that was it. Even to this day, when I hear a German voice I experience a myriad of emotions.

I have been told that, as I am the last survivor of the massacres, I should commit to paper what I saw and experienced. I've tried before and failed. What words can you use to describe such things? The only way I can put myself back into that horror and come out the other side of it sane is to tell you the whole story of my life and, when I come to the black awful, shadow that lurks in the depths of my mind, I will remember the joyful and happy life that I had there on Monte Sole with all of my family and my young friends.

Chapter 1

My name is Bruno Verdi. My friends on the mountain call me *Naso* on account of my Roman nose. It was common for all of us to use nicknames instead of our given names, but never in front of our parents. I was born in the village of Marzabotto, which lies about 10 miles south of Bologna on the wooded slopes of Monte Sole. I live in a three-bedroom terraced house just outside the village with my with my parents Moreno and Carla and my three brothers, Ricco, Benito and Gianpiero, who we called Pippo. I also have a little sister, Lisa, who is not quite two years old yet and is my father's undoubted favourite. My father is the village cobbler, and thankfully, there is enough work for him mending shoes and repairing other leather goods for the local people to provide for his family. Most people paid him in chickens and vegetables, so at least we always had shoes on our feet and food in our bellies.

Pippo stuck his head round my bedroom door, 'Are you not up yet Naso? Come on, it's eight o'clock and we've got our football game today.' I was lying daydreaming in bed when I suddenly remembered that we had a match with the boys from the other villages down in the meadow outside Marzabotto. 'Sorry Pippo, I forgot. Give me two minutes,' I said as I jumped out of bed and reached for my trousers. I hurriedly dressed in my oldest clothes, ran into the kitchen and grabbed a piece of bread off the plate on the table. Mum saw me and pretended to aim a slap at me. 'Bruno, you'll be late for your own funeral,' she shouted to me as I ran out the door to join my waiting siblings.

2

Pippo was my oldest brother at sixteen. Benito was fourteen and I was thirteen. Ricco was the youngest at twelve, and, as usual, was busy protesting to anyone who listened that he was fed up with wearing our old cast-off clothes.

The other boys were all waiting on us to start the game. It was September 1944 and the war seemed a long way from us. We all knew that the Stella Rossa partisan brigade was not only active on the mountain, but also in charge of our whole region and were looked upon as the guardians of the area, so we all felt safe from the war raging in the towns and cities close by.

The date was Thursday 28th September 1944 and little did I know that I would never play football with any of these boys again.

Italy had won the last two world cups before the war; in 1934 and 1938 and, like all small boys, we wanted to emulate our heroes. We selected our two captains by popular vote and then got down to the serious business of selecting the teams. Pippo, who was one of the captains, always picked his three brothers, and the other team captain, Marco, who was from Monzuno, always chose his two brothers. By the time the bargaining, shouting and manipulation was over, there were usually two teams of about twenty boys each. Marzabotto had about twenty boys playing today and the nearby villages of Monzuno and Grizzana supplied the rest. We ran around and played for hours with all the energy and enthusiasm of the young, happy and oblivious to the darkness that had descended on the outside world. Our only concern was to score a goal and if necessary, cheat to stop the other team winning.

It was about midday when we eventually stopped playing. We were all exhausted with the exertions of the day and with the afternoon sun at its highest and fiercest we said *ciao* to our friends and slowly wound our way back home to our own villages. We knew that our families would want us to help them with a few of the chores that all country boys were used to.

We had just arrived at our house that Mamma appeared at the door. 'Pippo, go and help your Papà with the handcart and take some shoes and boots over to Monzuno. I've got a list here of people expecting a delivery. Make sure that old Graziano who runs the market stall doesn't try to pay you with rotten vegetables like last time.'

'Oh Mamma, can't Benito go this time? I'm too tired to push the cart.'

'No, Benito has his own chores to do, so get your lazy backside moving and get home in time for supper.'

'What about our lunch Mamma?' Mamma handed us all a salami panino, 'Eat this as you do your work.' Pippo sullenly headed over to his Papà's workshop muttering to himself whilst taking a bite of his panino.

Mamma carried on giving out her orders just like all Italian *mamme* were used to do. There was no doubting the fact that Mamma was in charge of the house and ran it like her own little empire.

'Benito, go over to Aunt Lisa's farm and give her a hand with some jobs. She promised to pay you with some fresh eggs, so don't crush them or fall on the way back. Do you understand?' Benito smiled at this. He always enjoyed going over to his Aunt's farm. When all the work was finished, his Aunt Lisa would set the table for him and his Uncle Luigi, and give them a real man's meal. It was so different, he thought, from his own house where he had to guard his plate and keep a wary eye on his food in case his thieving brothers tried to steal some. His Uncle Luigi would always give him a glass of his homemade red wine during the meal and sometimes a cigarette after he had finished. As Aunt Lisa was heavily pregnant with their second child and found the heavy farm work tiring, Mamma had offered the boys as help for her during this time.

Mamma carried on with her orders. 'Bruno, go and get the axe from the woodshed and chop up some wood for the stove. Don't make the cuttings as big as last time, when they wouldn't fit into the stove and I had to do it myself. Understand?'

I felt my face going red at the sarcastic comments my brothers were shouting at me, so I moved quickly down the path to the woodshed.

Mamma turned her attention to young Rico. Next to Lisa, he was her favourite and he knew it. 'Rico, my little lamb, go to the edge of the woods and pick up some more kindle for the stove. There's a bag in the kitchen with a shoulder strap you can use.' She ruffled his hair as she spoke. Rico smiled, with the angelic smile he knew his Mamma loved. 'Make sure you don't carry too heavy a load,' she said, 'I don't want to see you struggle.'

'Okay Mamma, I'll be back as soon as I can.' He picked up the wood bag and headed for the door. As he stepped outside, I stuck out my leg and tripped him up. Rico fell to the ground, dropping his panino in the process, and crying as if the roof had fallen in on him. 'Mamma, Bruno tripped me and I fell.' He yelled out at the top of his voice. Mamma came running over and picked him up with one hand whilst, for the second time that day, aimed a slap at my head.

'You get on with your chores, Bruno and leave your poor brother alone,' she shouted in a shrill voice. Rico pulled a face at me from behind her back and made a rude gesture.

Later on that night, the entire family, with the exception of Benito, gathered round the large kitchen table for supper. Papà sat in his usual place and coughed for silence. We all joined hands and waited for Papà to pray. 'Thank you Lord for your provision, bless it to us now we pray. Keep us safe this night and through the next day. Amen.' 'Amen' we all chorused, as we reached for the bread together, slapping each other's hands aside.

We had all completed our primary schooling and, in liking with the other children on the mountain, we had left school at the age of twelve. Secondary education was not something that mountain people usually entered into. We had our farms, livestock, olive groves and vines to look after, so secondary education was just a frivolous luxury that we couldn't afford and we considered unnecessary to our way of life.

After dinner was over, Papà sat with us round the table that night and had a glass of his home-made wine. These were the times that I enjoyed most of all, our family discussions. Papà told us the story of Mussolini and how the great man had let his people down. At first, when he had come to power, all the Italian people adored him, except for the communists and the Mafia who he hunted down with a vengeance. He was the Duce: the leader. He provided work for his people and restored the international standing of a young nation not long unified. Then, as time went on, he made mistakes. Bad mistakes that brought the hated Germans and the war to Italy. Now, the people in the towns were hungry and furious at him for deserting them for his safe haven in Lake Garda, protected by the detested *tedeschi*, the Germans.

I told Papà that I remembered having to give the fascist salute in school at the start of the morning lessons. The teacher would shout out: '*Eia, Eia*' and we would all answer in unison, '*Alalà*'. I asked 'Papà, what did that mean?' He smiled, a sad smile, before answering, 'It didn't mean anything, just gibberish and nonsense. Much the same as fascism itself.' Benito spoke up, 'If we aren't fascists now Papà, will I have to change my name?' Papà looked up at him and said, 'Benito was a name to be proud of before Mussolini came to power, and it will still be a name to be proud of after he has gone.'

I asked him, 'Papà, when will the Germans leave Italy? Daniello Petroni in the village said he heard his father say that the Germans are doing *rastrellamenti*[1] in the villages below Monte Sole and killing anyone they find. Is that true?'

Papà took his time to answer me. He drummed his fingers on the kitchen table, and said, 'The Germans have taken up defensive positions on a line just south of Monte Sole. The Allies are attacking it as we speak and will eventually break through. The Germans have thrown all they have into the line to defend it and cannot allow the partisans to attack them in the rear. They can't fight two fronts at once. I think they will have to do more *rastrellamenti* in the area to stop the partisans. They may eventually come here.'

---

1 House-to-house searches, looking for enemies of the dictatorship.

The room was silent until Pippo said. 'Are we in danger Papà?'

Papà raised his two hands palm up in a gesture that said 'I don't know.' 'We should be safe on Monte Sole with the Stella Rossa watching and protecting the area. If there is any sign of the Germans coming up the mountain, then we will go into the woods and hide until they leave. With the Allies on their tail, the Nazis will not want to hang about and be captured.' With a grave look on his face he then said, 'If they do come and you have time, run into the woods and hide up a tree until they have left. Is that understood?' We all looked at each other with uncertainty. We had never seen Papà so serious before. Pippo stood up and said, 'If they come, Papà, I'll just throw Rico at them. He could fart for Italy and they would run at the first smell.' We all laughed at this, whilst Rico playfully aimed a kick at his elder brother.

Before long, it was time for bed. It was my turn to help Aunt Lisa and Uncle Luigi with the milking on the farm tomorrow, so I had to leave the house at 4.30am. Pippo was learning how to cobble boots with Papà in the workshop. Papà had great hopes that he would take over his business in due course.

Benito and Rico had the task of fixing some roof tiles that had come loose the week before during a high wind. They were pleased with this as it wouldn't take long and they could catch up with the football in the meadow.

We all said goodnight to each other. Mamma and Papà shared a room with baby Lisa, Pippo and Benito shared a room at the back of the house and I shared one with Rico.

Soon the house was quiet.

Chapter 2

September 28th 1944

Major Reder was proud of his position and growing reputation in the SS. He now commanded a Battalion of his own. The 16th Waffen SS Panzer Grenadiers. His expertise lay, so his superiors told him, in the clearance, and if possible the extermination, of large bands of Italian partisans, the Communist militias that were now the scourge of the Wehrmacht. They didn't fight you like real soldiers; they attacked you by ambush or by the sabotage of transport links. They had no honour and deserved to die the most violent deaths. The SS in particular viewed this type of warfare as the work of civilian criminal gangs who had no right becoming involved in armed conflict against them.

Reder first came across this type of warfare in Russia. The German Army was successful there in combating this kind of terror by employing ruthless tactics against them.

Unfortunately, he had lost his left arm in Russia during the fighting there in 1943, and after a period of convalescing back home, he was sent to Italy to help with the growing menace of the partisans there.

He had just returned from Tuscany where, in August, units under his command had 'cleared' the area of partisans in the village of Sant'Anna. They had entered the village after completely surrounding it, and had left again three hours later leaving over five hundred of the villagers dead. They had murdered, raped, and mutilated men, women and children, in the worst ways imaginable. In the list of the slaughtered was a twenty-day-old baby that was taken from its dead mothers arms by the SS and used as a football. In another incident, a seven-month pregnant woman was shot and her unborn baby cut from her womb and butchered.

Major Reder reflected on the events. It was necessary, he thought, to bring order to the area. It may appear brutal to the onlooker, but the results spoke for themselves. Reder reasoned that these reprisals, brutal as they were, brought a sense of fear to the Italian population in general and helped to cut off support for the partisans. For every German Soldier killed by the partisans, he had promised reprisals of up to one hundred Italians killed, and so far had kept his promise.

As he dressed, he looked at himself in the mirror. He had been recommended for promotion to the Führer for doing his duty, and he revelled in his growing reputation in Berlin for getting the job done.

He wasn't unduly worried about his stump of a left arm. In his service to the Fatherland and to Hitler, he would gladly have given his life.

Reder had received fresh orders that day from the Wehrmacht headquarters. They were concerned about the increasing amount of Partisan activity that was attacking them from the rear and causing them a tactical problem in how to deal with it. The source of this activity seemed to be coming from the direction of Monte Sole. Field Marshall Kesselring, the overall German commander in Italy, had personally given the order to eradicate this problem in as ruthless a way as possible, to serve as a reminder to others of what would happen to them if they became involved with the partisans or offered them support.

The German's last line of defence, the Gothic line, was being hard-pressed by the Allies, and Kesselring needed all his forces in the line to defend it. This Partisan menace was causing badly needed resources to be diverted from the main fighting at the front to combat them, and Reder had been ordered to take his unit to Monte Sole to completely eliminate this threat.

He was about to head to a meeting of his Officers and NCOs, to explain what the order meant in reality and to detail how the operation would take place. He thought out aloud,

'Thankfully, I can rely on my men not to be weak willed in carrying out this order.'

As Major Reder entered the large ornate room that served the Battalion as an operations centre, the assembled officers and NCOs immediately stood and with raised right arm gave the Nazi salute, *Heil Hitler*.

He raised his remaining arm in response, and crossed to the lectern set in front of them. He looked out over the thirty soldiers gathered there and nodded his head in approval. These men were the elite, the toughest and the strongest soldiers he had ever commanded or served with. Reder had served on the Eastern Front with some of the men in front of him and he knew they had what it takes to eliminate this Partisan menace without flinching. Others in the group had participated in the Final Solution in the concentration camps of Auschwitz and Bergen-Belsen, which were Hitler's industrialised murder camps for some six million Jews and political opposers.

Reder knew that they would obey also the order to kill the partisans and those who aided them with food and shelter without question. His eyes were filled with pride that the Fatherland could produce men of steel such as these. Silence filled the room as he prepared to speak.

'Soldiers of the Fatherland, we have been given another special task to carry out over the next few days. Field Marshall Kesselring himself has specifically asked for this unit to be at the forefront of the operation, and I have been honoured to accept the mission on your behalf.' The men murmured to one another and Reder waited until they settled back down.

'Starting at daybreak tomorrow we will attack the Monte Sole massif and clear the area of a band of criminals who call themselves the Stella Rossa: communist thieves, cowards and murderers who are attacking our positions in the line from behind. They number about fifteen hundred men, and our intelligence has reported them to be well armed. They are also supported by the majority of the local population, who view them as the guardians of the region. The main village, Marzabotto, has around six hundred inhabitants, and with the hamlets and farms around the massif, the total population is estimated at more than eighteen hundred men, women and children. Any questions so far?'

A blonde, well-built giant of a man stood up and clicked his heels.

'Yes, Kuller?' Reder said to Sergeant Hans Kuller, his Company Sergeant, who was only twenty-two years old and had been with him since 1943 when he was then a Private in the SS. Reder had become used to his abrupt manner; he saw it as part of what made Kuller an exceptional soldier. The first time they had met was in Russia during an action against units of the Red Army, when Reder was severely wounded by shrapnel in his left arm from an exploding mortar shell. Kuller had picked him up and carried him in his arms as you would a sleeping baby, whilst all the time he was under fire from enemy mortars and automatic weapons. He carried him to safety behind their lines and handed him over to Army Medics. When Reder eventually recovered and returned to duty he had requested that Kuller be transferred to his command. The request was accepted by the High Command and Kuller soon found himself transferred to Reder's unit and promoted to Sergeant. A close bond based on mutual respect was soon formed between them, though neither soldier ever took advantage of this friendship.

Kuller stood to attention and said. 'Are we being supported by other units, sir?'

'We are, Sergeant. Units of the Wehrmacht will provide mopping-up support on the perimeters, while we do the heavy work. There will also be a unit from the GNR – the Italian Fascist Black Brigade – working with us. I don't expect them to be very active in their duty, or to be as efficient or disciplined in their approach to exterminating these criminals as we are, so if they baulk at their clear duty then we will need to "educate" them properly.'

This caused a ripple of laughter across the room. There was no mistaking what he meant by "educating them". 'So, men of the Waffen SS, we leave our barracks at 0400 tomorrow morning. Transport will be waiting on us, and it should take us around twenty minutes to get to our marshalling point. The operation starts at 0430, so I want you to organise a check on your weapons and replenish with hand grenades, ammunition, mortars and whatever else your men will need for the work ahead now.' He looked around once more at their eager faces, shouted out *Heil Hitler!* and saluted with his outstretched arm. At this, all his men sprang to their feet, shouted *Heil Hitler!* in reply and gave the Nazi salute.

There was a buzz of expectancy in the room as the soldiers spoke for a few minutes before leaving to brief their troops on the operation.

Sergeant Kuller was bright-eyed and smiling at the thought of exterminating more partisans and their peasant supporters as he made his way to the SS barracks. He thanked God for the day he had run across Major Reder. He saw in him a perfect example of what an SS officer should be: brave, patriotic and zealous in his duty. He even envied him the loss of his arm, as he saw it as a red badge of courage. "One day," he thought, "I will be like the Major. In the meantime, I will do my duty as best I can, even if it means giving my life for the Führer."

He entered the barrack room where his unit was billeted and called his men to attention. There was a flurry of activity as they stood by their beds. Looking around the room he made sure he had the men's attention before speaking 'Soldiers of the Führer, we have been assigned a mission on Monte Sole early tomorrow morning. We have been tasked with clearing the area of Italian criminals, so let's have an early night as we leave at 0400 hours tomorrow. The order has come from the Field Marshall himself and he expects all of us to do our duty. We all know the danger these criminals pose so we will completely clear the area of them and their supporters. I want you all now to quickly check your weapons and replenish with sufficient ammunition and grenades for the work ahead. *Heil Hitler!*' His men responded by shouting out in return the Führer's name whilst standing rigidly to attention. A very pleased Sergeant Kuller turned and left the barracks, 'I don't have to worry about any of these men. They will all do their duty without hesitation.'

Chapter 3

As the first glint of the new day began to colour the edges of the dawn sky, I rose to leave for my Aunt's farm. I kept any noise down to a minimum to prevent wakening the rest of the family, so I walked around the kitchen barefooted. I had left my boots outside the front door and would put them on as I left the house.

Picking up a newly sharpened knife my father had brought in from his workshop, I cut off some cheese from the block Mamma kept in the larder; it was *pecorino*, my favourite, made with the milk from our own sheep. Crossing the kitchen to the breadboard I picked up a slice of fresh bread that Mamma had made just last night. I could still smell the freshness from it as I took a bite. I ate my breakfast in a hurry as I had to be at the farm for 5am to start the milking and it was now 4.30am. It would take me fifteen minutes to walk there and I didn't want to be late.

I quietly opened the outside door and slipped through it, carefully closed the door behind me and then put on my boots. I then made my way down the well-worn path to Aunt Lisa's farm.

After a few minutes walking I came to a bend in the path with open views down the valley, and looking down the slope I could see in the near distance smoke rising up from some of the hamlets further down the mountain. I held my gaze on the smoke and thought I could see what looked like small fires dotted around the area. "Must be the farmers burning vegetation and dead trees gathered from their ground clearances" I thought, and moved on down the path. I always enjoyed the early morning on the mountain, with the sound of birds and the noise of wild boar in the nearby undergrowth for company as I walked along.

Then, a new sound came to my ears. It was the sound of automatic gunfire and shrill screams rising up from the valley floor. I stopped and listened. There it was again, I wasn't mistaken, it could only be the Germans. I ran as fast as he could down the path to Aunt Lisa's farm, oblivious to everything but reaching my family to warn them of impending danger.

After what seemed a lifetime I came to a fork in the path, the left trail led to the farm. I paused for a second to catch my breath before running on. Just then, through the trees, I caught sight of some men in military uniform just ahead of me. I jumped into the undergrowth out of sight and cautiously crawled closer to the farmhouse.

The sight that met me chilled my whole being. Uncle Luigi was tied in a kneeling position on the ground with his throat cut. The soldiers had obviously made him watch as they raped his wife in front of him. His hands were tied behind his back by a rope. A wooden stake was attached to the rope and was tied behind his head, forcing it back to look over in his wife's direction.

Aunt Lisa was lying on the ground in front of him completely naked. Her stomach was cut from her chest down to her groin, and what appeared to be her baby was lying on the ground beside her. The soldiers had raped her and then cut her unborn child from her womb before leaving her to bleed to death. My cousin Moreno, who was twelve years old, was also lying dead. He had been shot through the back of his head.

I felt the bile rise in my throat. My stomach was churning at the awful sight before me. I fought hard to stop myself vomiting in case the soldiers heard me and came for me as well.

The soldiers were now busy torching the farmhouse, so I took the opportunity to crawl backwards through the undergrowth until I reached the main path again.

My mind raced. What now? I must warn Mamma and Papà, and I ran blindly up the path towards my home.

As I reached the bend in the path again I stopped for a moment. The fires I had seen earlier were now spreading along the valley floor in all directions. Smoke was rising like lazy plumes in the sky, drifting with the wind. My senses were all alert now. I could see men moving below me, and I could clearly hear the sound of automatic fire coming ever closer. The screams of the villagers were almost drowned out with the booming sound of grenades, or was that mortars? I turned to run up the path again, but stopped when I heard the sound of a vehicle coming towards me. I panicked, thinking "What should I do?" I jumped out of sight into the undergrowth growing along the edge of the mountainside once more. The sight of a German Army truck meandering up the path came into view. The canvas cover was down and I could see about a dozen soldiers inside chatting to each other quite normally. I could clearly make out their insignia; a skull - it was the SS. Even though I had never seen an SS soldier before, all the young boys in my school knew what their insignia was.

I wished at that moment that I had a weapon to shoot them with. Then the thought came to me that the next house they would pass on the way to Marzabotto was mine.

After the truck had driven past, I came out of the undergrowth and made a dash for the side of the mountain. I knew of a shortcut over the hillside that I could use to save time, and perhaps get to my home before the Germans did. All I could think of was to warn my family of the danger.

I frantically climbed higher until I came across the path through the undergrowth. I ran as fast as I could along it, with tears blinding my eyes as I stumbled and fell along the way. Although my heart was pounding like a piston in my chest, I refused to slow down. Eventually, I could see the chimney stacks of my home just ahead.

I pulled up sharply when I heard the sound of an explosion that seemed to fill the air, followed by automatic gunfire and what seemed like screaming. I ran forward at a crouch, hoping that no one would spot me while I was looking down on the house from the hills above.

My father was fighting a tall, blonde soldier who was wearing the uniform of an SS Sergeant who was gaining the upper hand. Papà was trying to hit him on the head with a rock he had picked up from the courtyard, but the blonde giant had pushed him away and thrown him to the ground. As Papà tried to get up the SS Sergeant stood over him, pulled out his sidearm and shot him twice in the body. I cried with horror as I saw blood pump out of my father's chest in what seemed to be a never-ending scarlet flow.

The sound of shouting from the house drew my attention. I turned my head towards the source just in time to see an SS soldier forcing my three brothers into our house at gunpoint. When they were inside, he shut the door, then threw a grenade through the open window. It exploded a few seconds later with a deafening booming noise and immediately set the house ablaze. As the flames reached the roof, fanned by the light wind, the soldier kicked in the door and sprayed the interior of the house with a few bursts of automatic gunfire, with the obvious intention of finishing off anyone still left alive.

Tears filled my eyes and I found it hard to breathe as I took in the dreadful scene unfolding before me.

Suddenly, I heard my *mamma*'s voice shouting from behind the house; terrified screams, such as I had never heard from her before. Different men's voices were also shouting things at the top of their voices in a foreign language and Mamma was screaming 'Stop! Stop! You're hurting me!'

I crawled slowly through the undergrowth in the direction of the shouting until I reached a safe position facing the back of the house, where I didn't think anyone would see me. The sight I saw there remains with me to this day. Four SS men had stripped my mother of all her clothing and she was struggling in vain to fight them off. They were holding her down on the ground and were taking it in turns to repeatedly rape her. I still feel an overwhelming guilt that I didn't try to help her. But what could I have achieved against heavily armed soldiers?

Eventually the tall blonde SS Sergeant came over and joined them in the rape as the other four stood back laughing as they watched. When he had satisfied himself, the SS Sergeant pulled out his bayonet and slit my mother's throat. I watched her lifeblood ebb away into the brown earth, turning it red. He then dipped his bayonet in my mother's blood and wrote something on the ground. A chill filled my whole body and paralysed me with fear. I felt an indescribable anger choking me as I tried to tear my eyes away from the horror scene before me, but I was unable to do so.

I wasn't sure how much time had passed before the soldiers left, but I was still there, lying in the long grass just staring through my tears at my mother's body, when the thought came to me 'Lisa! Where is she?" I raised my head and looked around me to see if the SS had left anyone behind, and seeing no one there I ran to the smouldering ruin of what was left of my house. I slowly entered and tried not to look at the carnage of what was left of my brothers' bodies. I frantically searched around and finally my eyes fell on a sad looking pink bundle in the kitchen sink. It looked like the same colour of pink as Lisa's dress. I walked over and recognised the dead body of my baby sister lying there with a bullet hole in her head. She had been crammed into the sink and then shot. What kinds of monsters were these *tedeschi*? Slowly, I reached over her small dead body and removed her gold chain and pendant from her little neck and put it in my pocket. I don't know why I took it, perhaps as a keepsake. To this day I'm still not sure, although I did find it helpful in later life.

I looked round at the scene of devastation that had been my home, filled with a sense of complete desolation and loss. I fell to my knees and screamed out at the top of my lungs again and again until I lost my voice and could scream no more. I felt the bile rise from my stomach and I spewed out a stream of vomit on Mamma's once clean kitchen floor. I lay on the cool tiles for a long time, not daring to move. I didn't want to leave the house. Where could I go to, anyway? My precious family were all dead, but as long as I was there, I didn't have to accept that fact.

Darkness began to creep over the mountain and it found me still lying there on the kitchen floor, still crying. Hours had passed by, but they had made no impression on me. Was I in a dream? Had it really happened?

It was like watching a film on a cinema screen and I was the principal actor. Nothing seemed real. How could such horror be a part of life and not belong to a nightmare? How could anyone cope with seeing such things and remain sane? I thought "I will survive this; I will overcome this horror and survive. One day I will avenge my family. As for the blonde one: I will find him and I will kill him."

I realised that I had to do something to come out of this dream-like state. Unsteadily, I stood up and walked over to the breadboard, lifted two loaves and put them in a bag. I then took a wedge of the Pecorino cheese and some salami and did the same with them. Mamma always had homemade lemonade in the larder, so I put a couple of bottles in my pack and left the house, taking care not to look at the dead bodies of my sibling lying in the ruins and growing cold. I paused outside for a few moments, said a prayer over my parents' bodies and read what the blonde killer had written on the ground in my mother's blood. Then I prayed for the souls of my siblings lying dead in the house before moving on. I vowed never to return to the house or Monte Sole ever again.

Chapter 4

Having nowhere else to go, I returned to my hiding place on the hillside. I just couldn't tear myself away from the place no matter how much I wanted to and I couldn't think where else to go. The events of the day had exhausted me, so I sat down on the warm ground and tried to plan what to do next.

Feeling somewhat hungry, I ate a little of the food I had brought with me and before too long my eyes felt very heavy and I fell asleep.

It was a silly thing to do. No sooner had I done so than I was awakened by a terrible nightmare. I tried to sleep again but the nightmares were always there. They always had the central figure of a tall, blonde-haired man, standing laughing over my family. I realised that I had to move away from the house, but I wasn't sure where to go. I picked up my meagre belongings and turned away from the scene of my hellish nightmare, and in the black mountain night I walked down the path I knew so well and headed for the village of Marzabotto. I felt I just needed contact with other people that I knew.

Usually, at this time of night, the village would have been asleep, however tonight there were people gathered in small groups all over the main street. I saw my father's friend Pietro talking to some people and I ran over to him. I grabbed him round the waist and let my tears erupt in loud sobbing cries. Pietro reached down and lifted me up in his arms. 'Bruno, what's wrong? Where are your parents?

I couldn't answer him; the words that confirmed my family were all dead just wouldn't come out of my mouth.

Pietro slowly nodded his head as if understanding without hearing any words.

'Did the Germans come to your house Bruno?'

I nodded.

'Did they harm your family?'

Again, I nodded.

Pietro took a deep breath before asking me, 'Are any of them still alive?'

I looked up at him for the first time and said in a clear voice, 'They are all dead. I saw it happen to them and to my aunt and uncle at the farm.'

Pietro held me close to him and said, 'Bruno, you can stay with us tonight until we think this thing through. The Germans were also here today and killed a lot of villagers; however, I don't think they will return tonight so we should be safe enough to get some rest and have a talk in the morning.' He took me by the hand and we walked through the village to his house. I saw that some villagers were openly weeping on the streets, and I realised for the first time the extent of the killings the Germans had brought on us.

Pietro told me that the Germans had forbidden anyone, on pain of death, to bury any of the dead villagers. The Parish Priest, Don Francesco, had tried to bury some of his own parishioners but was discovered by the SS. They executed him on the spot without mercy.

Eventually, we arrived at Pietro's house, a small terraced villa facing the village piazza, and only a few houses along from the Church. His wife, Giovanna, made a panino for me, before showing me to a small attic bedroom for the night. Giovanna was very kind and made sure that I was comfortable there. After eating my panino I was so exhausted that, as soon as my head hit the pillow, I was fast asleep.

I was wakened early in the morning by the sound of shouting in the street below. I jumped out of bed and when I looked out of the attic window, my heart skipped a beat. The Germans had come back again, and were rounding up the remaining villagers into the piazza. I felt so afraid; however, I knew that if I didn't act quickly to escape they would soon discover me up here in an attic bedroom with the only way out through the lower part of the house.

Then I saw him again, the giant blonde soldier. He was in charge and was separating the men from the women and children. Blood rushed to my head and once more, I felt physically sick. I knew what this man was capable of - if I didn't get away from him, I was certain I would be killed.

I heard the outside door being kicked open and a German voice in the house shouting "*Raus, Raus!*" to Pietro and Giovanna, as he ushered them out. I heard them downstairs, searching for anyone who may be hiding in the downstairs rooms.

I thought for a moment. How can I escape before they search here and find me? In desperation,n I opened the attic window on the opposite side of the room and looked out. I saw that the roof tiles there had a gentle slope and could quite easily be climbed onto. I pulled myself up onto the window ledge and lifted myself out onto the roof. I quickly reached behind me and pulled the window closed, then cautiously climbed up to the chimneystacks and perched between them out of sight from the soldiers below. As I huddled there, I heard the attic widow scrape open and the sound of German voices talking to each other. Eventually the window closed again.

From my vantage point, I saw the Germans herd the women and children into the cemetery beside the church. The cemetery was of typical country design, with tall stonewalls on three sides and a padlocked metal entrance gate to the front. One soldier broke the lock off the gate with his rifle butt to allow the women in. The women were all shouting to each other as they searched for their loved ones in the crowd. The children were screaming and trying to hide. A soldier calmly set up a machine gun at the entrance to the cemetery and, once ready, he waited on the order to open fire. When the women and children saw the machine gun, their screams grew louder.

Some women tried to climb up the walls to escape but were picked off by rifle fire from a group of soldiers standing close by. I closed my eyes and put my hands over my ears to try and cut out the loud chatter of the machine gun and the screams of the dying. Then there was silence, and when I opened my eyes and saw the pile of dead bodies in that small space, I felt a wet sensation spread between my legs.

The blonde SS sergeant walked amongst the dead, stopping every so often to move a body, checking if there was anyone alive underneath it. Anyone he found still alive he shot twice in the head. His pistol shots echoed loudly in the still air. Other soldiers then came and threw the dead bodies ever higher on top of each other until they looked like some sort of macabre art form of twisted arms and legs sticking out of tortured flesh.

Meanwhile, on the other side of the piazza, I saw the men being marched off into the woods. Amongst them were some of the boys I played football with. The contrast to the women in the cemetery was quite stark. There was not a sound from them as they walked along, as if they were resigned to their fate. I didn't see what happened to them, but I did hear the chatter of machine guns coming from their direction and eventually the soldiers returning without them.

About another twenty people, men and women, living on the outskirts of the village, were rounded up and escorted under gunpoint to the village church, protesting as they went. Some of them put up a struggle but they were soon subdued with a rifle butt or a shot to the head. The soldiers then took some of the boards from a nearby fencing and nailed them to the solid oak doors of the Church with the aim of stopping anyone from escaping. Some soldiers took dry tinder and placed it around the church then set it alight. It didn't take long for the flames to engulf the timber-framed building and I could clearly hear the sound of screaming people hammering on the doors. Soldiers stood by the entrance to prevent anyone still alive from escaping. Soon the sounds coming from the church were no more. An eerie silence hung over the village, broken only by the crackling noise of burning wood and the smell of death.

The Sergeant then stood back, surveying his handiwork. He looked up at the clear blue sky and watched the smoke from the fire drift lazily upwards, carried along by the slight breeze.

Gripped once again with sheer terror, I clung desperately to the chimneystacks around me, afraid that the soldiers would hear the sound of my heartbeat, or the staccato noise of my breathing. I was so frightened that my bladder gave way once again and a small trickle of urine flowed slowly down the tiles in front of me. I clung tightly to the chimneys as if my life depended on it. My hands were bleeding and lacerated as the rough brickwork tore them.

The *tedeschi* were killing everyone they could find. They were exterminating Italian lives as easily as if they were killing a chicken for supper.

I stayed up there on the roof until I was convinced the soldiers had left before I climbed back into the house through the attic window. I sat on the bed and sobbed. I shouted out aloud, 'Why God, why have you allowed this to happen? These were all good people who didn't deserve to die!' Of course, God didn't answer, but to the mind of a thirteen-year-old boy, he should have had.

I reasoned that I couldn't stay on this mountain any longer and that I should leave immediately. There wasn't much point in trying to seek out my other relatives and friends because if they weren't already dead, they soon would be. I thought of Bologna. It was only ten miles away, and I could easily walk that in an afternoon. Perhaps I could find shelter there with some charity or even find some work in a restaurant. I would take with me any food and clothing I could from the house and, if I was lucky, even find some money. My mind was beginning to switch off from the horrors I had witnessed over the last few days. Perhaps it was a coping mechanism I was developing, but I knew I had to leave as soon as possible before the Germans returned. I walked slowly downstairs, not sure of what awaited me there, but to my relief the house was empty. I looked around the kitchen then took a bag and loaded it with food from the larder. I opened a drawer in the downstairs bedroom and took some clothing from it. A pair of trousers, a pullover and a shirt that belonged to Pietro. I didn't care if they fitted or not, they were clean. I found some money in a jar on the kitchen table. Giovanna probably used it to pay for the household items she needed on a daily basis. I counted it before putting the notes carefully in my pocket. It was enough to buy me food for a few more days.

I then noticed a shotgun that Pietro used for hunting boars sitting in a corner by the outside door. I picked it up and checked it for cartridges. I already knew how to use a shotgun with some accuracy. My father had taken us hunting in the woods every Sunday before lunch, and he had made sure that all of us were familiar with the weapon. I also found a box of cartridges in a sideboard drawer, and I put those in my bag as wll.

When I was ready, I left the house and headed warily down the street in the direction of Bologna. I kept my eyes firmly fixed ahead, as I didn't want to look to the left or right in case I saw the dead bodies of the villagers lying there, and perhaps recognise some of them. The stench of death was in the air, and the smell of burning flesh that filled my nostrils made me feel sick.

I had only walked a few metres along the road when I saw some military vehicles blocking the road ahead. I threw myself to the ground and crawled to the end of a building for cover. I knew I had to get off the road before the Germans saw me, and the only place to go was up the steep hillside behind the village. I crawled along until I reached the grass verge and crawled my way quite high up the hillside to safety.

I now had time to think about what had just happened and the violent massacre of people close to me I had witnessed for the second time.

My young mind could not take in the total extent of what had happened.

As I lay there, I heard a rustling sound in the long grass behind me. I again felt absolute fear fill me and I sunk lower into the ground, hoping that my pounding heart wouldn't betray my presence. The sound of a moving body crawling towards me grew ever louder. I pointed my shotgun in the direction of the sound and waited. A face appeared through the grass and spoke softly in Italian to me. 'Don't be afraid, I'm with the Stella Rossa. I saw you coming off the road and hiding up here. What's your name?'

To my relief I recognised the man as one of the partisans who frequently came to the village to visit his girlfriend. He was about twenty years old and dressed in a British Army jacket and an Italian infantry hat with a red ribbon tied round it.

'My name is Bruno Verdi,' I managed to answer in a shaky voice.

'Well Bruno, my name is Italo Arcari. Lower your weapon, stay here and don't wander about. The *tedeschi* have a patrol out searching the hillside for stragglers.' As if to emphasise this he pointed to his Sten gun, 'and if they come near us I'll be ready.'

We lay together on that hillside until we were sure all the German vehicles had left the area, and even then, we continued to wait, and wait. I wondered what for. After some time, the partisan's body stiffened as he saw a German uniform below us crawling up the mountainside in our direction. Italo whispered to me, 'It's all right; this is their usual tactic after a *rastrellamento*. They drop off one or two soldiers to see if they can flush out anyone who escaped and are still hiding from them. If they do, then the soldiers finish them off. They then leave and are picked up further down the road by their comrades.' I could only see one soldier moving below me, 'Are there any more?' I whispered.

'There's probably another one covering his back with an automatic weapon,' he said as he cocked his own Sten gun.

Italo watched the German crawl his way up the hillside in a zigzag pattern for a further ten minutes, then, as if bored with the game, the German stood up and walked back down the way he had just come. Italo breathed a sigh of relief at the narrow escape. 'He's probably seen enough and thinks there are no more survivors here,' he said, holding a shaking gun.

The German soldier had reached the road, and was joined there by another soldier who had remained hidden all this time in the long grass.

Italo laughed. 'These Germans are so predictable in what they do. They have no imagination. They always have to follow the book.'

For the first time in days, I smiled.

'What do we do now?', I asked the partisan.

'Well, I think we should take advantage of the rest and have something to eat. What do you think, Bruno?'

I admitted that I did feel quite hungry, so I rummaged in my bag and pulled out some bread and cheese.

'Do you think they will come back?' I asked.

Italo thought for a moment or two. 'I don't think they will come back to Marzabotto. Two soldiers being dropped off is usually a sign they have finished operations in an area. Although I don't think they will have finished the *rastrallemento* on the mountain itself. They may come back tomorrow for operations on the other side of the mountain. They caught the Stella Rossa by surprise yesterday and almost finished us all off. The remains of the brigade are now scattered all over the place and we are not a credible fighting force anymore.'

'What will you do now?' I asked.

'I'll go to Bologna and join the partisans there. This war should not last much longer now and I want to be involved in the fighting when the *tedeschi* eventually surrender.'

'Will the partisans take me as well? Those German bastards murdered every member of my family and I want to kill as many of them as possible,' I said, lifting my shotgun to emphasise my point.

Italo looked at me closely. 'I'll take you along with me to speak to them, but I honestly don't know if they will think you too young to join them. How old are you?'

I stood up to my full height and said in as deep a voice as I could, 'I'm fifteen years old and I can fight as well as anyone. Just give me a chance to prove it.'

Italo smiled, then said, 'Well then little tiger, we'll rest and settle down here until it's dark, then we'll head along the road to Bologna. If we see any vehicle lights, we'll leave the road and hide. There won't be any night patrols out after what's happened here so we should be fine. As far as I know, Bologna is still in German hands, so we'll have to be careful entering the city.'

And so, I left my childhood behind on the verdant slopes of Monte Sole. It seemed to me that my rite of passage from childhood to adulthood had been almost instantaneous. My nightmares continued, but gradually became less intense and easier to bear. However, in my quite moments, I can still hear the sound of screaming voices.

The partisan band was based in the mountain region near Bologna and they were always looking to recruit new members, although they took great care over selection in case of infiltration by fascist agents. When they found out what had happened to my family they had no problem in accepting me into their band, and as Italo had already proved himself with the Stella Rossa, we both joined together.

I was with the Bologna 8th Garibaldi Brigade of partisans until the war ended in April 1945, some seven months after I joined them. They never found out that I lied about my age, although they may have suspected it. I was involved in several operations against the Germans and never once did I show any mercy towards them. During that time, I was constantly on the lookout for a tall, blonde SS Sergeant, but our paths never crossed during those eventful months.

The partisans taught me how to handle all different types of weapons, and I proved to be a quick learner. I did find out though, that the German *rastrallemento* on Monte Sole had lasted for four days, and that the final death count numbered over eighteen hundred people, including forty-five children under two years old. One of them was my Lisa.

I had never felt hatred against people on this scale before, but I now experienced an overwhelming compulsion to eliminate every German I laid eyes on. Over the next few weeks I became eaten up with a desire to kill Germans and not to stop until they were all dead or they had killed me. My company commander noticed that I was being eaten up with hatred and took me aside.

'Bruno, I realise that you have every right to hate the Germans and to want revenge for what they did to your family, but you must be careful. Many good men have felt the same as you do and threw caution to the wind in their attempt to get at the Germans and ended up dead. Don't let this hatred consume you to the point that you lose your sense of reason. You are no good to me or to our cause if you continually burn with this anger. It could threaten us all. Do you understand what I mean?'

I nodded my head in agreement. 'I'll try to change. Italo has already spoken to me about it. He told me to let my anger simmer and not continually boil over.'

'Good lad that Italo, that's sound advice. Make sure you take it to heart.'

Life in the partisan camp was very structured and based on strict military discipline. We had our own cooks and medics as the regular forces would and everyone was always very busy working around the camp. We even had our own ranks and a distinct military structure that was necessary for efficient organisation. The only official activity that I detested were the political lectures, usually from the communist commissars, that all partisans in our band had to attend. Even though we were called a Garibaldi Brigade, the name was not an indication of our political affiliation, though most Garibaldi Brigades were communist. If anything, we were mainly non-political and we took these mandatory lectures in a light-hearted manner.

The only reason that our leader allowed the communist commissars to operate in the camp was because of his agreement with the Italian communist partisans under the control of General Tito in Yugoslavia to supply us with arms. The payback was Tito had agreed to do so, through the local network of Garibaldi brigades, if he allowed the politicisation of the band with commissars attached to carry out the work, and for us to be absorbed into the communist network of Garibaldi Brigades fighting in Italy.

There was another unofficial activity that took place in the camp on an irregular basis, and that was the visits that took place from some local prostitutes from Bologna. When I first saw them I wondered why they were there, however I soon came to understand that their function was to boost morale. One night, during a visit from these girls, I found myself sitting alone at a camp fire when Marisa, one of the prostitutes, sat down beside me. I found her to be very friendly and extremely talkative, and before too long the inevitable curiosity on my part turned into active participation. The experience of losing my virginity that night was one I shall always remember. Marisa treated me with tenderness and understanding, and as for my part, I felt that I had passed that night into the ranks of manhood.

The autumn turned to winter, and a cold winter it was that year. The snows came early to the mountains, and perceptibly changed from a serene white dusting that covered the countryside and the mountains around us to deep snowdrifts that hindered all movement on the mountain and the surrounding area. Gianni reasoned that if the snow impeded us moving around, then it would also impede the Germans. He decided to give some of the men with families in the area some leave time, which was gratefully accepted, but left the camp much quieter than usual.

Not having much to occupy me, I found myself dwelling on the massacres and on my family. As I focused more on my dead family and friends, I experienced a tremor in my hands which quickly spread to my whole body. I found myself shaking like a leaf from head to toe. I felt tears well up within me like a pent-up force and suddenly erupting with a passion and fury that surprised me. Some of the partisans heard me scream out and came running over to me. I found myself being held down by them as I continued sobbing, violently shaking and screaming out to the heavens. The partisans were concerned in case I hurt myself and they held me down until I became calmer. After about ten minutes I began to relax and returned to normality. I later realised that this episode was the result of all the horror I had experienced for such a young person, even though it was a delayed reaction. I had become a closed book since the events and even when I had witnessed the second massacre, I had shown no sign of it having affected me in anyway. I was told by the camp medic that what I had experienced was a healthy sign, and was probably the first stage of emotional healing. These days, you would probably call it post-traumatic shock; however, in those days, the older men called it shell shock: a delayed reaction to a violent traumatic experience.

Whatever normality was, I welcomed it. Although, when I look back on those times, I wonder how "normality" could be achieved for a now 14 year old orphan living in an armed camp high up in the Italian mountains, being trained to kill Germans.

The heavy snow had also disrupted our food drops, as the Allied supply aircraft wouldn't drop their loads in case the supplies were lost in the snowdrifts and never seen again. Consequently, we took to hunting the scarce game in the woods. I was surprised , at how easy it was for me to show my comrades my proficiency, thanks to my papà's training . I hoped that when it came to hunting Germans I showed the same measure of skill.

My first taste of action was just before Christmas on an operation we had set up just outside Bologna to ambush German military vehicles moving men and materials further north to set up new defensive positions. Our leader, Gianni Bellucci, who previously had been a Colonel in the Italian Army, was an excellent soldier and all the partisans under his command were highly disciplined. Gianni was well liked by his men and he in turn treated us all with respect. He put me to work with a group who were setting up a machine gun post hidden in nearby woodland, which had a clear view of the main road. My orders were to wait until the machine gun opened fire, and then I had to pick off any Germans trying to run or take cover in the undergrowth. I was given a heavy British-made Lee Enfield bolt-action rifle and, even though I was feeling very nervous over my first taste of action, I couldn't wait to kill my first German.

I didn't have to wait very long before I heard the rumbling sound of heavy transport coming our way. I saw a convoy of about ten trucks, all in olive green with military insignia painted on the sides, moving at speed along the main road in an attempt to put off any snipers lying in wait for them. As they approached us, the first truck hit a buried landmine and was blown over onto its side, which effectively blocked the road ahead. There was another explosion almost immediately after this as our men threw hand-grenades at the last truck and successfully disabled that as well. With the two trucks on fire, and blocking the road at either end, the German soldiers on board had no alternative but to seek cover where they could. As they dismounted, our men opened fire with their machine guns, and most of the Germans were cut to pieces. Some of them ran into the undergrowth and managed to return fire with whatever light weapons they had. That was where I came in. With shaking hands I looked along my rifle sights and fired as fast as I could into the *tedeschi* to great effect.

Eventually, after a short-pitched fight, the remaining Germans held up their hands and surrendered. There were about eight of them. They threw their weapons down on the ground and walked out into full view, with their hands on their heads. The problem was that, as we lived a frugal life in the mountains, we had no facilities for taking prisoners. Some of the partisans motioned with their weapons at them, and pushed them up against one of the remaining trucks under armed guard while Gianni had a discussion with some of the other leaders on what to do with them. There appeared to be no alternative to shooting them because we may have been recognised from our visits to Bologna and by letting them go free we could be putting our own families and friends in danger. We drew lots and three partisans were selected to execute them. When the soldiers realised that they were about to be shot, one of them fell to his knees and began to pray out loud. Another took out a photograph of his family and began to shout '*Kinder, Kinder!*' This visibly disturbed the partisan firing squad. They looked round at Gianni as if wanting him to change his mind. Gianni picked up his rifle and joined the firing squad; I suppose this confirmed again the kind of leader he was. Eventually they opened fire on the Germans and I watched them fall to the ground like rag dolls. This was the first time I had witnessed our side doing this kind of thing and it didn't sit well with me. It reminded me of the slaughter on Monte Sole. After all, we were the good people and they were the bad guys. It blurred the edges of our moral high ground and I didn't like it.

After the ambush, Gianni told me that I was personally responsible for killing about three Germans with my rifle and, even though I was pleased by this news, the execution I had witnessed rather spoiled it for me. I didn't really want to kill Germans in this way. I wanted to kill them in combat; otherwise I felt that I was no better than they were. I needed to believe in our moral superiority, although back then I would not have expressed it in those words.

I was very quiet on the march back to camp until Gianni came up and put his arm round me. 'Bruno, listen to me. I wish we could fight a clean war under clean rules, but the Germans don't recognise our status as combatants. They see us as criminals, armed gangsters, and that's why they kill our families and friends and local villagers in an attempt to stop us. We couldn't take the chance in releasing those soldiers.'

Chapter 5

One morning in early February, Gianni called me aside. 'Bruno, we need you to go on a mission to Bologna for us. It may prove to be very dangerous as the Germans are becoming very nervous over the partisan attacks and they are checking identity papers at random on the streets. Do you want to go?'

I immediately accepted the mission, 'What do you want me to do, Gianni?'

'It's less likely the Germans will stop a young boy, so, I want you to make contact with a local doctor; his name is Roberto Galassi, and he works at the hospital. Tell him we need more medicines as soon as possible, especially first-aid supplies, and to leave them at the usual place for our pickup in seven days' time. Give him the password "*vinciamo*" and he will know you are genuine.'

I felt so honoured to be trusted with such an important mission that I didn't give the danger aspect a second thought. I knew that if I was caught by the Germans I would probably be tortured before they killed me, as it had already happened to some captured partisans from our Brigade. They had been visiting their families in one of the villages nearby, when a fascist informer recognised them and reported them to the German authorities. The Germans came during the night and took them by surprise. They tortured the men for three days trying to find out about the partisan's future operations and where their base was before they shot them.

I filled a backpack with some food, put my revolver on top so that I could easily reach it in case of an emergency, and set off down the mountainside for the road below. I reckoned that I could walk the distance to Bologna without any problem and arrive there by noon. If I heard the sound of approaching vehicles, I would immediately dive into the undergrowth as I had been trained to do, and wait until they had gone before returning to the road.

When I was about a mile from the outskirts of the city, I left the road and climbed up the mountainside until I had a clear view of the road ahead. What I saw there filled me with dread. The Germans had set up a heavily armed roadblock with about fifteen soldiers and they were checking everyone's papers before letting them pass. Behind the roadblock sat two soldiers on motorbikes attached to sidecars, with their engines running. They were obviously prepared to chase after anyone or any vehicle that tried to break through their cordon. How can I get past this? Maybe if I climbed higher up the mountain I could get around them. On the other hand, if I waited a few hours they may leave.

I decided to wait and see what happened, and if they were still there by mid-afternoon, I would try to get around them. I lay back on the grass and with the autumn sunshine warming my face I closed my eyes. It was inexcusable, but I must have dozed off.

The sound of engines starting up and people shouting in German woke me up. I saw the Germans leaving and heading back into the city. I waited for a while longer before I ventured onto the road and began walking towards Bologna again. As I approached a bend in the road ahead, I saw two motorbikes sitting with their riders, parked just off the road and partially hidden by trees. They must have moved to their new positions when I fell asleep on the hillside. The Germans always left behind two soldiers to catch anyone who may have been waiting for them to leave and I had walked into their trap. I should have been watching to see if the motorbikes had left with the rest of the soldiers or if a German truck had stopped just out of sight ahead to wait on their men returning from their search of the area.

The soldiers saw me and immediately raised their machine pistols at me. 'Stop, show your papers,' one of them shouted to me in Italian as he walked forward. I stopped walking. I had no German ID papers, only my Italian ID card showing my name and address on Monte Sole. I reached into my pocket and pulled it out. The soldier stared at it and began shouting in German to me. I didn't understand a word of what he said but I knew what he wanted. Eventually, the other soldier came over and roughly pulled my backpack off my shoulders and opened it. He pulled out my gun and showed it to his comrade. They spoke together for a moment as they decided what to do with me, before one of them turned to face me.

It felt as if my head had exploded as he hit me with his machine pistol. I fell to the ground and tasted blood filling my mouth. I was dragged to my feet and tied with rope before being roughly pushed over to where one of the motorbikes with sidecar was parked. I felt my feet leave the ground as I was lifted inside it. For good measure, they slapped me a few more times round the face and head. I never knew that blood could taste so salty.

They took me into Bologna to the Gestapo Headquarters and threw me into a cell. I lay on the floor on top of damp straw. I was very frightened. I had heard many stories from the partisans on the Gestapo's interviewing methods, such as pulling out their victims' fingernails with pliers, and I was terrified of what lay ahead for me.

When my eyes became more accustomed to the poor light in the cell I could see that the straw was not damp with water but was wet with blood. I wondered what poor creature it belonged to, and if he was still alive. I shivered, not just with the chill permeating through my cell, but with fear of the unknown. Then, two black uniformed SS men came into the cell and pulled me to my feet. Without a word they took me from my prison, one on each of my arms. They dragged me along a corridor to an interview room where I was pushed into a seat in front of a large wooden desk. They then disappeared into the shadows round the walls, although I was still very conscious of their presence. I could feel my heart beating in my chest and I resolved not to show any fear.

Sitting behind the desk was a Gestapo interrogation officer dressed in his black uniform and smelling sweetly of cologne. In Italian, he asked me my name and I answered him, 'Bruno Verdi, sir.'

There was a long silence following this, and it unnerved me.

'Where do you live Verdi?' He asked me in a gruff voice.

'In Marzabotto, on Monte Sole, sir.'

'Are you with the partisans?' he asked, looking at me for the first time. He had small beady eyes set in a soft round face. He looked like a bank clerk and probably would have been completely unsuited to proper soldiering. He resembled a vulture feeding off human flesh.

'No, sir. I'm not.'

'Then why were you carrying a gun in your backpack?'

I answered without hesitation, 'I found it in Marzabotto after the *rastrallemento* there and I kept it to protect myself. These are difficult times, sir. I was alone and afraid.'

The Gestapo officer stared at me with those cold beady eyes that seemed to pierce right through you, reading what was going on inside your head. I was scared. Eventually he came from behind his desk and stood in front of me and said, 'I don't believe you, Verdi. There has been no one living in Marzabotto since the *rastrallemento*. Where have you been since that time? How you have fed yourself and kept yourself so clean? The answer is that you are with the partisans. It also means that you know where their base is.'

He leaned over me and said in a very quiet voice 'If you don't tell me the truth, I will have you taken from here to a nice country house where my friends will make you talk by attaching an electric current to your testicles. Do you understand, Verdi?'

My heart was pumping at a fast rate and my mouth felt very dry as I answered him.

'Sir, I don't know anything about the partisans. I am an orphan and I have been living alone on Monte Sole. Please believe me.'

He punched me two or maybe three times in my face and head and I passed out.

When I came to, my head and face were throbbing with pain and I could only see out of one eye. I was sitting in the back of a car with an SS guard beside me. I was being driven along a country road to, I presumed, the Gestapo interrogation centre in the country. I once again began to protest my innocence to the SS guard beside me, only to be greeted by a backhanded slap across my face. 'Only speak when you are spoken to,' he bellowed in my ear. Once again I tasted blood.

Suddenly, there was the unmistakable sound of a British Spitfire flying above us. The two SS men started shouting at each other over the roar of its engines and the car accelerated faster and faster, as the Spitfire banked steeply and prepared to make a pass over us. With a screech of tyres, the car entered a bend in the road at speed. At that moment the plane opened fire with its machine guns, raking the car from front to rear with its heavy calibre bullets and immediately killed the driver. With the driver dead the car sped out of control, skidded off the road into the undergrowth and hit a tree before overturning onto its roof. Overhead, I could hear the sound of the Spitfire's engines fading into the distance, apparently satisfied with its work. I had been thrown to the floor before the attack when the car had accelerated into the bend and it had probably saved my life. I looked round for my SS guard and saw that he had blood gushing from a head wound where he had made contact with the wooden dashboard. He was sprawled semi-conscious between the front seats. I seized my chance to escape. I crawled forward through the shattered windscreen onto the roadside, taking care to avoid the broken glass, and pausing only for a second to remove the dead driver's handgun from his belt. Once outside and standing on the road, I cocked the weapon and shot my SS guard twice in the head through the side window. I couldn't risk him regaining mobility and following me.

I looked around at the surrounding countryside and tried to get my bearings. I didn't know where I was but, according to the position of the sun and the time of day, I reckoned

I was on the right side of Bologna. I painfully climbed up the mountainside for as long as I could manage, and only stopped when I was out of breath. It seemed like I had been walking for hours and the upward climb was beginning to tell on my legs. When night eventually fell I broke off a thick branch from a tree and used it as a blind man would a white walking stick. From my earliest days I had been used to the black nights that fell so quickly on the mountains like a dark blanket covering the woods, so I felt comfortable enough in the darkness, but I also knew the dangers of walking in it without a torch. After a long time walking in the pitch-black night I thought I must be pretty close to the partisan's camp so I kept walking in a straight line and sang out my name hoping that a perimeter guard would hear me. I stumbled a few times in the dark and once or twice almost lost my balance as I wandered too close to the mountain's edge.

Eventually, I came across some of my fellow partisans on patrol duty guarding the tracks leading up to our camp, and after a warm welcome and a brief conversation, two of them helped me back to safety.

I was greeted by my comrades like a returning hero, even though I had failed in my mission. Gianni debriefed me on my escapades and told me that when news had reached him of my capture and subsequent interrogation, he had feared the worse for me.

Once I was cleaned up and after a few days' rest, I felt suitably refreshed and ready to resume my duties, although I was still sporting a bruised and swollen face and stiff limbs as a memento of German hospitality. One positive note from the operation was that I now felt the other partisans accepted me as an equal despite my young age and this certainly gave me more confidence for future missions.

When Italo returned from his patrol, he made a point of seeking me out. When he saw me, he gave me a big hug and a kiss on both cheeks. 'Well little tiger, I heard you have sharp claws, well done.' With a smile on his face he said, 'Pity your memory was not as sharp as your claws, as you forgot about the German tactic of leaving two men behind.' He gave me a playful tap on the shoulder and said, 'Good to see you back, comrade.' That was the first time he had called me that, and it filled me with a sense of pride. I was also too embarrassed to tell anyone the truth that I hadn't forgotten about the German tactics but had simply fallen asleep and hadn't been watching what they were up to.

With the Allies pushing the Germans back, it wasn't long before they took up defensive positions on Monte Sole, a natural fortress to defend. We received orders to disrupt their supply route from the north, and we moved into position for this. The fighting was furious with no quarter being given from the Germans when they captured partisans, and we reciprocated, killing every German we captured. Such was the nature of the bloody conflict we were engaged in.

Where we differed from the South of Italy was in the civil war we were fighting. Our enemy was the Fascist Brigate Nere, the Black Brigade militias. We were not only fighting the Germans, we were also fighting the Italians who had remained loyal to Mussolini's Repubblica Sociale Italiana which was based around the Lake Garda area. To complicate matters even more so, the Royal Italian Army was fighting on the side of the Allies, and was being used almost exclusively in a combat role against the Brigate Nere. It was a sad affair that Italians were killing Italians and I wondered then what it would lead to after the war. Could these open wounds heal sufficiently to give us a healthy Italian body?

On 24th April 1945, units of the Polish Independent Brigade were the first Allied troops to enter Bologna. The Poles were surprised and not very happy seeing Communist partisans in the city, and they shouted abuse whenever they saw us marching in column. We understood these feelings because The Russian Red Army was now occupying Poland, and Polish freedoms and independence were being brutally repressed there.

These units were followed a few hours later by contingents of the British 8th and American 5th Armies. Liberation had eventually arrived, and the local population greeted the Allies with jubilation. Street parties were being organised everywhere and there was a real feeling of unity and joy as the war was passing us by.

We wanted to continue fighting with the Allies, but we were ordered to stand down and disband. We were of the opinion that the Allies didn't want bands of armed communists operating at their rear. Our leaders tried to convince the Allies to allow us to join forces with their regular troops but we were ordered again to lay down our weapons. If we wanted to continue fighting, then we would have to join the Royal Italian Army on an individual basis.

We found out after the war that the British were afraid of a Greek situation developing in Italy, where armed communist fighters, the ELAS, had attempted to overthrow the Greek government with an armed coup following the German retreat in 1944. Their stated aim was to set up a communist Republic. With around 100,000 armed fighters they almost succeeded before they were put down by the British Army.

On the 28th of April, we heard the news that Mussolini had been captured at a partisan checkpoint on the road to Lake Como, at a small town called Dongo. He had been taken overnight to a remote farmhouse by another group, together with his mistress, Clara Petacci, who had also fallen into the hands of the partisans.. The following morning they were taken outside into the courtyard, put against a wall and shot. The partisans then put the dead bodies into their van and, under orders from partisan headquarters, took them to Milan for open display. They travelled up the Corso Buenos Aires, the main thoroughfare in Milan, to the Piazzale Loreto where they hung them upside down from an Esso Garage scaffolding.

The local people reacted furiously at the sight of them hanging there. One old woman fired a revolver four times into Mussolini's body. With tears streaming down her face, she shouted at him, 'You killed four of my family you murdering bastard! they were in your army, so here's a bullet for each of them.' Another man held his child up to Mussolini's face and urged the child to urinate on it. Others beat the dead bodies with anything they could lay their hands on. They blamed Mussolini for leading them into a disastrous war, and for the German occupation of Italy that had almost destroyed the country. Many blamed him for personally getting too close to that maniac Hitler and for also listening to his ranting.

With Mussolini dead, the war in Italy came to an end but the killings continued. Reprisals throughout the north of Italy against the Fascists or anyone suspected of being a Fascist took place. Before the killings stopped, over thirty thousand Italians had been killed, either by the partisans or by ordinary Italians. I suspect quite a few old scores were settled during those days. The reprisals took place mainly in the north of Italy with very few killings happening in the south of the country. What I didn't understand was that the Allies stood back and allowed this to happen. I don't think that particular wound has ever been healed. Even to this day the country, underneath a thin veneer of unity, was still divided between the right and left.

When the war ended and the partisan brigades were disbanded, I was left on my own. I wasn't fifteen years old yet and I was left to fend for myself. I knew that the Allied Military Government (AMG) had set up some sort of refugee relief system to meet the demands of the many homeless people in the area, including the many orphans who roamed the streets. The various charities were overwhelmed with the sheer volume of people seeking help and so the AMG offered extra assistance. One of their refugee houses was an old convent converted as a shelter for use by homeless men of all ages, and I ended up there. The charities fed us there every day. At 6am we were all given a breakfast of bread and cheese washed down with coffee, and at 7pm we were fed an evening meal which was usually pasta with something.

I quickly realised that, if I wanted to get on with my life, I would have to get out of the shelter during the day to find some work. Most of the men were just lying around the building during the day feeling sorry for themselves, and I didn't want to end up that way. A lot of them were drinking heavily, and the alcohol combined with the boredom of the day was leading to some bitter fights developing between residents.

I used the shelter as a base just for sleeping in and eating, and during the day I went out looking for any kind of work. I did this for several years, odd jobs anywhere ranging from waiter to labourer until I was eighteen. That was when I volunteered for the Italian Army as a regular soldier. Since I had first joined the partisans at the age of thirteen, I had matured into a strong young man. I was now just under six feet tall and I weighed around twelve stone. My active life in the mountains with my comrades had helped me to fill out and I now felt that I could face just about anything. My previous experiences serving as a partisan came in very useful, especially when it came to infantry training, and I was very quickly promoted to the rank of Corporal.

I was stationed around Rome for a while and was relatively happy with my life in the military, although I still missed my family very much and grieved for them every single day of my life. I did the usual things that young soldiers did. I drank a bit too much, I chased the bar girls and I sometimes visited the brothels. I was trying to live my life to the full and not mourn what I had lost on the mountain all those years ago.

One day, as I was walking through the city, I saw an exhibition advertised outside a local museum. It was displaying memorabilia and old photographs from the war years from both the Axis and Allied Armies.

Having nothing better to do I went in and wandered amongst the collection. One section was dedicated to the Wehrmacht units that had been stationed in Rome during the conflict. I looked at some old photographs in frames hanging on a wall under the heading 'SS Units attached to the Wehrmacht' and there he was, the tall, blonde Sergeant. Numbly I stared at the old photograph of my mortal enemy, until I felt the same old fear build up within me. As I began to physically tremble, an elderly man standing beside me asked if I was feeling all right. I nodded to him, 'Just recovering from the flu, I'll be all right in a moment.' I again looked closely at the photograph and read the identity label underneath it, Sergeant Hans Kuller, 16th Waffen SS Division Reconnaissance Battalion. At last, I knew his name.

I stood for some time just looking at his face. Old memories of my family's personal tragedy and of the villagers of Marzabotto came flooding back to me. Tears welled up in my eyes and formed little rivers of grief running down my face. Now that I knew who he was, I resolved to find him and to kill him. Not able to look at his face anymore, I turned away, and as I did so, another photograph on the wall caught my eye. It was in a frame on its own. It was Major Walter Reder, the 16th Waffen SS Commanding Officer. I recognised him from his pictures in the local newspapers of the day. Major Reder had been tried by a military court in the town of La Spezia in 1951 and had received a life sentence for war crimes, which was to be served in its entirety, in the Military Prison in Gaeta, near Naples. At least he had been captured and some form of justice served, but Kuller was still free. There and then, I made a vow, that even if it would cost me my life, I would find this animal, this murderer, and kill him.

I served in the Army for 7 years until I was twenty-five, when I then left the military and headed back to Bologna to start a new life there, hopefully for the first time without the intrusion of guns or violence.

I had a small army pension that would help pay the rent on a little flat I liked in Via Roma, near the city centre. My next goal was to find work, so I applied for a job as a waiter I saw advertised in a local paper for the Hotel Principessa and was surprised to find Italo, my old Partisan comrade, doing the interviewing for the job. He was now the headwaiter for the hotel and he was delighted to see me. We hugged and kissed and spent the interview time catching up on old times. I was offered the job on the spot, and was asked to start the following morning at 7am sharp. I was to shadow a more experienced waiter for the first day, who would help me learn the ropes, and after that, I would be on my own.

Italo took me to meet the waiter I would be shadowing so that I would not be wasting anyone's time the next day. He introduced me to a girl about my own age whose name was Maria Fabiani. She was a bubbly type of person with long brown hair and was really quite good looking. I liked her straight away. I realised after the first two or three days that there was a mutual attraction between us, and after a few weeks in the job Maria and I started going out together. At first, we would just go to a movie after work and then, after a while, we progressed to going out for meals, followed afterwards by long chats over a coffee or a glass of wine at the Bar Regina, a trendy bar near the church of Santa Maria Delle Stelle in the city centre. We would sit and talk into the small hours about anything that came into our minds, laughing and joking over the silliest of things. Sometimes we would just sit holding hands and enjoying each other's company, but most of the time we sat talking about the things of the day. By this time, I was a confirmed communist atheist and Maria was an innocent Catholic conservative. I would kid her on about religion and she would pretend to pray for me. We would laugh at our differences, however, I wondered if her parents would laugh too, if I ever got to the point of meeting them.

It was a Monday evening in May and I was sitting in the Bar Regina waiting on Maria. Italo had arranged it so that we had our days off at the same time and we would usually spend them together. Maria came into the bar with her usual smile lighting up the room like a bright ray of sunshine. When she sat down beside me I could tell that she had something on her mind. After a while she said, 'Bruno, would you like to meet my parents on our next day off?' She shifted uneasily in her seat and before I could answer she continued, 'They are dying to meet you.'

Of course, I readily agreed, but I could tell there was something else on her mind.

'What is it Maria, what's troubling you?'

Maria was reticent to continue. Eventually, she plucked up the courage to say, 'My parents were asking me about your family Bruno and I had to tell them I don't know anything about them or anything about your background. It got me thinking that we have never spoken about your past and I wondered why.'

I was stunned. It had become such a way of life for me not to think about the events on Monte Sole and to try to blank out any thoughts of my family that I hadn't thought about the effect on Maria of never mentioning them. I held her hand tightly in mine and kept my gaze on my wine glass, afraid to look at her. 'Maria, it's not what you think. I find it very painful to talk about my family because of what happened to them. Have you heard about what the SS did on Monte Sole during the war?'

She nodded, 'They killed everyone there.'

'I witnessed my own family, every last one of them, being butchered by the SS just outside Marzabotto. I lost all of the members of my family in that *rastrallemento*. Mother, father, brothers, sister, even my aunt and uncle with their own family, so you can understand why I never talk about them. I even lost all of my friends and neighbours. Maybe one day I will tell you the story, but I think I have told you enough for you to understand.'

When I looked up again at Maria, she had tears running down her face. She picked up a tissue from the table and dried her eyes.

'Bruno, I had no idea. I'm so sorry for bringing this up please forgive me.'

'How could you possibly have known Maria, there is no forgiveness necessary, so let's have a glass of wine and put this behind us.'

We kissed and I felt the warmth of her lips and knew from that moment that I loved this girl and that I would spend the rest of my life with her.

On our next day off, we headed for the bus station and took a bus to Maria's parents' house. I had been invited there for lunch and I was feeling very nervous. This was the first time I had been in a family gathering since before the massacre and too many memories of my own family mealtimes were filling my mind. Maria held my hand as we knocked on the old oak door of the small town house. 'Remember Bruno, my father's name is Placido and my mother's name is Laura. Just be your usual good-natured self and they will love you.

The door was opened by Maria's mother who gave us both a big hug and asked us in. Her father was a tall man with a distinguished look about him, which was emphasised even more so by his grey hair and neatly trimmed beard. He politely shook my hand and offered me a glass of wine.

Over lunch, the subject of the war came up and Placido asked me if I had been involved in it. I simply answered yes.

He told me that he had fought with the Italian Army in North Africa and had been wounded in action fighting the British near Benghazi. He had been shipped out to a military hospital in Sicily for recuperation until the Allies landed and he was made a prisoner of war until 1944. The more the wine flowed the more Placido wanted to hear of my own military involvement. After more prompting, I finally gave him the story of my war, although when I spoke, I couldn't look him in the eye.

'I was only thirteen when the SS came to my village and murdered all my family. They killed my parents, three brothers and my baby sister. I also saw them kill my uncle and aunt and my young cousin. I watched the slaughter from a nearby hillside unable to help any of them. My mother was raped before my eyes before the SS slit her throat and killed her. My aunt had her unborn baby cut out from her womb and both of them were killed. When the slaughter had finished, I left Monte Sole and joined the partisans in Bologna. I fought the Germans until the war ended in April 1945. After a few years of different jobs, I volunteered for the Italian Army until I left that last year for the hotel.'

There was an embarrassed silence round the table. Placido put his arm round my shoulders and gave me a warm hug. 'You have seen much, Bruno, and suffered much. This has helped to make you the man you are now. I want you to consider this family as your own family from now on.' He gave me another hug and pushed a glass of wine into my hand. 'Maria tells me that she is in love with you and that you are in love with her, so I raise my glass in approval of this love. *Salute*!"

We all clinked our glasses together and I laughed out aloud at this unexpected acceptance into the family. That was how

I came to have this new love in my life, which changed me from being a loner to a man who cared with his whole life for another person.

Placido and I became great friends and we spent many hours talking about the things that a father and son would normally have talked about. He became almost as close to me as my father had been and this feeling was reciprocated as he treated me as the son he never had. Maria was delighted at our closeness and it seemed to confirm in her eyes that her love for me was meant to be.

Maria and I often spoke about her moving into my small flat in Bologna and eventually she made the break from her parents' house. We planned to get married in a few months' time with the wedding service being held in the church of Santa Maria Delle Stelle in Bologna, and the reception in the hotel Principessa. Even though I was an atheist, and would have preferred a civil ceremony, I realised that Maria needed the whole church experience to feel that she had been properly married. I asked Italo to be my best man and I was pleased that he agreed and said he was looking forward to the day. He had never been one for marriage and still considered it a bourgeois concept invented by the capitalist system to control the individual freedom of expression of the proletariat. Personally, I think he just wanted to bed as many women as possible without commitment.

Maria and I wanted to start a family straight away, which led to the conversation about where to live once married, as the flat was too small for children. Maria asked me about the properties in Marzabotto, 'Bruno, you have your family house outside the village and you are probably the legal owner of the farm as well. Do you think you could ever live there?' I was taken aback by this. I had never thought about living in Marzabotto and didn't think I could even visit the area, never mind living there. 'Maria, don't ask me to do this. The very thought of living there fills me with dread. I just couldn't do it.'

'I thought as much Bruno. What do you think about selling the house and the farm? What we could get from the sale may help us buy a place of our own in Bologna. What do you think?'

It sounded a sensible idea, but I just wasn't ready to talk about selling the properties just yet. I didn't want to talk about anything to do with Marzabotto; it was still too painful for me.

'Give me some more time Maria. It's still too fresh in my mind.'

'Bruno, it's 1958. It happened fourteen years ago. I know you still feel the loss, but what about when we have a family? Will you push them away when they ask about their grandparents and other family things, or will you be able to tell them about the good things you did on Monte Sole with your family and friends? You don't have to forget your family Bruno; it wasn't their fault they died, and it wasn't your fault either; however, it certainly will not be the fault of any children we may have in the future.'

I stood facing her open-mouthed. Maria was right. It was time to start living a normal life again and to try to put the horrors of what I witnessed on Monte Sole behind me. I could never forget what I saw, but I didn't need to have this dark cloud hanging over me and depressing me whenever I thought of my family. It was time to start a new life and hopefully a new family.

I contacted a estate agent in Bologna and sought his advice on what to do with the properties. Later on that day, I shared with Maria what he had told me.

'No one is living in the villages and farms on Monte Sole since the massacre and the Allied air raids that followed later. The Germans didn't leave there until just before the war ended when the whole mountain was targeted by Allied heavy bombing that eventually forced them out. Since then, vegetation has overgrown almost all of the ruins so it would be highly unlikely that anyone would find it an attractive proposition to buy there. There is also this shadow of the massacre hanging over the villages and you know how superstitious people can be.'

Maria gave a deep sigh, '*Que sera, sera* Bruno. Maybe in time it will change.'

As I stood in the church waiting on Maria, I glanced over at Italo who was standing there with a grin on his face.

I whispered in his ear, 'What's so funny, Italo?' He leaned over and whispered back to me, 'When we chased the girls together Bruno, you were always the one they fancied, so it's a joy for me to see you off the market from now on.' We laughed and hugged.

When the music played the entry anthem 'Ave Maria' everyone in the church stood as Maria and her father walked slowly down the aisle. I had never seen such a beautiful woman; she was radiant. The afternoon sun shining through the stained glass windows of the church seemed to focus solely on Maria as she walked towards me. Her smile matched the radiance of the sun itself. I knew without a doubt in my heart that I was in love with this woman and would be till the day I died.

Chapter 6

When the war ended, Hans Kuller was still in uniform and stationed near the Austrian border. He and the rest of his SS comrades knew that they had to very quickly decide what their next step was to be. Major Reder had already escaped to Germany and Kuller was thinking about leaving that very night for his home town of Munich in Bavaria. First, he would enter Austria and then make his way there. They were now having an open discussion in their barracks on what to do. Sergeant-Major Palframan stood up to address his comrades.

'The options are very clear, comrades. We are the SS, and in following orders, we had to do what many people would now view as war crimes. We can leave for Austria as an organised unit and disband there, or we can leave from here in civilian clothes individually.'

Kuller stood up to reply. 'You can all do as you wish. However, for me there is no alternative. I leave by myself tonight in the uniform of the Wehrmacht. My reason for this is very clear. If we leave from here as a disciplined body of SS soldiers, we will be arrested by the Americans or the British for alleged war crimes and put on trial. That trial may have one end: our execution. I will leave by myself in the uniform of a soldier of the Wehrmacht returning to his homeland. There will be many such soldiers on the road and I hope to go unnoticed amongst them.' He stood to his full height, gave the Nazi salute, and walked out the door.

It was early evening when he put on the uniform of a Feldwebel, a Sergeant in the Infantry and was about to leave the barracks for the vehicle compound when he came across some of his SS comrades in the courtyard. 'Hans, listen. We will have a better chance of escaping if we all leave together as Wehrmacht soldiers returning home. We all have fake ID and we can take a Wehrmacht truck for transport. What do you say?' Hans thought for a moment. 'What about the partisans? They may attack us if they see a small military unit.' His friend, Peter, an SS trooper, replied 'Even the partisans are not so stupid. Why would they risk their own lives to stop five or six German soldiers returning home? There are thousands of them swamping the roads still armed and trying to escape a POW camp.' Hans took his time in answering, 'All right lads, but we have to leave now. If partisans or allied troops stop us we will have to fight our way out as our IDs are not that good and may not stand scrutiny.'

They made for the vehicle compound and commandeered a military truck with no unit markings on it. Peter volunteered to drive and Kuller sat up front with him. The other four SS soldiers sat inside the truck with weapons primed and ready for action should they meet any trouble. They reckoned they were only about fifteen miles from the Austrian border and, if things went well, should be across it in a few hours.

They were beginning to relax when an explosion seemed to open up the road in front of them. This was quickly followed by the sound of small arms fire and voices shouting. The men in the back shouted 'Partisans!' and began returning fire. Kuller and Peter opened their doors and jumped out of the vehicle onto the roadside. Already standing there waiting for them on the road were about twenty men dressed in a variety of military clothing and holding sub-machine guns aimed at them. The leader of the group shouted, 'Sergeant, tell your men to stop firing or we will shoot to kill.' Kuller immediately shouted to his men, 'Cease fire, cease fire!' The SS men in the truck stopped shooting, and came out throwing down their weapons and raised their hands above their heads. The Partisan leader then said to Kuller and Peter, 'Lay down your side arms and raise your hands as well.' They did as they were told. The partisan leader said, 'We are the 10th Garibaldi Brigade, my name is Vittorio and we are authorised to check all transport heading to Austria for escaping Italian fascists, Nazis or SS personnel. I will need to see your identification papers and search the truck for anything suspicious.' Kuller could feel the tension in the air as the Italians went efficiently about their business. Eventually, the truck was cleared and Vittorio walked up to Kuller and asked him in German for his papers. Kuller and the rest of the men handed over their papers without a word. Vittorio took some time examining them before saying, 'Where are your orders for returning to Austria, Sergeant?' Kuller gave a short laugh and said, 'Orders, what orders? We just want to go home. The war is over and you have won, Vittorio. Just let us go home.' Vittorio seemed to accept this. 'Well, Sergeant, you can all go home. However, you will have to walk. We still have fascist militia to fight and we will need your weapons and transport for that. The border is only a few miles along the road and it is manned by British troops. They will see you are taken care of. Thank God, it's not the Russians. They are less friendly and are not taking any German prisoners.' Kuller thanked him. Turning to the rest of his group he said, 'All right, we can go home now, let's go.' Eventually they reached the border post, where they were strip-searched by British troops who then processed them into a POW camp where they would be eventually interviewed by the Military Police.

It did not take them long to find out that Kuller was in fact an SS Sergeant in the 16th Waffen SS. However, as there was no war crime listed against his name, they could not hold him for very long, and after some six months in a special SS prisoner of war camp in Nuremburg he was set free. The other SS men he had escaped with were found out to have been on the SS staff in the death camps in Poland and were put on trial. They were all convicted of crimes against humanity and were imprisoned for varying terms.

Kuller thanked his lucky stars that his unit had left no survivors on Monte Sole to come forward and testify that he was not only present there, but was one of the SS leaders. The British knew that his unit had been active in the killings but could not prove he had been with them at the time. He smiled as he made his way into Vienna to start a new life. His first thought was to find work and earn some money, which he did at a bakery near the city centre. The owner of the bakery had lost a son in the war and needed some help with his business. He took one look at Hans with his straight back and height and asked him if he had worked in a bakery before. Hans had helped an old uncle a few times in his bakery in Salsburg when he had visited with his family before the war when he was a boy. When he mentioned this to the baker, he jumped on this and offered Hans a job.

Kuller worked at the bakery for three months, sleeping in the back shop on an old mattress to save as much money as he could. The baker gave him his keep and a small salary, which Kuller managed to save for the next part of his journey. Eventually, he decided he had saved enough for his travel expenses and other costs to give him a start in Munich. The next morning, he said his farewells to the baker, thanked him for his help and left.

It was January 1946 when Kuller arrived in Munich. His first impressions of his home city on the bus ride left him feeling angry. There didn't seem to be a building standing. He found out later that Munich had been targeted seventy-seven times with heavy bombing raids during the war, and it had left the city with very little infrastructure. Everywhere he looked, he saw ruined buildings and people huddled in what was left of their homes. Long queues were lining up at the soup kitchens the Allies had set up to feed the population. He walked with a heavy heart along what was left of the once wide avenues of the city to his parent's house on Friedrich Strasse. When he got there, he stopped outside the ruined building of what had once been his house and just stared at the wreckage. 'This was my parent's home. Where are they? What happened to them?' He felt a fury welling up inside him, but it wasn't aimed at the Allies for what they had done to his city, or what he could see in front of him. It was the Jews he blamed for all of this. Those damn Jews are responsible. Hitler was right. If there had been no Jews in Europe left to speak against us in America and Britain there would have been no war.

He was about to walk away when he heard his name being called. He turned to see an old woman he recognised as a neighbour of his parents'. 'Hans, is that you? Thank God you're safe.'

'Mrs Prellwitz, it's good to see you again. Tell me, do you know what happened to my parents? Have they moved away?

Mrs Prellwitz joined her hands together as if in prayer. 'They were killed in the last bombing raid. It was early morning and most of us were still in bed when they came. There was no warning. The bombs just suddenly fell. We had no chance. I was pulled from the wreckage with just a broken leg but my husband was killed.' She started crying.

Kuller walked away without a word.

'I'll find somewhere to rent, then I'll get a job' he thought. 'I've got enough money saved to last a little while longer. Maybe there's a vacancy in a bakery; I've got the experience to handle that now.'

He walked away without another thought for his parents. As far as Kuller was concerned, they were just another casualty of war and he had seen plenty of those.

Chapter 7

It was in 1960 when I found myself nervously sitting in the Maternity Hospital waiting for news. Maria was in the delivery ward having our first baby and I was feeling very anxious about the whole experience. What added to my nervousness was she had been in there for over twelve hours and I wasn't allowed to see her. The doctor had said that the baby was tangled up in something or other and it was going to be a complicated job setting it free. It was moments like this that I felt my lack of a proper formal education. Because I had left school at the age of thirteen, I found myself ignorant of understanding things like how the human body worked. The doctor had mentioned things I didn't understand but knew that I should, so I nodded my head as if I did.

I heard the sound of a baby crying and it sounded as if it came from behind the green swing doors facing me. I sat upright in the chair and wondered if it was mine.

Then, a doctor came out to see me. 'Well, Signor Verdi, everything went very well, although your wife is very tired and she is resting at the moment with your son.' It took a moment for this to sink in.

'A son, doctor? Are they both all right? When can I see them?'

The doctor laughed. 'Yes, they are both fine and I can let you see them both for a few minutes today, but that's all. She really does need rest.'

I got off my seat and followed a nurse into a small side room. Maria was lying in bed with our new-born baby in her arms and she indeed looked exhausted. Her hair was soaked in sweat, but through her tiredness I saw a look of joy in her eyes as she gazed at her baby. I walked up to them and gently kissed Maria on her cheek before kissing my son on his head.

'Are you happy Bruno? I knew you wanted a boy first so I thought I'd surprise you,' she said in a weak voice. I just looked at my son. I couldn't take my eyes off him. I stretched out my hand and very gently held his hand in mine.

'Maria, I couldn't be happier. Let's call him Moreno, after my father, and we'll call our next child after your parents.' Maria nodded. I could see that she wanted to rest, so I kissed her again and left.

Moreno proved to be a great blessing in my life. I loved to hold him in my arms and tickle his tummy. His squeals of delight filled our new home with the sounds of family love. We had now rented a three bedroom terraced house that wasn't far from Maria's parents' house. The rent was a large chunk of our salary and, with Maria now only working part-time, we didn't have much left over at the end of the month. I was also studying for the civil service exams that were held every year, and if I passed them, I hoped to be accepted as an administrator with the local Council. The pay was much better than I made at the Principessa and there was even a pension at the end of your working life.

My friendship with Placido had deepened and it came as a shock to us all when he had a stroke that took his speech away from him. This once animated man became a quiet figure sitting in his armchair in the kitchen. He seemed to lose heart quite quickly and it was no great surprise to the family when he died the following year; a great sadness fell over us all for quite a considerable time. Maria was concerned at her mother being alone and I knew without asking that she wanted her to move in with us. And so she did. Now we were a real Italian family.

Moreno was growing up to be a real country boy with a love of fishing, hunting and the outdoor life. One time, when he was about fourteen years old, we went hunting together for wild boar in the wonderful countryside surrounding

Bologna. Wild boar is a very dangerous animal to hunt. They can suddenly charge you from their hiding place and maul you with the horns on their snout, giving you a nasty gash. We also knew that over the years some hunters had been killed by them. Moreno thought that it added a little spice to the hunt.

As we entered some dense undergrowth with our rifles at the ready, I was charged by one from behind. He caught me with his horns with such force that I was propelled to the ground, injured in my right leg. As I fell, I saw Moreno calmly raise his rifle and take aim as the boar charged once again, this time at him. He fired, and the animal squealed as it dropped dead literally at Moreno's feet. He rushed over to me and looked at my wounds, which, thankfully, were not really that serious. I had two deep gashes on my calf which were bleeding quite freely. Luckily we had some ointment and bandages in our backpacks, which - with a snort of Brandy from my hip flask - soon had me limping back to our car, dragging behind us a large dead boar. I was so proud of my son that day. How he had stood in front of a charging boar calmly taking his aim had taken great courage from him. Needless to say, we lived well off the carcase and the storytelling for quite a long time.

As he got older, he began to ask more questions about his family and the massacre on Monte Sole. I found it very difficult to talk to him about these things, and only gave him curt answers and so I suspect he asked his mother for more details.

Moreno, according to his school reports, was considered an average student and therefore had decided not to stay on and try for university. So, when the time came for him to leave school at the age of eighteen and find a job, he was delighted. It didn't take him long to find work. A large estate outside Bologna was looking for an estate warden, and to his delight, he was successful. His job was to control the wildlife on the estate that could endanger the farm stock; foxes in particular. He was also to prevent poachers stealing fish from the river, and laying traps for the wild animals, and because he loved the countryside so much, this was his dream job and I was happy for him. Maria was also happy as it meant he would continue staying at home, at least for the meantime.

It was early in 1980 when Moreno and I had our first real conversation about the events on Monte Sole. It was after our evening meal and I was sitting at the table enjoying an espresso when Moreno said, 'Papà, I went with some friends to Monte Sole yesterday and I visited Marzabotto. We also went to the cemetery at Casaglia.'

It was strange hearing those names from my son's lips, and I wasn't sure what to say in return. I looked at Moreno in silence as he continued. 'I understand, Papà, that you still feel the pain of what happened, but I wanted you to know that I also feel the pain. It was my family as well.'

He got up from his seat and hugged me. I felt the tears well up from deep within me and I cried on his chest like a baby. This was my twenty-year old son telling me that he felt the pain as well, and that I wasn't alone in it anymore. I had carried it for thirty-six years, and it's true what people say that a burden shared is a burden halved. I cried on his chest as I had never cried before. What had been bottled up inside of me came flooding out in a torrent of tears. I found that I was now able to talk to him about the massacre in a way that I could not with anyone else because it was also his family, his blood, as well as mine, that was spilled that fateful day. Even though my son and I had always been close, this was a new bond being forged between us. A bonding of two men joined by a common tragedy and I have to say it did help me a little further along the road.

I was in the habit of visiting my local market once or twice a week when my shifts in the hotel allowed it. I liked to cook with fresh vegetables and various rare cuts of meat that were sometimes difficult to find in the shops. I also enjoyed the banter with the stall holders and I usually passed some time talking to some of the local people I knew. One day, as I was standing at a stall waiting to be served, a stranger pushed his way past me and began shouting, quite aggressively, in broken Italian to the stall holder. Old Franco, the stall holder, had apparently made a mistake with the stranger's change and he was now enraged. I had known Franco for many years and I knew that he was as honest as the day is long. I listened to the stranger's accent and realised that he was German. I could see that Franco was quite shaken by the verbal abuse the German was giving him so I decided to intervene. I tapped him on the shoulder and said, 'Please don't shout at the old man like that, it's obviously just a mistake.'

The German turned to face me and with anger filling his eyes said, 'What the hell has this to do with you? This old thief owes me money, so just clear off.'

He gave me a shove which moved me back a few feet. The thought ran quickly through my head: *the days when Germans could come to Italy and act like this are over. I'll teach him a lesson.*

A red haze came over me and, before I knew what I was doing, I sprang forward and struck the German with two powerful punches to the face. He went down and I stood over him and said, 'Don't think you Germans can come to Italy and do what you want anymore. If you need more convincing, then just stand up.' I peeled a few lira notes from my pocket and threw them at him. 'This should cover Franco's mistake. Take it and go home.' The German just lay there on the ground looking at me in amazement, but he had the good sense to stay down. I turned and walked away. My mind was churning. Did I hit him because of his attitude to Franco, or did I hit him because he was a German? Would I have been so angry if he had been an Italian?

I reckoned that there was a mixture of both in there, but the one thing I couldn't deny was that I enjoyed thumping him.

At last, the news that I had been hoping for came through. I had passed my civil service exams and had been accepted as a junior administrator in the department of employment in Bologna. The salary was a lot more than what I had been earning as a waiter at the Principessa, including my tips, and it meant that we could now afford things that we never could before. Another factor was I would not have to work crazy shift hours in the hotel anymore. When I told Italo that I was leaving, I could see that he was sorry to lose me, however we promised to keep in touch and to meet regularly for a coffee or a glass of wine at one of the many bars in the city.

It was a Saturday morning in 1984 when we were having a morning coffee together in a new Café not far from the city centre when we saw in the newspapers that Reder had written an open letter to the Italian Government apologising for the atrocity on Monte Sole and asking for forgiveness from the Italian people. This was followed up over the next few weeks by a campaign orchestrated by the Catholic Church and the Austrian Government to have Reder released back into society. Italo and I watched this develop with great interest. We even discussed if Reder was released if we should attempt to kill him, or whether he had paid enough for his crime with the thirty-three years to date he had spent in prison. It was only idle talk, but it brought to my mind Hans Kuller. If I could find out where he was, then I would go there and kill him with great pleasure and without a moment's hesitation.

Italo seemed to voice my thoughts, 'Would you kill Reder if you had the chance?'

I thought for a moment. 'He wasn't on the mountain during the massacre. I know he did the planning and gave the order for the *rastrallemento* but he has served a long prison sentence as a punishment for that.'

'What about Kuller?'

'He's a different matter. He killed unarmed civilians for pleasure, not just once but probably hundreds of times. He killed them in the most horrific ways imaginable, and he made no distinction between men, women and children. He deserves to be killed and if I could find him I would kill him without a second thought.'

'It's strange, Bruno, that we were killing these people legally during the war, but as soon as some Generals signed a piece of paper ending the conflict, our fight against them had to stop, even though some atrocities personal to us still go unpunished.' He took a sip of his coffee as we sat together in a silence, only broken by the murmur of voices around us.

I was the first to speak. 'The signing of that paper could change me from being a heroic partisan to a murderer in the eyes of the State. It's all a matter of perception and timing. I believe that my quest for justice was thwarted by this so-called peace, and that I cannot personally find peace until Kuller has paid for his crimes.'

We held each other's gaze for some time and I felt Italo's eyes burn deep within me, until he finally spoke. 'The Stella Rosa partisans who were killed that day were armed fighters and knew well the risk they took fighting the *tedeschi*, but the villagers were different. I knew many of them as friends.' He stopped speaking for a moment as he choked up with emotion. 'I promise you Bruno, if we find out where Kuller is, I will go with you to kill that piece of shit and, if need be, I'll be prepared to be called a murderer by the State.'

We stood up and embraced each other as the tears ran down our faces, merging into one. I sometimes look back at that moment and think how it was so like the ancient initiation ceremonies of pricking fingers and merging blood to symbolise the bond of a familial blood line. We had always been friends but now we were as one, with the same desire to see justice finally won for our friends and family.

Chapter 8

Kuller soon found a job in a small bakery not far from where he was born. The owner was someone Kuller knew from their Nazi party days in the city and who Kuller knew was still sympathetic to the extreme right wing ethos. He worked hard in the bakery and soon earned the owner's respect. He was even offered a room over the bakery in the family house, which Kuller readily accepted.

He also saw an opportunity to ingratiate himself further by making advances to the owner's daughter, who was not exactly a pretty girl. One night, when they were in the house alone, Kuller made his move and after a few drinks he seduced her. The girl, whose name was Gertrude, was so overjoyed at such a handsome man finding her attractive that she readily entered into an affair with Kuller. It wasn't before long that she found herself pregnant with his child. Gertrude, with Kuller not far behind her, approached her father with the news. The father, being a pragmatist, realised that he had two choices for his not-so-attractive daughter. The first being a daughter with a child and no husband. The second being a daughter with a husband and a father for the child. He quickly gave them his blessing.

In Kuller's eyes, there was no such thing as romance or love: only duty and honour and so he proved himself a good provider for his family. The baker, who was getting on in age, turned a blind eye to the occasional bruising he saw on Gertrude's face and body. After all, what a husband and wife did in private was no concern of his.

For Kuller, the world around him had turned into something he despised. What with the partition of his beloved Fatherland into two separate countries and the Jews being allowed to return to Germany, he strongly felt the injustice of it all. Now the Jews even have their own country called Israel, which was supported by Americans and the United Nations. What next? A Jewish Chancellor in Germany?

The one thing that he really looked forward to was the quarterly gathering of his former comrades in the SS. The 16th Waffen SS Old Comrades Association. They met in hotels throughout West Germany and Austria with the strict rule that no outsiders were allowed to attend, especially members of the press. After one such meeting in 1978 in Frankfurt, Kuller and a few ex-comrades were drinking in their hotel bar in the city centre, and were still in celebratory mode after their meeting, when he saw a man wearing a Jewish skullcap walking past them in the bar. Kuller, fuelled by alcohol, threw all caution to the wind and attacked him. He never even spoke a word to him. He waited until he was just passing before he turned to face him and smashed his glass tumbler on the bar and thrust it into the Jews face, much to the amusement of his other comrades. The Jew fell to the ground in agony and Kuller, apparently not satisfied with the result of his unprovoked attack, stood on the man's face grinding the glass further into his wounds. The police were called and Kuller was arrested. He was handcuffed and spent the night in a police cell. The following morning, he appeared before a Magistrate and pleaded guilty. He was given a three-year sentence. The Magistrate said in his summation of the case, 'In all my years on the bench I have never witnessed such savagery. Your victim is permanently blinded by your attack and faces life as a disabled man. I am also appalled by your lack of contrition and I have no hesitation in sentencing you to the maximum sentence I am allowed by law to give; a three-year prison term to be served in all its entirety.' Kuller showed no emotion as he was led away. *There was a time in this country when I would have received a commendation for what I did!* – he thought – *Curse these Jewish vermin and their allies. They have deceived the world into thinking they are the victims of a conspiracy against them, when the truth is they are the ones who have formed a world-wide Zionist conspiracy to control the worlds banking systems.*

For Kuller to be in the disciplined environment of a prison was no great shock or ordeal. Because he had spent many years as a disciplined soldier taking orders, he felt no great discomfort meeting the requirements of the prison regime. His fellow inmates were unsure of how to approach him at first because of his obvious size and strength, and he simply became known as "the quiet man" to the prison population. Kuller's approach to prison servitude was simply to do his time and to do it without bitterness. He was guilty as charged but in his eyes, he couldn't understand all the fuss surrounding the attack: after all, it was only a Jew he had assaulted.

He took to physical exercise as a duck takes to water. He found it the perfect release for his pent-up frustration at being cooped up in prison.

One afternoon, as he was training, a new guard he hadn't seen before came on duty in the gym. Kuller watched as he made his rounds introducing himself to all the inmates exercising there. When he came to Kuller he stopped and said, 'Hello, what's your name?' Kuller looked at him and stopped his training on the barbells. 'My name is Hans Kuller, guard. What's yours?'

The guard gave a smile and said 'My name is Guard Cohen.'

Kuller stared at him with obvious hatred in his eyes. 'Are you a Jew?'

The Guard's smile vanished as he said, 'Is that a problem, Kuller?'

'It certainly is, I didn't think we had missed any of you bastards so it's a surprise to find one left.'

Cohen moved closer to Kuller and said, 'Remember, Kuller, the roles are reversed now. I'm in authority here, not you bloody Nazis.'

Kuller smiled at him, 'How could I forget, Guard Cohen. Just watch your back.'

Cohen turned on his heels and walked out the gym.

Later that night, Kuller heard the sound of voices gathered outside his cell. His instincts told him it meant he was in trouble. He had just stood up to face the door, when it opened and Guard Cohen stood there with three other guards. Cohen turned to Kuller's cellmate and said 'Take a walk with the guard; we want to have a chat with your friend.' When the prisoner had left with his escort, Cohen turned to Kuller saying 'Is there anything else you would like to mention about me being Jewish, you piece of shit?' Kuller laughed in his face, 'Pity your people didn't show the same bravery when they went to their deaths like lambs.'

Cohen and his two companions entered the cell and closed the door behind them. They then set about Kuller with their batons, taking care not to hit his face. The blows fell on his shoulders, sides and midriff until Kuller fell to the ground winded and in pain. He never cried out or asked them to stop the beating. It just wasn't in his makeup to ask for mercy. Cohen then kicked him a few times in the groin, just as a parting gift.

When they had finished with the beating, Guard Cohen stood over Kuller and said, 'Is there anything else you would like to say, Kuller?'

Kuller slowly pulled himself up to a sitting position and looked Cohen directly in the eye before saying, 'No Guard Cohen, I've said all I ever want to say to you.'

Cohen and his friends left him on the floor and locked the cell door after them.

When his cellmate came back, he asked Kuller what had happened to him. Kuller stared at him before answering, 'I fell off the top bunk and I think I must have broken a few ribs.'

Word soon got round the other prisoners that Kuller was a marked man with the guards. He never told anyone what happened that night, and he never gave an opinion on any of the Guards. He just bided his time for an opportunity to strike back.

As he lay in his cell, he worked on a plan and finally after a few days he was ready to put it into action.

Every morning, at the beginning of the working day, the prisoners had to stand outside their cells for inspection by the guards, and Kuller had worked it out that it was Cohen's turn to inspect the prisoners every fourth day. His cell was on the upper floor at the end of a row beside a metal staircase leading to the ground floor, and on the appointed morning when Cohen was inspecting the prisoners, Kuller was standing waiting on him approaching him. When he did, he briefly stopped in front of Kuller and said, 'Well, is there anything you would like to say to me?'

Kuller just shook his head and just stared at the ground.

As Cohen walked past him to use the stairway, Kuller timed his move to perfection. He stuck his foot out in front of Cohen's legs, causing him to stumble and fall head first down the staircase. He bounced a couple of times off some metal treads and lay on the ground with his neck sitting at a strange angle.

Kuller could see that the fall had killed Cohen outright. The prison authorities interviewed all the prisoners on the upper floor and asked them what they had seen. No one had noticed anything unusual and certainly hadn't seen Kuller's leg trip the guard. When Kuller was interviewed, he told them he had seen nothing except Guard Cohen flying past him down the staircase. The prison authorities held an official enquiry into the "accident" and even though they suspected Kuller's involvement, they couldn't pin anything on him. The official verdict on Cohen's death was that it was accidental and that no prisoner was involved. Kuller kept quiet on the "accident" and never even hinted to anyone that he had anything to do with it. In his own mind, he thought thatmust be the only benefit that democracy offers, that you are innocent until proven guilty.

Once again, the prison grapevine told the story that he had killed Cohen and that the other prison guards involved in the beating would be next.

Kuller was approached in his cell soon after by one of the guards who had taken part in the beating. He said to him, 'Kuller, I don't know if what they say about you is true, but I know your past history in the SS. I'm a married man with a family and I don't want an accident happening to me.'

As a final retort he added, 'I also served in the military and, like you, was also an infantry soldier at Stalingrad.' Kuller studied him for a moment in silence before saying to him,' 'What you did to me was out of loyalty to a comrade. Misplaced loyalty to a Jew over a German, but you still showed commendable loyalty. I would have done the same as you did. Don't worry about any accidents happening to you.' The guards thanked him and was about to leave when Kuller added, 'Tell your other friends that I also respect their loyalty in this affair, but to never again choose a Jew over a German, especially one who has served his country.'

Kuller spent the rest of his sentence being respected as a man not to be trifled with by prisoners and guards alike, and he never had any further problems.

He was released in 1981 and immediately returned home to be with his family. His wife, who wasn't sure what to expect from her returning spouse, was greeted by a slap round the head for not having a meal ready and waiting for him, and so life returned to what passed for normality in the Kuller household.

At the next meeting of the Old Comrades Association, Kuller was treated as a celebrity who had upheld the values that they all espoused. He was asked to give an impromptu speech to the gathering which he readily did.

'Dear comrades, the honour you give me is indeed touching. You all know that because of the Jewish menace, we now find ourselves with a divided country and Bolshevism living next door to us. Let us not forget what our Führer taught us, the values of purity of race, obedience and honour. It is our sacred duty to re-educate the German people in this and to remain faithful to our oath.'

The room erupted with wild cheering and hand-clapping. Former SS soldiers thumped the tables and impromptu singing broke out. Kuller felt elated as the words of the Horst-Wessel-Lied rose up all around him. As he gave the Nazi salute, tears filled his eyes as his comrades followed his example.

Sometime later in 1984, as he was driving in Munich with Gertrude sitting beside him, he was involved in an accident when another car came speeding out of a side street and crashed into the side of his vehicle. Thankfully, no one was injured. Kuller got out of his car and approached the other driver, who by this time was inspecting the damage to the vehicles. The driver was very apologetic to Kuller, 'I am so sorry, sir. It is my fault entirely, please accept my apology.' This seemed to pacify Kuller until it came to exchanging insurance details. Kuller looked at the man's name in amazement, 'Your name is Goldman. Are you Jewish?'

Herr Goldman, not knowing the fury that was about to fall on him answered, 'Yes I am. Is that a problem?'

'Problem, problem,' roared Kuller, as he stepped forward and punched Herr Goldman in the face with such ferocity that he was knocked to the ground. As Goldman tried to get up Kuller kicked him repeatedly in the face, on his body, anywhere he could. Gertrude tried to stop him but Kuller slapped her round the face a few times, knocking her to the ground as well.

He began shouting out as the blows rained down on Goldman, 'There was a time when we could treat Jewish scum like you anyway we wanted.'

Eventually he stopped. A crowd had gathered on the pavement watching with amazement what had happened. Kuller helped his wife to her feet and they walked away towards their car. They drove off without another word. When the police arrived, Mr Goldman couldn't tell them who his assailant was, as he had no idea of his name. In the small crowd that had gathered, apparently, no one had thought to take down Kuller's licence number. Even though Kuller had lived in the area with his wife for many years, no one admitted to recognising him. The description given of a tall blonde man could have fitted a high percentage of the German male population in the town, so Kuller was not traced. He realised that the damage to his car was a giveaway, so he visited an auto-body shop belonging to a former comrade and the car was repaired with no record of the work being done and no questions asked.

When the police, on a routine enquiry, asked the owner of the auto-body shop if he knew anything about a damaged black Volkswagen Beetle, he just shrugged his shoulders and said no.

Herr Goldman was in hospital for some time with a fractured jaw, broken limbs and ribs. However, the greatest damage done to him was that once again he had become frightened to walk German streets as a Jew.

Kuller first heard the news that Walter Reder could possibly be released from his Italian prison from someone at the Old Comrades meeting. Apparently, Reder had apologised to the Italian Government through an open letter. Kuller laughed at this and called it nonsense, a mere ruse by Reder to help him in his campaign for release.

He wrote to Reder congratulating him on his expected release and to ask him if he would when freed be the guest speaker at a reunion dinner of the 16th Waffen SS Old Comrades Association, which would be held in his honour in his home city of Vienna. Reder answered that he would be delighted to, and also that he was pleased to hear from others that sergeant Hans Kuller was still being faithful to his SS oath. Kuller laughed. *I knew that Walter Reder could not change. Even after all these years of imprisonment, this man of steel is still the same. His beliefs have not diminished and the flame of National Socialism still burns true in his heart.*

In 1985, the news that Kuller was waiting for arrived. It was announced in the German press that Walter Reder was to be released within the next few weeks. Kuller was overjoyed with this news. He even took Gertrude out for a meal to celebrate, much to her surprise. He contacted as many of his closest ex-SS comrades as he could and organised a party to celebrate Reder's release and to plan a reception in his honour in Vienna. He even contacted the Austrian Defence minister Herr Frischenschlager to tell him that the last Austrian prisoner of war, incarcerated in an Italian jail, was about to be released after thirty-four years. Herr Frischenschlager, who had been completely unaware of Reder, or his imprisonment up to this point, promised to meet him with full military honours on his arrival at the airport. His office even informed the Austrian television stations of the event in order to get the greatest publicity. The minister saw this as the dawn of a new era for Austria. The past forgotten and the future lying wide open. The only thing missing in all of this hype was that Kuller conveniently forgot to mention to the minister that Reder was not a prisoner of war but was in fact a convicted war criminal who had been sentenced to life imprisonment in a military court in Siena for the massacre of Italian civilians on Monte Sole and Sant' Anna di Stazzema.

Finally, the big day arrived. The Defence minister was in attendance with a military band. The television cameras of Austria's three television stations were ready and waiting for Reder's plane to appear. The ranks of newspaper journalists were waiting to hear from Reder's own lips, the returning war hero, how it felt to be free again.

At last the plane landed and the official delegation, comprising of the Minister of Defence, the Mayor of Munich, the Colonel of Police and the local military Commander all lined up to meet their guest of honour. To the side of the runway, Kuller and his Old Comrades Association stood to attention to receive their distinguished and beloved leader.

The moment Reder appeared at the head of the steps that were covered in red carpet to suit the occasion, the band struck up the Austrian national anthem. Herr Frischenschlager stepped forward to shake Reder's hand and introduced him to the assembled dignitaries, who then followed on behind as Reder inspected his Old Comrades honour guard.

Kuller face was beaming as Reder approached him and warmly shook his hand before embracing him. The television cameras mounted on their mobile platforms captured every word and every moment and transmitted it throughout Austria to the delight of the population. There was even a link-up with RAI Italian television for their early evening news bulletin. Reder was still big news. Even more so now that he had been accepted by the Austrian establishment in the person of the Minister of Defence as a returning war hero. The Catholic Church even presented him with a hunting lodge in the Austrian Alps as a temporary home until he was settled, and it wasn't too long before the Austrian government, on behalf of the Austrian people, gifted him a home of his own. It is interesting to note that it was around this time that Reder rescinded the letter of apology he had written to the municipality of Marzabotto and to the Italian people in general, stating that as a soldier, he had merely done his duty and followed orders, therefore he felt no guilt or remorse.

The feelings of outrage and disbelief in Italy at Reder's rehabilitation and integration into Austrian society sounded loud and clear in the Italian media. It was universally condemned as unprecedented and dangerous for a tried and convicted war criminal to be feted by the Austrian government, people, and media in such an outward display of affection. It was an insult to the Italian people and to the memory of those slain.

Vatican sources in Rome and the hierarchy of the Catholic Church in Italy and Austria then went into overdrive and were instrumental in bringing to an end the ill feelings generated by the Austrian government's actions.

Chapter 9

I was sitting at home with my family and had just finished eating my evening meal and was enjoying my after dinner espresso. I called out to Moreno, 'Would you switch on the evening news, please.' Moreno picked up the remote control and the screen came to life. It was filled with a newsreader presenting the news of Reder's release and his reception at the airport. The picture then changed from the newsreader in the studio to the airport runway at Vienna.

I sat in shock and watched the screen in silence. Maria came in from the kitchen and sat beside me, holding my hand. Moreno turned the sound up.

The presenter on the ground was describing the scene as Reder inspected his honour guard. I froze as I recognised Kuller shaking his hand and embracing him.

'It's him, Kuller.' I stood and shouted out aloud. Moreno reached over to the cassette recorder and turned it on to record the events so we could watch it later. 'He's a little fatter and his hair is greyer, but that is Kuller.'

I stopped talking to take in the scene in front of me. The presenter was interviewing Reder on the runway before he left with his friends.

'I understand that your Old Comrades Association is arranging a special reception for you, Herr Reder.'

'Yes they are. It's on Friday night at the Hotel Bristol and I understand that most of my old comrades in arms will be there. I am looking forward to that.'

'What does it feel like to return to your homeland as a war hero so many years after the war ended?'

'I served my country and did my duty to the best of my ability and the honours I was presented with then are still relevant today in my eyes.'

In the background, the honour guard was being dismissed and some of them were heading over to where Reder was. I watched transfixed as Kuller appeared over Reder's shoulder. Reder looked round and saw them, then said to the TV presenter, 'These were my men. They served with me in battle.' He pointed to Kuller 'This man was my sergeant, Hans Kuller. He also served the Fatherland and did his duty as required.'

The screen changed back to the TV studio and the newsreader with a different news item.

Moreno looked at me, waiting for some reaction from me on seeing Kuller. I was very quiet. *He's too quiet for his own good. I wonder what he's thinking of.*

I got up from my seat and reached for my jacket. Without a word, I put it on and left the house. I drove around the city for a while before I eventually stopped outside the hotel where Italo worked. When I walked in, I saw Italo standing at the main doors to the kitchen looking thoughtful. I wondered if he had seen the news bulletin as well.

'Italo, did you see it?' Italo looked at me for a few moments before saying, 'We have to talk, Bruno. I'll take my break now and we can go for a coffee down the street.' We walked along together in silence, both of us thinking the same thing, both planning things in our minds. Every so often, our eyes would meet and we both knew.

We sat at a corner table and drank our coffee in silence until I said. 'Can you get the time off. The reception is being held in two days' time so we would only need three days to do it.'

Italo nodded. 'You would need to phone in sick for those days, Bruno. We can come up with a definitive plan as we travel to Vienna.'

I asked, 'Do you still have your gun?

Italo nodded. 'Do you still have yours, Bruno?'

'Yes, I've kept it in good condition just in case I ever found out where Kuller was.' I pulled out a railway timetable from my pocket and put it on the table. 'I picked this up last week. It shows a train leaving early tomorrow morning, and with a change in Austria, it arrives in Vienna at three in the afternoon. Kuller will probably have a room booked at the hotel Bristol where the reception is being held. We can also book a room there by phone or we can hit him before or after the event then leave. What do you think Italo?'

Italo thought for a moment or two. 'It sounds all right to me, except how do we know Kuller will not be sharing a room with someone else?'

'We don't. We can ask at the hotel reception what the situation is and change our plan to suit. I'll also tell Maria that we are going fishing for a few days up north. She probably won't believe me, but what can she prove?'

'Have you thought Bruno how we are going to kill him?'

'I have a plan forming in my mind. I'll share it later once I've thought it through myself. In the meantime, I think it's better if I go home now, as Maria will be worried about me after seeing the news. I'll see you at the train station tomorrow morning. Oh, by the way, I nearly forgot. We better get dressed as if we are going to the reception. We don't want to stand out from the rest, do we?'

The two friends stood and embraced each other. Italo looked searchingly at me before saying, 'I know you lost everything on Monte Sole, but I also lost many comrades and people I knew as friends. Don't think you can't trust me to see this through.' I nodded, 'I trust, you my friend. This has been a long time coming and no matter how it turns out, I know we will see it through together.' We embraced once more and then parted.

When I returned home, I was met by an anxious wife and son. 'Where have you been?' said Maria.

'Just driving around trying to get my head straight. I passed by the hotel, saw Italo and arranged a fishing trip over the next couple of days. I think it will do me good just to get away from all this.'

'Are you planning something stupid Bruno, like going to Vienna and killing Kuller?'

I looked her in the eye and said, 'It did cross my mind, but what would it achieve now, after all these years?'

'Promise me on your mother's grave you are not planning something against him.'

I gave a sigh. 'I promise you on my mother's grave I will not go to Vienna to kill him or anyone else. I just want to get away from all of this for a few days with my best friend.'

This seemed to satisfy Maria. She kissed me on the lips and said, 'I know you won't break that promise, Bruno. I think a fishing trip is just the thing you need.' She left the room a lot happier than before. I turned to Moreno, who all this time had been studying me. 'What's wrong, son?'

Moreno said, 'I know you too well dad, you're going to Vienna to kill him and I want to be there when you do it. I won't say to mum, but I want to go with you.'

'Moreno, I won't try to fool you. We leave for Vienna tomorrow morning; however, it is impossible to take you with me.'

Moreno scowled, 'Tell me why.'

'I need you here to look after your mother in case I don't return. Anyway, you haven't been involved in anything like this before and I can't take the risk of Kuller getting to you first. He's killed enough of my family. This man is a brute, and it will take brutish methods to kill him. He can smell danger.'

Maria came back into the room, saw us both in deep conversation, and asked, 'What are you two talking about?'

'I'm trying to convince dad to let me go with him fishing but he said no. He wants to be alone with Italo.' He made a "I know something" face and laughed.

I smiled at him and mouthed 'Thank you'.

The train proved to be quite crowded that morning. Italo and I moved along the carriages until we found two aisle seats beside each other. With people all around us, it was impossible to discuss anything about our mission. I said to Italo, 'Let's just spend the time thinking of what's ahead of us and we'll discuss it later.' He agreed.

I settled down for the long trip and began to focus on Kuller.

He will probably be in the company of around one hundred ex-SS comrades. Men who have lived and fought together over a number of years. *We are going to walk into the hotel, kill Kuller and leave again without being noticed. Apart from that, we don't have any idea yet on how to do it.* I shook my head in disbelief at this and looking round I caught Italo smiling at me. 'Not so easy Bruno, eh?' I smiled back at him.

Our journey was in two parts, as we had to change trains for Vienna once we arrived in Austria. It was around 4pm, later than expected due to maintenance work on the line, when our train pulled into Wien Westbahnhof railway station, the magnificent heart of the Austrian railway system built on two levels. We used the integrated underground system to make our way to Karntner Ring where the hotel Bristol was situated near the State Opera House. In any other circumstances, it would have been a treat to go to the opera together. We were both lovers of Puccini and that night *La Bohème* was being performed.

We had agreed beforehand that because we didn't know what to expect inside the hotel, it wasn't possible to come up with a definite plan of action, so we would just have to react to whatever we saw inside or to any situation that developed. One thing in our favour was that neither Kuller, Reder, nor any of the Old Comrade's Association knew us by sight or by name.

We walked inside the hotel and went up to the reception. Italo, who could speak good German after his years serving them in the hotel trade, booked us in and was handed a key for room 485 on the top floor. He then asked the receptionist for a sheet of hotel paper and a pen and stood to the side of the main desk. He wrote on it 'Looking forward to seeing you later.' and signed it with a single letter "R". 'What's that for?' I asked him.

'Just a ploy to find out Kuller's room number.'

'Why did you sign it "R"?'

'I'm pretty sure amongst all this crowd there would be someone he knows whose name begins with "R", so I don't think it will alert him and put him on his guard."

He gave the note to the receptionist and said 'Would you put this in Herr Kuller's key box, please?' The receptionist took it saying, "Certainly, sir." 'As we watched, she turned and placed it in one of the key boxes behind her: number 118.

We then walked to the rear of the reception area and sat down in two large armchairs away from any eavesdroppers. The only other people there were an elderly Italian couple speaking softly to each other. The man was about eighty years old, clean shaven and used a walking stick. He was dressed in a light coloured suit and shoes and smiled our way as we sat down. His wife was of a similar age, well dressed and held her husband's hand as she spoke to him. We sat away from them and continued our conversation.

I spoke first. 'His key was still there so he isn't in his room yet. I think we should go up and prepare a surprise for him.'

Bruno rubbed his chin as if in deep thought. 'What if he comes in with friends?'

'We'll face that if it happens. It's just as likely he'll come in alone.'

'Let's do it then,' said Italo.

We got up and made for the stairs rather than the lift. Less chance of someone remembering our faces. We went first of all to our room to leave our bags and to retrieve our weapons. We made sure that our guns were loaded before we put them in our trouser waistbands. We walked down the stairs to the first floor and casually strolled along the corridor. Room 118 was about half way along.

Italo studied the lock on the door. 'Thankfully it's not one of the modern electronic key cards. It's a key lock.' We each put on a pair of thin household gloves to prevent leaving any fingerprints. Italo pulled a set of keys from his pocket and tried a few different ones in the lock before he found the right one. The lock turned with a faint click and we were in.

'Where did you get the keys from?' I whispered to him in the darkened room.

'Just one of the perks of being the head waiter of a large hotel,' he answered in a soft voice. 'These are what we call "master keys".'

When our eyes became adjusted to the dark, we had a look round the room. Kuller had left a fresh white shirt and a light grey suit hanging up in the built- in wardrobe built in the window wall.

'That's a stroke of luck; he hasn't changed yet for the reception.' I said. 'He'll be coming back here to do that soon.'

'He is on his own as well. No sign of anyone sharing with him,' said Italo.

We decided that I should wait in the bathroom, beside the outside door so that when he came in I would surprise him from behind. Italo would hide behind the window curtains and face him when he came in. We took up our positions and settled in for the wait.

Chapter 10

Kuller was in the hotel bar having a few drinks with his old comrade, Werner Brenst. He was a tall man with a ramrod straight back and a thick head of grey hair, who came from an old Viennese family. They had served together in Russia and Italy, and had seen many of their old comrade's die in the Russian snows and on the green mountains of Italy. Kuller had first met him on the retreat from Stalingrad, when the Soviet army was pushing the Germans into a costly retreat. They were marching together through the thick snow at the rear of their squad when Werner tripped over something hidden there and fell face first onto the ground. As Kuller bent down to help him up, a Russian tank appeared out of nowhere and opened fire with its cannon and machine gun, killing everyone in their squad except them. Kuller had kept Brenst from getting up. He had often thought if Werner had not tripped that day, they would also have been left lying in the snow covered wasteland that was Russia. They dived into the snow to hide from the tank, and waited until it had moved on. Altogether, some forty men had been killed that day.

They were now busy toasting their good luck with Schnapps, a custom they had developed through the years when they met up at functions like this.

Werner was in a more sombre mood than Kuller had seen him before. As they ordered another drink, Kuller asked what was troubling him. Werner thought for a moment before saying, 'Do you ever wonder if we always did the right thing, Hans?'

'What do you mean "the right thing"?'

'I mean the Jews and the Italian civilians. Back then, it seemed the right thing to do, but today. I don't know.'

Kuller took a sip of his Schnapps before saying, 'Everything we did was under orders. If it was wrong, then it was the High Command that was wrong, not us.'

Werner gave him a searching look. 'Do you really believe that, Hans? We were part of an extermination process that killed millions of innocent people. We must take some responsibility for what happened. Back then, we didn't know the bigger picture but now, with all the newsreels and films from the inside of the concentration camps there is no place to hide.' He took a sip of his Schnaps before continuing. 'I also feel ashamed for what we did in Italy. There was no need to be as cruel and ruthless as we were'.

Kuller looked at his old friend with pity. *The propaganda and lies had gotten to him. The Jews were the problem back then, and they are still the problem today. Their greedy thieving ways are still causing problems in the world. Look at the land they stole from the Arabs to form the illegal state of Israel. They kicked out of their own homes anyone who stood against them. They took land that had belonged to Arabs for over a thousand years and laid some fictitious claim to it. And this fool thinks we were ruthless.*

Werner continued, 'Even the events on Monte Sole. I look round and see Reder who spent thirty-four years of his life paying for that crime. The world condemned our actions then and still does now.'

Kuller looked around the room and wondered how many more of his old comrades were losing their ideals. He looked at Werner and said, 'I believed back then we were men of vision and courage and that, in the near future, Germany will need men like us again. Our country is divided into East and West, our youth are undisciplined, and Bolshevism is on the move again. Stay strong, Werner, and you will be able to help the fatherland when the time comes again.' Werner wearily nodded his head as if he wasn't too sure of his friend's views. Kuller looked at his watch and said to Werner, 'Time for a shower and to get changed for tonight. I'll see you later on.' He took

Werner's hand and they embraced. He rose to his feet a little unsteadily, smiled at Werner and headed for the reception. Werner sat for a while thinking over their conversation. *Was there an alternative then? Could I have refused the orders? I don't think these re-unions are helping me; I'll probably make this my last one. I don't like reliving the past, it doesn't relate to the present and to who I am now. I am Austrian not German, and this is my home city and the Capital of an Independent country once again.*

At the reception desk Kuller looked at the pretty receptionist with hungry eyes 'My keys please, Fräulein. Number 118.'

The receptionist handed him his room key with the note. She kept her eyes down and made no comment. She was used to men on the lookout for any easy lay and she usually just ignored them, but this one was different. She sensed bad vibes coming from him and she instinctively knew he was trouble.

Kuller opened the note and read it with a puzzled look on his face. Who wants to see me later? The only "R" he could think of was his mistress Renata who was back in Munich. It couldn't be her. I didn't tell her where I was going. Oh, it could be that fool Richard who was quartermaster sergeant with Headquarters Company. That's just the kind of thing he would do, leaving little notes around the place. He was always very meticulous in what he did. He had a little laugh to himself.

He put the note in his pocket and headed for the lift. The door opened, he entered and pressed the button for the first floor. He never paid any attention to the old couple who stopped the lift door from closing and joined him in the lift. When the lift door opened at the first floor, the elderly couple watched him with mild amusement as he staggered his way along the corridor to his room. They also got off on the first floor and walked slowly along the corridor arm in arm.

He put his key in the lock, opened the door to the room, and stepped inside.

I heard him enter and waited until he switched on the light before I stepped out from the bathroom and pressed my gun against his head.

'Don't move a muscle, Kuller; if you do I'll shoot you down like a dog', I said in Italian.

He froze, and waited. Italo came into view from behind the curtain and made a point of raising his gun so Kuller could see it. I searched Kuller for any weapons he may have on him. When I was satisfied he was clean, I took his wallet from the inside pocket of his jacket and then pulled the jacket down over his arms to prevent him making an unexpected move. My heart was thumping wildly in my chest. I couldn't believe that I had a gun aimed at Hans Kuller.

Italo told him in German to move over to the bed and to lie down on it. We reasoned that it was unlikely that he could launch an attack on us from a prone position and with his arms behind him. Up until this moment, Kuller had been silent but now he spoke for the first time. 'Who are you and what do you want?' Italo answered him, 'We are survivors of the Monte Sole massacre and we want your life.' Just for a moment, a look of fear flickered in his cold blue eyes. 'What has Monte Sole to do with me?' He asked in Italian.

I crossed the floor so that I stood in front of him and said, 'I saw you that day, Kuller. I was a witness to your savagery. You killed all of my family and then you raped my mother before you slit her throat and killed her. You have to pay for that.'

Kuller looked at me with hate in his eyes. If he could have reached me, he would have killed me. He spat out at me. 'We never raped Italian women, it was forbidden by our officers. The only women we raped were the sub-human Jewish shit we sometimes came across. No one gave a toss about them.'

I could feel the rage building up inside of me and I was ready to explode. I raised my gun and put it against his head. 'My name is Bruno Verdi. If you translate my name to German, it would translate as *grün*, green. A name used by many Jewish families such as mine. After you killed my mother, I saw you dip your bayonet in her blood and write "Jew" on the ground. You killed my uncle, who was the local Rabbi, but first you tied his head back and forced him to watch as you raped his wife. Then you cut her unborn child from her womb and killed him as well.' Kuller's face was white with shock. His cocky aggressive behaviour melted away as he remembered the killings. He lay very still on the bed with only his eyes darting from Italo and back to me in quick succession.

I continued, 'The women wore a Star of David round their necks which identified them as Jewish, even my baby sister, who you also killed and stuffed like a piece of meat into our kitchen sink wore one.' I reached into my pocket and pulled out a gold chain with a small gold Star of David dangling from it. 'I took this from my little sister's dead body and now after all these years I have come for her revenge. I want you to look at this chain and understand that it is a Jew who has come to take your life away.'

When I looked over at Italo, he was standing with a look of incredulity on his face at what I had just said.

All this time Kuller was lying very still on the bed. It was as if he realised that he was about to die and was now showing his fear. 'Is it money you want? I can pay you a tidy sum, just don't kill me!' he whimpered.

I laughed at the sight of the brave Teutonic warrior begging for mercy.

'How you die depends on you, Kuller. With a bullet through the head with some dignity as if you had committed suicide, or you can die with a bullet through the heart dressed in these. At that I pulled from my inside coat pocket a pair of frilly knickers and a lacy bra I had bought in Italy before I left. 'If you choose the second method then I promise you that your family and your comrades will see photographs of your corpse wearing them. If you choose the first method then there will be some honour in it for you. All you have to do is leave a note admitting the part you played on Monte Sole and that you can't go on any longer hiding from the atrocities you committed in the war. Make your choice now.'

Italo turned to me and gave a short laugh. 'When you said you had an idea of a plan, I should have guessed you had it all worked out.'

I smiled at him, 'I've had this worked out for quite a few years now. If sergeant Kuller won't co-operate with us, then

I want you to shoot him in the heart. I promised Maria I wouldn't kill him, and I would like to try to keep that promise. We can dress him up in the bra and panties after he's dead.'

I turned to Kuller, 'Time's up, sergeant. Make your choice. I wonder what your comrades will think of their big brave SS sergeant wearing a bra and panties. Perhaps a lover's quarrel with a male friend that turned violent?' I watched Kuller go red in the face with anger.

Kuller seemed to quickly regain some of his bravado as he looked at me and said, 'I am the master of ceremonies at the reception tonight and if I don't turn up they will come looking for me.'

'Kuller, the reception starts at seven-thirty and it's now 6pm. I reckon we have at least an hour to see this through and walk out the door. No more stalling - what's it going to be?' As a final persuader, I asked Italo to place his gun against Kuller's chest. 'It makes no difference to us what you choose just so long as you are dead,' Italo said, bending over his intended victim, and blowing him a mock kiss, 'We will make it look like a lovers' quarrel.'

The overpowering smell of urine filled the room as Kuller wet himself and began to shout out for help. We had already discussed what to do if he tried to alert his friends by shouting. Italo pulled a silk handkerchief from his jacket pocket like some stage magician and stuffed it into Kuller's mouth. The room fell silent again. 'I'm going to count to ten and then my friend is going to shoot. Bra and panties or your brains on the bed. One…two…three…four…five…' Kuller became very agitated and was trying to speak out. I pulled the scarf out from his mouth and he said, gasping for air, 'I'll do it. I'll write the note and take the temple shot.' 'When I let you up Kuller, if you try anything funny I will shoot you down.' Italo said as he bent over to help him get to a sitting position. I watched carefully, and covered him from a distance with my gun.

Italo pulled his jacket off and handed him a writing pad and pen. 'Just write what I tell you to write and remember, I read German.'

Reluctantly, under instruction Kuller wrote:

Dear Gertrude and my dear comrades,
All these years I have been living a lie and I can't go on any more. I have decided to take my own life tonight with the comfort of knowing that all my old comrades are in this hotel with me.
What I did on Monte Sole and Sant' Anna was very wrong and I ask forgiveness from God and my family for these deeds.
Please understand.
Hans.

Italo read the letter a few times to make sure that there were no mistakes before he told me it was fine.

We must have taken our eyes off of him for only a second, but for a killer like him, a second was enough. He sprang up from the bed with all the agility of an acrobat and kicked out with his left foot giving me a heavy blow to the head. As I went down I heard the sound of Italo's gun firing. I lay there on the floor stunned for a few moments until my head cleared.

As I got up, the first thing I saw was the horrific bloody mess splattered all over the headboard that reached as far as the window curtains. Italo was standing with the gun still in his hand staring at Kuller's dead body. 'I was lucky' Italo said, turning to face me. 'I managed to press the gun against his temple before firing. It should look like a suicide.'

I took in Italo's appearance. He had blood and gore all over his shirt. I thought for a moment before saying to him 'Italo, go into the bathroom and clean yourself up. Wrap your shirt up in a towel and we'll take it away. Put on one of Kuller's, your both of a similar size.'

I looked again at the dead body of the man I had sought for all these years. I wish I could say that I felt relief or some other similar emotion but the truth was I felt nothing, no emotion whatsoever. It was as if we had just killed another animal on one of our woodland hunts. Perhaps in my mind he wasn't human after all; perhaps I saw him only as a wild dangerous animal that needed put down. I continued staring at Kuller when there was a knock on the door that brought me out of my contemplative state.

A soft voice called out in Italian, 'Bruno, Bruno Verdi, open the door.' Italo came out of the bathroom with his gun in his hand. We looked at each other mystified as to who was there. I said to Italo, 'Carry on and get cleaned up. We don't have much time before they'll come looking for him. I'll handle the door.' The voice then said 'Bruno, we used to call you *Naso*, open the door.'

Now I was really spooked. The only people who used my childhood nickname were people who lived on the mountain and knew me from my childhood.

I took the gun from Italo and crossed to the door. Slowly I opened it, and standing there, much to my surprise, were the elderly Italian couple I had seen downstairs.

The old gentleman smiled at me and said, 'You had better ask us in Bruno, the sound of the gun shot was quite loud and I don't think we should be standing out here in the corridor.'

I stood back and let them enter the room. The first thing they saw was the dead body of Kuller lying sprawled out on the bed with his brains blown out. I had my gun levelled at the couple, not sure of what to do next when the old man spoke.

'You won't remember me Bruno, but I remember you. I recognised you straight away in the hotel lobby. My name is Graziano Sambucci. My father, who was also called Graziano, ran the vegetable stall in Monzuno and used to pay your father for cobbling his shoes with his produce.' I suddenly remembered him. He was in his late thirties when the massacre took place. 'What are you doing here, Graziano? I don't understand.'

Graziano looked again at the dead body on the bed and said, 'We came to kill him. My wife, Ivana, and I have waited all these years for revenge and then we saw him on the television. We made plans to come here and kill him. We have taken the room next door to him, and we thought we would kill him tonight after the reception.'

'How did you plan to do it?'

He opened his jacket to show a large stiletto shaped knife in a sheath attached to his belt. 'This is razor sharp - it doesn't take any strength at all to use it.'

At this point Italo came out of the bathroom, all cleaned up from any blood stains and wearing a fresh shirt. 'Italo, this is Graziano and his wife Ivana, they lived on the mountain and they also escaped the massacre.' It was a weird way to greet anyone, with a dead body lying on the bed and lots of blood, clearly visible from where we were standing, sprayed around him.

Graziano raised his hand for silence, as we were all talking at once. 'Perhaps we should leave here immediately as some of Kuller's friends may come up here at any moment. We have the room next door, so we should all go there and discuss this further.' We all agreed. I walked over to the bed and tidied up around Kuller. I put the note he had written on his chest and the gun in his hand, and then left with the others. I couldn't quite believe that we were all acting so matter-of-factly with a murdered body on the bed with his brains all over the place.

As I closed the door to Kuller's room I closed the door to a lifetime of hatred, anguish and revenge. The strange thing was I still felt no elation over his death, in fact I felt nothing. It was as if we had just killed a fly on the wall and walked out without giving it a second thought.

Once in Graziano's room we all sat down and tried to relax a little. Graziano poured us all a glass of red wine from a bottle he had brought with him. After taking a sip he looked at me, smiled, then said, 'I remember you well, Bruno. They used to call you "*naso*" because of your Semitic features. Your family was the only Jewish family on the mountain, and was very well respected. Your uncle Luigi was not only a friend to me, but as a Rabbi, I confided in him the things that troubled me rather than confide them to the Priest. I heard what happened to your family and until today I believed that you were killed as well.' He paused for a second to take another sip of wine. 'It was a shock to see you in the hotel lobby. I didn't speak to you then because I didn't know why you were there. You could have been visiting or just sightseeing, but when I stood outside Kuller's room I heard your conversation through the door, and then I heard the shot. I knew for sure then.'

'How did you survive the massacre?' I asked them.

Ivana spoke for the first time. 'When the Germans came that day, we were out walking together in the hills. My father-in-law was looking after our two children at home. We heard the sound of shooting and loud screams coming from Monzuno and we ran back to see what had happened. We were too late. The SS were just leaving our house. The bodies of our children and old Graziano were lying dead in the courtyard. We hid in the long grass and watched them loot our house before setting it on fire. The leader was a tall blonde SS sergeant who we found out many years later was Kuller. We were more fortunate than you Bruno, my brother in law and his daughter were in Bologna when it happened, so we thank God they were spared.'

Graziano interrupted her. 'We swore to find him and kill him. We also thought that we were the only survivors of the slaughter, until today. That is probably the reason why I love my niece like a daughter. She is the last of my blood.'

I stood up and embraced them both. We were all hugging each other when we heard the sound of loud banging on Kuller's bedroom door. This was followed by someone shouting, 'Hans, Hans, open the door. It's Werner.'

He continued knocking and shouting for a while and then the clamour stopped.

Italo said, 'He's probably gone to report to reception. He must have checked if Kuller had picked up his key. Someone will be up shortly to open the door, so I think we should get our story straight before the Police visit us.'

I said to Graziano and his wife, 'Where do you live now?'

'Bologna, a small apartment on Via Venezia.'

'When the police ask us what we are doing here, tell them that we know each other from way back and that we all live in Bologna now. Italo and I are here sightseeing and you have come for a city break as you have never been before. We all decided to meet up at this hotel. That should be enough to satisfy them.'

I could hear the rustle of a key in Kuller's door and the sound of raised voices in his room. Soon, in the distance, I could hear the noise of police sirens coming ever closer. Ivana's face was very white. She was obviously feeling the strain. Graziano seemed to take it all in his stride and showed no visible signs of anxiety as he refilled our wine glasses. Italo and I were surprisingly calm. I said to Italo, 'Where's the shirt with the blood on it?'

'I've still got it here in the towel.'

Graziano stood up and pulled out a suitcase from underneath the bed. 'Put it in here, Italo, beside my dirty clothes. We can dispose of it later.'

Ivana walked over to the television and switched it on. 'This seems more natural for a group drinking wine to have some background music.' She searched for a radio station. The sound of soft jazz came from the set. We could have left the hotel but that would have seemed very suspicious to have booked in and then vanished. No, this was probably the best approach, so long as we kept our nerve.

After about an hour there was a knock on the door. Graziano rose to open it. Standing there was a Police Officer. 'I'm sorry to disturb you, sir but could I take a few minutes of your time?'

Graziano smiled, and said in accented German, 'I'm sorry, I don't speak German, only Italian.' The Police Officer nodded in understanding. 'Does anyone here speak some German?' Italo stood up. 'I speak a little, Officer. Can I help you?'

The Officer said, 'May I come into the room?'

Italo said, 'Of course, Officer' and he opened the door wider.

The Officer said, 'There has been an incident in the room next to yours. Someone is dead. Did anyone from your group hear anything unusual such as a loud bang, like a gunshot?'

Italo translated what the Officer had said. We all exhibited the appropriate shocked expressions and said the right things. Italo gave a sigh and said, 'I'm sorry officer; we've all been sitting here for much of the afternoon just talking and drinking some wine. We didn't hear anything unusual. I'm sorry we can't help you.'

The Officer once again nodded his head in understanding. 'I will need to take your names and addresses for the record, just a formality, you understand.' We gave him our addresses in Bologna and he then left us alone.

Italo was quite sure that would be the end of our involvement. I said that I felt the police and the coroner should give a verdict of suicide without much of a problem as all the indications for that were present, such as powder burns to the temple area, suicide note and no signs of a forced entry or a struggle.

Graziano was acting as if he was preoccupied with something else on his mind. I asked him if anything was wrong. He looked at me and said, 'What would you say if I told you that there will be more of these Nazis dead before the night is out?'

Italo stood up and said, 'Bruno, I don't want to be involved in anything else, our work here is finished, come, it's time to leave.'

Ivana said, 'If you leave the hotel now it will look suspicious and the police will track you down and arrest you for mass murder.'

I was stunned at these comments. *What have they done? Have they poisoned the food?* My mind was racing as it quickly scanned the possibilities. Graziano calmly raised his hand above the loud babble of voices asking questions and demanding answers. 'Let me explain what we have done. We have planted four hand grenades attached to a mechanical device and timer in each of the four corners of the Ballroom. When the reception is at its height they will detonate and hopefully kill as many of them as possible. At the appointed time the device will pull out the rings and there will be synchronised explosions.'

This was met by silence. Italo and I looked at each other and struggled to find words. Eventually I blurted out, 'You can't do that, Graziano. You will be killing people who were not involved in the killing of our families.' He looked at me with disdain in his eyes. 'You can't moralise with me, Bruno. You have just killed a man in cold blood and in the eyes of the law you are a murderer.'

'Yes, that's true, but I know that he was guilty of murdering my family. I saw him do it. There is no doubting that fact, but to murder people because they are attending a party here is insane.'

'Insane, is it? These people downstairs are veterans of the 16th Waffen SS. They were present at the massacres of Sant' Anna and Monte Sole. All told, a total of over two thousand five hundred Italian civilians, men, women and children, were slaughtered by them. Tonight they attend a party to celebrate the release of their leader who is now free to breathe the fresh air of freedom. Whilst they are celebrating, the Italian civilians they massacred are turning in their mass graves crying out "who will avenge us? We cannot party or breathe fresh air again." And I answer them that I will. There is insanity here, yes I agree, but it is the insanity that allows over one hundred known killers to go unpunished whilst our friends and families who were completely innocent lie dead.'

'There will be innocent people who will also die. Waiters, chefs and other staff. What about them? I'm sorry Graziano; I'm going to the police.'

'And what will you tell them when they ask you how you know about this? Will you tell them that you found out after killing Kuller?'

Italo took me by the arm. 'Calm yourself Bruno, there's nothing we can do. If we go to the police we will be charged with murder. Even if we try to find the explosives ourselves we don't know how to disarm the mechanism.' He shook his head in dismay, 'All this explains why Ivana and Graziano took Kuller's dead body in their stride when they saw it. For them he was only the start of the killing, whilst for us it was the end.'

'Why have you told us all of this? You didn't have to.' I said to the old couple.

Graziano put his arm around my shoulder as if trying to placate me.

'You may have wandered near the scene of the explosions and been injured. Or you may even have entered the Ballroom to see Reder. I couldn't take the chance, enough Italians have died because of those scum.'

Italo said to me, 'Bruno, let's go to the reception and book out. Tell them we are disturbed at the thought of the dead body and the Police activity next door, and that we want to cancel our booking. That way it won't look suspicious to anyone.'

I agreed. We said our goodbyes to the Sambuccis and left.

We were silent as we passed by our room and picked up our bags.

The girl on the reception apologised on behalf of the hotel for the 'terrible events that have taken place' and willingly cancelled our reservation and refunded the deposit we had paid.

We took a taxi to the train station and went to a coffee bar there as we waited on our train. 'I don't feel comfortable just walking away knowing that many people will die tonight, Italo.' I said over my espresso. Italo nodded. 'No one in their right mind would be comfortable with this, but what can we do? I don't want to go to prison as a convicted murderer because we saved the lives of some SS killers.'

We sat in silence for quite a while until I said. 'What about an anonymous tip-off to the police? That way we can do the right thing without being compromised.'

Italo looked at me for some time before saying, 'The police may probe a little deeper into who would try to kill over one hundred ex SS soldiers and discover that their unit was involved in the Italian massacres of 1944. They may then check the hotel guests and find that four of them came from the Bologna area where the biggest massacre took place and that two of them had been with the partisans. They may then think that those two then had the knowledge of working with explosives and perhaps the motive to kill them. Further when they find out that you came from Monte Sole and that I was with the partisans there, I think we would be facing a life sentence.'

I saw the sense behind Italo's argument, especially when he added, 'The person making the phone call would have to be me, a German speaking Italian with a pronounced Italian accent. Now there's a good clue Bruno, eh?'

Every way we looked at it, we found a problem. If the bombs went off in the ballroom, we would eventually be implicated.

Even if we wanted to go back and try to find them ourselves, we didn't know how to disarm the mechanisms. Eventually we just gave up thinking of a way through it and sat in silence waiting on our train back home. I looked at my watch and noticed that it was 7.45pm and that in about 45 minutes we would know if we were accomplices of a mass murder or merely of one killing.

Chapter 11

Walter Reder had considered cancelling the reception and was sitting with some of the organisers in his hotel room discussing what to do. The general consensus was that they should continue the evening albeit with a more muted approach. They all were of the opinion that Kuller would have wanted it that way; why else would he have waited until the evening of the reception to commit suicide. Reder suggested that Werner Brenst should be the master of ceremonies in place of Kuller, to unanimous acceptance. With the meeting at an end, Reder stood up and said, 'Gentlemen, we should now go to our rooms to get ourselves ready for this evening. Our minds are obviously on what has taken place here, but once again we will do our duty to a fallen comrade and follow through, painful as it may be.' They all stood ramrod straight as if on parade and left the room.

At precisely 1915 hours Reder and his comrades entered the ornate ballroom of the Hotel Bristol. Overhead the elaborate crystal chandelier glistened and shone like twinkling diamonds. The rows of tables were covered with white starched linen, the serviettes were black and placed in silver rings engraved with a skull. To the uninitiated this would have not much relevance, however to everyone attending the dinner the symbology was all too clear. Black was the colour of the SS uniforms they once wore with pride and the engraved skull on the serviette ring was a reference of the cap badge of the SS. The flag of the West German republic was proudly draped over the top table, and behind it on the wall was a banner with the slogan 'Death or Dishonour' stencilled in large black gothic lettering.

Reder led the way to the top table where he was met with a warm handshake by the Austrian Minister of Defence. Out of respect for the Minister, the Austrian National Anthem was given priority before the German anthem, and when they had finished playing, the guests sat down.

Werner Brenst remained standing and waited until everyone had settled before speaking. 'Herr Frischenslager, Herr Reder, Mayor Muller, Colonel Haus and assembled ex-comrades of the 16th Waffen SS, I warmly welcome you to this reception being held in honour of our old Commander Walter Reder (or, as we once knew him, Major Reder) being released from his internment as a prisoner of war.' The sound of thunderous applause filled the room as Reder stood to accept the salutation. Brenst continued, 'Sadly our evening's proceedings have been somewhat marred with the news that our dear friend and old comrade Hans Kuller took his own life this evening. I would therefore invite you all to stand for a minutes silence out of respect for him before we continue the evening's festivities in the way that he would have wanted us to.'

The one hundred and fifteen people in the room stood for a minute in complete silence and then broke into instantaneous applause with some of them shouting out 'Hans, Hans.'

Werner Brenst raised his hand for order before continuing, 'The format of this evening will be as follows. First, we will have our banquet meal which has been specially prepared for our guest of honour and includes all his favourite foods. After a short interlude, we will hear some words of welcome from the Minister of Defence, Herr Frischenslager, followed immediately by our guest of honour Walter Reder.'

Once again thunderous applause greeted the mention of his name.

Walter Brenst then sat down and took a drink of Schnapps from his almost-full glass. He was confused and felt decidedly uneasy over his friend's death. It was only a few hours ago that Kuller had told him to be strong; and now he was dead. Apparently suicide. Could this really be the case? How could someone change so quickly from being bullish to the depths of despair in such a short time? He shook his head and thought, 'The man must have been deranged.'

Gertrude Kuller was gazing out of the lounge window of her house at some local children playing outside in the morning sunshine when she noticed a police car pull up slowly in front of her gate. She watched with growing interest as the two police officers got out and looked around them at the other houses before they settled on hers.

As they walked up to her door, Gertrude had a sinking feeling that something was very wrong with her little world and that she was about to find out what it was.

She opened the door at the first knock.

The older of the two officers took off his hat before saying' Frau Gertrude Kuller?'

Gertrude felt her throat dry up, and could only nod her head at him.

'May we come in please?' Said the younger policeman.

Gertrude held the door open for them and led the way into her small but tidy lounge. 'Take a seat please,' she heard herself say in a calm, low voice.

When they were seated, the older officer said to her, 'Frau Kuller, I am Officer Palframan and this is my colleague, officer Schroeder. We are herewith some grave news, I'm afraid.'

Gertrude stiffened in her seat and gave a little gasp. 'Please tell me what's happened.'

Palframan shifted uneasily in his seat before continuing. 'We have received notification from the Austrian police that your husband, Hans Kuller was found last night dead in his hotel room in Vienna.' He paused, as if uncertain what to say next. 'First reports indicate that he appears to have committed suicide, although we will have to wait on the autopsy results to be certain.'

Gertrude stared at the officer without saying anything. When she eventually broke the silence, she said, 'Are you sure he's dead? Could there not be a mistake?'

Palframan shook his head, 'He was identified by his army comrades, so there is no chance there's been a mistake.'

Gertrude was aware that the officers were looking at her for some reaction, but she just didn't feel anything. She felt completely normal, as if she was having a coffee and a chat with them about the weather. Slowly it dawned on her that she was now a free woman. Free to take up her life again and free to regain control of the bakery. She restrained a smile from appearing on her face. 'I am free from that bullying monster forever,' she thought. 'I'm also free to encourage that nice butcher, Peter, who likes to flirt with me.'

She shook herself out of her day-dreaming and said to the officers. 'Thank you for coming and telling me. I suppose you'll let me know what arrangements I'll have to make.'

The funeral had attracted quite a large turnout; however, Gertrude didn't really care if no one had turned up. She was dressed from head to toe in black as any self-respecting widow should, but she couldn't wait until the funeral was over so she could go away on holiday to Spain with her close friend.

She stood at the graveside and gave out the appearance of a grieving widow to everyone there, crocodile tears included. She looked round the assembled mourners and her eye rested on Peter. Peter caught her look and winked. She smiled to herself behind her hand. She couldn't wait to meet him at the airport later on. A little shiver of anticipation ran through her *as she thought* 'I am starting a new life with a new man, and I will never make the same mistakes again. The bakery stays in my name, no matter how good he is in bed.'

Chapter 12

We sat on the train beside each other sharing a cheese and salami panino and feeling the stress of the moment. I looked at my watch and said, 'Italo it's 8.30 pm. If the grenades have exploded they will have done so by now.' Italo pulled out a hip flask of grappa, took a long drink and passed it to me saying, 'Bruno, there's nothing we can do about it, so let's just try to relax and go home to whatever awaits us there.'

The journey seemed to go on forever. The train clacked and swayed its way home as if it parodied our obvious gloomy mood. When we eventually arrived at Bologna in the early hours of the morning, we said our goodbyes, and with heavy hearts made our separate ways home.

The house was dark and I fumbled for my key. Perhaps too much grappa or too much stress, I couldn't tell. Much to my surprise, Maria opened the door and greeted me with a big hug. 'Welcome home *amore*, did you have a good trip?'

The following morning when I got up, the first thing I did was to switch on the radio and tuned into the news station. I didn't know what to expect with the planted grenades. *Did they detonate or not? If so, were there many fatalities and injuries?* To my amazement, there was no mention of any incident involving explosions in the Hotel Bristol.

Over breakfast I decided to phone Italo to arrange a meeting.

'What's wrong Bruno? You're very quiet this morning.' said a sleepy Maria, as she sat down beside me at the breakfast table.

I looked up and smiled at her. 'I'm still thinking about Kuller. It's difficult to let it go knowing he's so close by,' I lied to her.

'Well, you don't have to worry about him anymore,' she replied, as she casually threw down her newspaper on the table.

I picked up the paper and read from the open page she had pointed to. The headline read, "SS colleague of Major Walter Reder, Hans Kuller, commits suicide at SS reunion party in Vienna."

I read the headline with unbelieving eyes. So it hadn't all been a dream. I acted surprised as I read the article. There was no mention of explosives being found in the hotel.

Maria looked at me with suspicion written all over her face. 'Do you know anything about this, Bruno?' She asked, as she gave me an inquisitive look.

'Why should I know anything about his suicide, Maria? Do you think I sat there and watched him shoot himself? This is the first I've heard about it or even read about it.'

Maria reached for my hand and looked me in the eye, 'Tell me you didn't kill him, and swear it on your mother's grave and I'll never doubt you again.' I reached out for her other hand so that I was holding both of them, before I said to her, 'Maria, I wanted to kill him with every fibre of my body, and I had even thought about trying to, but I swear to you on the graves of all my dead family that I never laid a hand on him and I certainly never killed him or forced him to shoot himself.'

Maria looked at me steadily in the eye before she smiled and gently said, 'Do you want more coffee, Bruno?'

After making a hurried phone call to Italo, I showered in our little bathroom, and I found myself scrubbing my body repeatedly with the sponge as if the events of the previous day had left some indelible marks on me that perhaps other people could clearly see that I had killed in cold blood.

When I met Italo later on that day in the Café Romano on Via Mazzini, I could tell by looking at the dark bags under his eyes that he had enjoyed as much sleep as I had. After ordering a coffee at the bar I sat down beside him. I looked at Italo with an inquisitive look, 'Well then, Italo, we got away with this one, or so the papers report, but what do we do with Graziano and his homicidal ideas?'

Italo gave a mock growl, 'Why should we bother about some SS murderers being bumped off? We just killed one ourselves, for God's sake, so let's not get too moral about him.'

I couldn't believe my ears. Italo was condoning mass murder.

'We just can't sit back and allow Graziano to kill on a mass scale. Innocent people would get killed as well, we have to stop him and disarm those grenades.'

Italo was silent for a moment before saying, 'Bruno, I agreed with you about Kuller and that we had to take him out, but I can't agree with you about your view about Graziano. I don't care if he kills every Nazi under the sun. If there is collateral damage and some innocents die, then that is just war. I'm sorry, my old friend, but I just can't help you in whatever you're planning. Besides, the grenades are probably very old and there is no guarantee that they will even detonate.'

I could understand Italo's position but I could not accept it. Graziano would not stop until he had killed as many of these Nazis as he could and he had to be stopped.

After small talk with Italo, I left him and walked the short distance to the local library. It was quiet in there and I needed some time to think this through without distractions. I remembered that Graziano had told me he lived in an apartment on Via Venezia and I thought it might be a good idea to visit him there and try to dissuade him from any further attempts at killing, and to persuade him to disarm the grenades before innocent people died.

I felt better in myself at coming to that decision and decided to give Graziano a visit the next day.

When I got back home Maria wasn't in, so I made an espresso with *sambuca* and sat down in front the television to watch the afternoon news bulletin. Reports were coming in of an explosion in an Austrian hotel that had killed, on first counts, some thirty people, with many more reported as injured. Video footage flashed across the screen showing a raging fire engulfing the building, with many fire engines and crews in attendance fighting the blaze. An onsite reporter was saying that massive explosions had originated in the area used for conferences around two-thirty that afternoon and had ripped through the hotel Bristol in Vienna with devastating effect.

I sat stunned and watched the unfolding scenes with incomprehension and horror. All these innocent people dead and many more injured because of some old man's vendetta against some SS killers who still remained alive and unhurt.

I turned my attention back to the screen. The reporter was interviewing a senior police officer about the incident. I turned the sound up to listen.

The reporter asked, 'Do you think this was a deliberate act of violence or was it, perhaps, a gas explosion or some such similar accident?'

The police officer, looking suitably sombre, replied, 'First reports would indicate that there were a series, maybe up to four, individual explosions closely following each other, and emanating from an area not associated with a gas mains. Also the type of detonations and the damage caused would be more indicative of explosives, like grenades, than a large one-off gas explosion.'

'In your opinion, if this is indeed a terrorist incident, who do you think could be responsible for such an act?'

The police officer thought for a moment before answering. 'Once we have time to investigate more fully all the possibilities we will be in a better position to answer that question; however, if it is a terrorist group that's responsible for this then it could probably be Badder Mienhoff or an affiliated group.'

I stretched over to switch off the set and sat there too stunned and shocked to even think clearly. After a while I was startled out of my blank state of mind by the ringing of the phone. It was Italo.

'Bruno, you were right, have you seen the news?'

'I've just been watching it.'

'What do you think we should do now?'

'The first thing Italo is not to talk on the phone about specifics. We can meet for a drink later on tonight, or we can even meet in the park over on Via San Martino for a walk and talk.'

'I'm working until 8pm tonight, but I can meet you about eight-thirty in the park. See you then.' With a click the phone went dead. I sat and stared at the receiver in my hand for some time before I lowered it onto the cradle. We had now become involved in mass murder and I was feeling very afraid.

Chapter 13

Walter Brenst was sitting in his small conservatory looking over his notes, trying to make sense of the jumble of information he had unearthed since the death of Hans Kuller. He had always felt that something was very wrong with the whole affair. Ever since Kuller's death he had been concerned at the sudden change of mood that Kuller apparently went through that night. From defiance at the new order of things in Germany, as demonstrated by their last conversation together, to despair, as his state of mind showed by his suicide and the note he left behind.

'All this took place in a one hour time-frame. I just don't buy it,' he thought.

His mind wandered back to his notes and he read them through again. 'What am I missing here? There must be something I'm not seeing,' he thought as he scanned the sheets of paper in front of him.

He picked up another sheet with a list of the hotel's guests for the night of the Association dinner. As he looked through the list of names, he stopped at three that stood out from the rest of the guests. Arcari, Verdi, and Sambucci. 'These Italian names stand out from the other German ones,' he thought. He looked at their addresses and noticed with mild excitement that all three names came from the same city in Italy, Bologna. He also noticed that two of the names, Arcari and Verdi, had booked in for an overnight stay, but had cancelled their reservation and had left the hotel shortly after Kuller was found dead. *They had not stayed overnight, why? They travelled from Italy to Vienna to a hotel, and then didn't stay the night. Where would they leave at seven-thirty in the evening looking elsewhere for a room for the night? It didn't make any sense.* He looked at the third name; Sambucci. Mr and Mrs Sambucci had the room next to Kuller's and had left the hotel the following morning. They had only booked in for one night, which wasn't unusual in itself, but when looked at as part of the overall picture it formed a pattern.

Brenst remembered Bologna from his days with the 16th Waffen SS. He knew it to be the area where his unit had massacred many Italians and had been the main cause of Walter Reder's conviction and imprisonment.

'Could this be the answer to the riddle?' he thought with growing anticipation. 'Is it just a coincidence that Italians from that area were guests at a hotel where Reder was being feted? And where Kuller, who was instrumental in the massacre, was staying?' He focused his mind on this new line of thought. 'If this is the answer then why didn't they go after Reder as well? He was the overall planner and leader of the *rastrallemento*, so why wasn't he targeted as well?'

He sat bolt upright in his chair as the answer came to him in a flash. 'They tried to kill us all by bombing us. The bombs were supposed to go off when we were all there together at the dinner but for some reason they didn't detonate until the day after. They were avenging the deaths of loved ones who were killed by us on Monte Sole.'

He felt his hands tighten on his notes. 'I'm lucky to be alive. They tried to kill us all.' He took control of himself. He was a man who had faced death in battle many times before and he could face this the same way now.

'Why did they target and murder Kuller separately from the rest of us?'

As he asked himself the question, he immediately knew the answer.

Kuller was one of the leaders in the field and was known for his merciless brutality. He had never been charged with war crimes, but Brenst knew that, in many people's eyes, he deserved to be.

He went over the notes again in case he had missed something else. When he had finished reading, he was convinced that he now knew enough about the operation against them to bring it to the attention of the police. He had thought about going after them himself but he knew that was just bravado. *Those days are past now.* He pondered whether or not to tell the Association, or even Reder himself, but he decided against it. Perhaps some hotheads may decide to take the law into their own hands and try to take out the Italians. After all, they weren't boy scouts, and they wouldn't take this lightly. No, he decided to inform the police and there was no time like the present. He put on his coat, shoved his notes into his pocket and left the house.

The desk sergeant looked up as Brenst approached him

'Yes sir, may I help you?'

'Yes sergeant, my name is Herr Brenst; I would like to speak to a senior officer please. I have some information on the bombing of the Hotel Bristol that may help you in your enquires.'

The desk sergeant looked at Brenst with fresh interest, 'Could you give me some more details, sir?'

Brenst took in the sergeant's appearance with mild disgust. He saw an officer who was due for retirement and who had let his appearance somewhat go. He was fat, his uniform was too tight for him, and his manner was slovenly. 'Thank god we had no one like him in the SS,' he thought, 'no style and certainly no substance.'

'Sergeant, the information I have is very sensitive and is live. With no disrespect to you, I think that it may be above your rank to be privy to it.'

The sergeant thought for a moment then said, 'Take a seat sir, I'll see what I can do.'

After a few more minutes a tall grey-haired officer appeared from a side door. 'Herr Brenst? Come this way, please.'

Brenst followed the officer into a small office with a window overlooking the city of Vienna.

'I am Inspector Michael Muller, senior officer at this station. Please sit down, Herr Brenst.' He pointed to a seat in front of his desk.

'I understand, Herr Brenst, that you may have information relating to the bombing of the Hotel Bristol. May I ask how you got this information?'

Brenst sat down and slowly crossed his legs. 'Inspector Muller, I was in the 16th Waffen SS and during the war part of our area of operations was in Italy, near the city of Bologna.'

'Please carry on, Herr Brenst,' said an interested Inspector Muller.

Werner Brenst told his story from the *rastrallemento* on Monte Sole to the bombing of the hotel Bristol, and when he had finished speaking, Inspector Muller sat behind his desk in silence, as he took it all in.

'It would certainly explain the hotel bombing. Our forensics people have found the fragments of what appears to be World War II Italian grenades in the hotel debris, so your story fits that. As for Hans Kuller, there have been unsupported suspicions about how he died, but being unsupported they remain only suspicions. This gives us a little more meat on the bone. I will speak to my superiors about this as soon as possible, Herr Brenst. In the meantime I would ask you to make an official statement relating all the facts you have told me about, and to sign it before witnesses. You understand that until I have that in my possession I cannot officially speak to my superiors or take this any further.' Brenst nodded his head in assent to this request. Muller pressed his intercom button and spoke into it; 'Please send a secretary in, prepared to take a statement.

Chapter 14

At eight-thirty that evening we met at a bench in the park, far away from anyone who could hear what we had to say.

I arrived first and sat quietly waiting for Italo. When he eventually arrived thirty minutes late, he appeared very agitated.

'What's wrong Italo? You look nervous.'

'Sorry I'm late; I've just had the police in to see me at the hotel asking a lot of questions about Kuller and various other things.'

I was stunned. 'It's probably just routine questioning,' I said, more in hope than belief. 'What did they ask you about?'

Italo gave a nervous shrug, 'They asked if I knew Kuller personally or had ever met him. They even asked if I knew him by reputation. I completely denied any knowledge of him. They then asked me about Reder and his connection with Monte Sole. I had to admit to knowing about him through recent TV coverage. They seemed happy enough with that, although I was blown away when your name even came up in questioning. They knew about your family being killed by the SS, and they wanted to know how friendly we were and how we first met. They asked me if I knew about Italian hand grenades from our time with the partisans, or had any in my possession. I denied anything that would have compromised us.'

'They're certainly fast off the mark Italo, but they can't prove anything, it's all just wind in the air.'

'Maybe so Bruno, but we have to be extra careful from now on. My main worry is that nut case Graziano. Suppose he goes for Reder and his gang again and is caught this time. He will have no problem singing out to the police about us. *It wasn't me mister, it was the big boys, they made me do it.*'

'We'll have to speak to Graziano about this and there's no time like the present. Come on.' We left the park feeling, for the first time, that this was all spiralling out of our control. We made for my car and drove to Graziano's flat; number 1A, ground floor on Via Venezia.

Graziano heard the knock on the door and looked at his watch. 'Ten thirty at night. This can't be good news at the door,' he said to himself.

When he opened the door and saw me and Italo standing there he was taken completely by surprise, although he quickly recovered his composure.

We stood at the door looking at each other for a while before Graziano invited us in.

'Is this a social call, boys?' said an ever cool Graziano.

'The police have been talking to Italo about Kuller. We think they suspect our involvement in his murder,' I said.

Graziano smiled as he sat down. 'Sit down, boys and rest your legs for a while. I have to say that they may suspect both of you of murder, but it certainly doesn't involve me. I wasn't even there.'

Italo, his face reddened with anger, stood up and pointed his finger at Graziano. 'You are as guilty as us, you lying bastard! If we go down then you do as well.'

Graziano smiled that annoying little smile of condescension that can infuriate a man to kill another. 'Prove it Italo, I'll deny everything.'

I said, 'What about the grenades you planted?'

Graziano shrugged his shoulders, 'What grenades? I don't know anything about grenades. Aren't you boys the experts in bombs and explosives? Haven't you killed using them before? I'm sure the authorities are aware of that. I only sold fruit and veg in mountain villages, which is not much of a training background for bomb making. Wasn't it you boys who were trained by the partisans in explosives and various other ways in killing people?'

Italo, holding his temper in check, tried another tack. 'Knowing that the police are sniffing around us, don't you think it would be wise not to aggravate the situation by planting any more bombs?'

Graziano laughed, 'Are you boys wired for sound or something? I don't know what you're talking about. What bombs?'

Without saying anything else Italo turned to leave. We could both see that it was no use even talking to the old man. Graziano didn't trust anyone and especially not us.

'Graziano,' I said, very quietly, 'don't try for the rest of Reder's gang or even Reder himself. You have already killed over thirty people and maimed many more. If you do try again I will take you down without a second thought, so don't try taking the moral high ground. You are a mass murderer and I will kill you to prevent you killing again.'

Graziano stood up and faced me; 'Bruno, you forget who these people are. Do you think you can stop me bringing justice to the dead of Monte Sole? To do that you will have to turn a deaf ear to your parents, your brothers and sister, and also to your other relatives. They cry out for vengeance Bruno, are you listening?'

We stood silently facing each other, and without another word Italo and I left the flat.

Once we were outside Italo said, 'That bastard is going to set us up for a fall. We have to take him down and make it look like an accident otherwise the police will screw us.'

I looked at my friend, 'We can't just go around killing people on spec, Italo. Even to protect more lives. I know what I said in there, but I couldn't just kill an old man who hasn't harmed us.'

'What if the police are thinking of pinning the murder of thirty odd people on us Bruno? What then? What if their evidence is based on Graziano's testimony? What if they charge him and he implicates us in exchange for immunity? Should I carry on, Bruno? Because I can think of a hundred reasons why we should get rid of him.'

'Do they include the scenario that if the police are watching us with undercover surveillance and possibly electronic as well, they may be slightly annoyed if they see us killing someone who may be their star witness in a multiple murder case?'

Italo stopped walking and stood still. He looked at me with an incredulous look on his face. I didn't say anything and waited to hear what he had to say.

'I remember you as a young boy hiding on the hillside outside Marzabotto, frightened and angry. I said I would help you Bruno, and you trusted me with your life. We saw things that took us into a hell where we shook hands with the Devil, but we survived; and now I'm asking you to trust me again. I know it's hard to believe but we have no option. We have our own families to protect, not just ourselves, and we should bear in mind that this murderer is as bad as they come. Never forget Bruno, he has already killed thirty people and is planning to kill many more. He has to be stopped, and we can't ask the police to do it.'

Reluctantly, I agreed.

We eventually pulled into the first roadside *trattoria* we came to and parked near the entrance. I wasn't sure if we were just being paranoid or merely careful but, for sure, we were both spooked. I wanted to make sure that if we had to, we could make a fast exit.

'You feel hungry Italo?' I said, trying to appear light. 'Let's try the pizza. This place has a reputation for making a good tomato and seafood.'

Italo looked at me with mock pity written all over his face; 'Don't feel you have to give me a pep talk, Bruno. I was the one who helped train you, remember?'

'Suitably scolded old friend, let's eat and then talk about what we do next.'

Our snack was rapidly devoured without much conversation passing between us.

We both knew that we had to do something about Graziano, but what?

Even if we killed him it still wouldn't get the police off our back. We passed it backwards and forwards between us for about an hour, and we were getting nowhere. The problem always came back to the police. How do we get them off our scent and onto Graziano?

The answer to our problem came unexpectedly to me as we mulled over the problem. 'Italo, we need to kill the two of them together, Graziano and Ivana, and make it look like a suicide. We need to get them to sign a letter admitting to the bombing and the killing of Kuller, and as they are now so full of remorse at their terrible actions they have decided to end their lives. That clears us of any involvement in the bombing and also gets us off the hook for Kuller's death as well.'

Italo said, 'Quite a good plan, but how do we get them both to write and sign the letter? Old Graziano is as tough as they come.'

I admitted I hadn't worked that part out, but I couldn't think of any other way of silencing the Sambuccis and getting the police off our trail.

'Bruno, doesn't Graziano have a niece on his brother's side that he treats like a daughter? Maybe we could put some pressure on him there.'

'Do you mean to threaten her?'

'No Bruno, to threaten Graziano with her death if he doesn't sign.'

'So you think that giving him the choice of killing himself and his wife or allowing his niece to be killed, that he will say "yes, I'll kill my wife and myself; let my niece live"?' We both burst out laughing at this ridiculous notion.

Even though we discarded this idea, there was some merit in part of his plan, perhaps we could fake a suicide note from them and work out some way to kill them so it looked like suicide.

We decided to sleep on it and meet again the following day.

Alone at home, I allowed my mind free licence to roam over these events.

What a twist of fate it was that was now proving to be the driving force in my life, that I should be striving to save the lives of the SS men who were responsible for the deaths of so many of my friends and possibly even my family; and that I should be plotting the murder of two old villagers from Monte Sole. Such irony could fail to go unnoticed and perhaps could even prove to be the thing that saved Italo and me from arrest by the police.

Comandante Vittorio Bertolini had just left a meeting with his two subordinates who had interviewed Italo Arcari. He was left with the impression that there could be something in this story of bombs, murder, and intrigue from Austria that had landed on his desk. Probably the next step would be to interview the other Italian national in the story; Bruno Verdi. He noted with mild interest that Verdi was Jewish and wondered if there was some connection with the SS massacre on Monte Sole during the war. Was this an act of reprisal? He decided to interview Verdi himself as he had probably been primed for police questioning through his friend Arcari and could prove to be a tough nut to crack.

His interest factor moved from mild to very interested when his research revealed that Verdi and Arcari had been together in the Partisan Brigade from Bologna, and that Arcari had originally been in the partisan band that was wiped out on Monte Sole. This information, coupled with the fact that he already knew that Verdi's family was massacred on the mountain by the SS, gave the investigation a new edge.

He would visit Verdi the next day.

Chapter 15

When I heard the officious-sounding knock on my door I suspected it was the police. Maria opened it and was greeted with the introduction, 'Good afternoon *signora*, I'm Comandante Bertolini.' I could see that Maria was taken by surprise as she let out a little gasp. Perhaps she had been expecting something like this to happen.

'Could I have a word with *signor* Bruno Verdi, if he's at home?'

At this, I went to the door and invited the Comandante in.

I thought the best place to speak to him was in the kitchen, so I sat there at the table in front of him and waited.

Bertolini took his time to speak. He shuffled some papers around in his briefcase in an apparent attempt to unsettle me.

'Signor Verdi, I'm investigating the death of Hans Kuller and the bombing of the Hotel Bristol. Are you familiar with these events?'

'Yes I am, but only what I've seen on TV or read in the papers.'

'Were you and your friend Signor Arcari not at the hotel the night Herr Kuller was found dead?'

'Yes we were, but with all the police activity and a suicide in the hotel it wasn't a good atmosphere to be in, so we left.'

Bertolini looked me straight in the eye and said, 'Why would you travel all the way up to Vienna and not stay overnight? Why should you come straight home because you were put off by the activity in the Hotel?'

Without hesitation I answered him. 'Comandante, we were there on a short visit, and by accident we found ourselves in a hotel full of ex SS comrades, plus a dead man who apparently committed suicide. We found it the least distasteful to say and we decided to leave. We didn't know where to look for a room at that time of night, so we went for a drink then caught the train home.'

'Why did you choose Vienna and that particular hotel at that particular time?'

At this point in our conversation, Maria walked into the kitchen and sat beside me at the table. 'I couldn't help but listening in Bruno. I never knew you were there at the hotel when it all happened.'

I knew she was secretly seething at me for lying to her, but at least she had the presence of mind not to show it in front of Bertolini. I held her hand in mind and gave it a loving squeeze. 'I was just explaining to the Comandante that it was a spur of the moment decision that didn't work out very well, Maria.'

Bertolini was watching us very closely, obviously looking for a weakness in my explanation. He said, 'Tell me about the Sambucci couple you met there at the hotel.'

I took a deep breath before answering, 'I knew them from when I was a boy in my home village before the massacre. I know you're aware about what happened on Monte Sole from your talk with Italo Arcari; however I knew the Sambucci's lived in Bologna on Via Venezia and I also knew they would be there at the Hotel Bristol at the same time we were going, so we had agreed to meet up there.'

Bertolini gave me a condescending look, 'Do you expect me to believe that four survivors of the Monte Sole massacre booked into the same hotel, on the same night that the SS unit responsible for the slaughter were having a reunion dinner, and that one of the main perpetrators of the massacre was found dead in his room by an apparent suicide. Also, the fact that the same hotel was bombed later by Italian WWII hand grenades that you and your friend Arcari were trained in using during your time with the partisans, and that thirty innocent people were killed. Have I missed anything out?' he asked in a pseudo-comical sounding voice.

I could hear Maria taking a sharp intake of breath. This was the first time that all of the details had been packaged up so neatly for her, and it was proving to be a frightening experience. There was the distinct possibility that her husband was a killer many times over.

Werner Brenst sat at home looking over what he had just written in his notebook. He was concerned over a few points in his unofficial investigation. The first one was he didn't trust the Italian police to follow this investigation through to its proper conclusion, and secondly, he was becoming more convinced that the older Italian, Graziano Sambucci, was responsible for the murder of Hans Kuller. He knew that he had the room next door to Kuller at the hotel, and that his family had been murdered by him on the mountain. In other words, he had motive and was in the right place at the right time. He suspected that the other two younger Italians were involved in the bombing of the hotel, but as that didn't immediately concern him, they weren't his prime focus. 'I'll sort out the old man first, then I will make the other two pay for trying to bomb us all. Yes, the old man was the one. He had killed my friend Kuller.' To Brenst, the military bond of those years was indissoluble, even after all of this time in civilian life, in his eyes, if Kuller had not gone down in the snow to help him up, and then stay down with him when the Russian tank appeared, he would probably have died with the rest of his squad that day. He felt he owed Kuller a brotherly debt for saving his life, and in the SS tradition he now felt the time was right to repay that debt with the taking of his killer's life. He now made plans to revisit Bologna, his previous killing ground, to kill again. This time it was for the honour of his comrade.

Chapter 16

Graziano was acting agitated and bad tempered. Ivana clearly knew the reason for his change of mood. He was concerned in case the two men returned to harm them. She watched him as he cleaned and loaded his old Beretta before putting it in the sideboard drawer in the kitchen.

He didn't talk about why he was doing this. He didn't have to. Ivana had known him long enough to recognise fear in his eyes. Like the day on the mountain when they had witnessed the massacre of their family. That day Graziano had the same look. A kind of fear mixed in with anger. He turned to face her. 'Ivana, until all of this is over I want you to keep the door locked at all times and to be careful who you open it to. OK?'

Ivana walked across to him and gave him a hug. 'Graziano, *amore*, we have been through so much together and we will see this through together. Don't worry so much, no one suspects us, we're in the clear. Don't worry about Italo and Bruno, they won't come for us or harm us.'

Graziano seemed to relax a little. 'Maybe you're right, maybe not, but we'll take extra precautions just in case.'

Maria had calmed down a little. She was now thinking clearly and wanted some more answers as she still wasn't sure of the truth. 'I want to understand why you lied to me about the fishing trip, Bruno, and why you couldn't trust me to understand why you had to go to find Kuller.' I tried to explain to her that I wanted to keep her out of this. This was something I had to do, but even feeling that way, I still hadn't killed Kuller. I had promised Maria that I wouldn't and I had kept that promise.

She had gone upstairs to be alone and I sought comfort in a bottle of grappa. My mind was in total confusion. 'Where do I turn now? Who do I speak to? What should I now do?' I just sat in my armchair and gradually emptied the bottle until I fell asleep. It seemed to be an easier solution. When I eventually awoke it was daylight and Moreno was sitting opposite me with a look of disgust on his face.

'Papà, this is no answer to the problem. Don't go down this road.' At this he got up and left for work. My head was throbbing and my throat was dry, so I went upstairs to probably face another hard time from Maria.

Werner bought his ticket at the platform machine before boarding the train. He wanted to get to Bologna for around sunset, do what he had planned and then return on the train back to Vienna the same night.

He had it set in his mind how this would go. He would force entry into the Sambucci's home and kill the old man. Bang, bang. Two shots, then out the door. He would be wearing a face mask so he wouldn't be recognised in case Sambucci's wife was there. He smiled to himself 'Once I kill him I will be even with Kuller and will be free of any commitment to the SS. I won't attend any more of their meetings. It's time to move on.'

Eventually the train pulled into the Bologna station and Brenst got out to a hatful of memories. He remembered herding the Jews from the area onto cattle trucks lined up in the marshalling yards and listening to their unanswered cries for help. He felt it was wrong then and now he felt disgusted by their actions. At that time it was war, but he could never reconcile war with what they did to the Jews. He heard the stories other SS men brought back with them from various death camps and pretended he didn't understand what they meant by exterminating them.

He remembered the layout of the city fairly well and decided to walk the short distance to the Via Venezia and the Sambucci's flat.

He felt the gun in his anorak pocket and experienced a sense of familiarity as he touched it. Very soon he would be at the flat and his training would kick in. *You don't hesitate from what you plan to do. Act confidently and get out as soon as completed.*

He saw the flats in front of him and he checked what he had written down in his notebook. Flat 1A, ground floor.

He walked up to the door and checked it was the right one. He knocked and waited. A gruff voice answered 'Who's there?' Brenst knocked again and this time the voice said 'Go away, I'll call the police.'

Graziano took his Beretta from the drawer and motioned for Ivana to lie behind the settee facing the outside door. Before joining her there he switched off all the lights in the house. He primed his gun and waited.

Brest knew that the element of surprise was now gone and that his prey was spooked, so he decided to go in hard. He pulled out his gun and took a run at the door, tensing himself for a shoulder charge. He hit the door full force and felt the lock give. He rushed into the flat and dived to the floor. Sambucci had turned out all the lights and was poised, gun in hand, behind the settee. Brenst heard the sound of two or three shots being fired at him and returned fire at the muzzle flashes. He heard a yell of pain as one of his shots found its mark. A wounded Graziano stood and ran at him firing on automatic with surprising speed for an old man and Brenst felt the rounds enter his chest. As he lay mortally wounded on the floor he loosed off a couple of shots at Sambucci, more in hope than anything else. As his eyes closed he thought he heard the sound of a body falling in front of him.

The noise made by the shootings attracted the attention of neighbours and passers-by who crowded round the shattered doorway of the flat and stared at the two dead bodies lying on the floor next to each other.

Someone had called the police and they were very soon in attendance. When they entered the flat they found Ivana Sambucci in a state of shock sitting on the floor against a wall. They called for an ambulance, but by the time it arrived Ivana Sambucci had died of a massive heart attack.

When Comandante Bertolini was informed that the two older Italians who had been at the Hotel Bristol were dead, and the violent circumstances surrounding their death, he had a feeling that the stranger in the flat was the key to many things. He ordered his team to liaise with the Austrian police over the dead man and to get his photograph and fingerprints to them as soon as they could.

When the results came back, he wasn't too surprised to find out that Werner Brenst was an ex member of 16th Waffen SS and was at the hotel the night of the reunion. He sat at his desk thinking, 'Why did Brenst want to kill Sambucci? What did he know or suspect?'

He picked up his phone and spoke to one of his team, 'Get me all the background you can on Graziano Sambucci and send a team to search his home and any other places he may have. Look out for anything that can be tied in with this case, or anything else that looks unusual.'

Before the end of his working day he had his answer. Sambucci's father and two of his children had been killed in the massacre on Monte Sole. He apparently wanted revenge for this and had intended blowing up the SS unit responsible at their reunion in Vienna when Walter Reder was their guest of honour. This was corroborated by three grenades his team had found in a lockup garage belonging to Sambucci. Tests showed they were of the same type and batch as the ones used in the bombing.

'So,' thought Bertolini, 'Brenst found his killer and so did we'

His thoughts wandered to Arcari and Verdi and he wondered what their involvement was in this, if any at all. He also wondered if Kuller's was really a suicide after all and if the two suspects he had marked down for killing him were completely innocent. Either way, he knew that unless he had more evidence he wouldn't be able to take it any further. With the Sambuccis dead, the evidence he needed had died with them, and it's not without probability that if Kuller was murdered, then it could have been the Sambuccis that killed him.

With a deep sigh he closed the case file, switched off his desk light and headed home.

Chapter 17

Some years had passed since the events of the Hotel Bristol and Maria had come to terms with the lies I had told her about that period. Moreno is all grown up now and is married to a lovely young girl called Monica. They have three children, Moreno, Bruno, and Carla, and they live on Corso Garibaldi in Bologna.

After the events of the Hotel Bristol I had experienced an emotional release that had led me to a more secure place within myself. I still have bad dreams, and I still hear the screams of the dying, but they are not as loud or as vivid. Somehow, even writing about the events on the mountain has been a cathartic experience for me.

I am now in my eightieth year and I am struggling to put the events of my life to paper, however my family have been very supportive of me.

I know that I am the last one from that experience still alive, as I lost my best friend Italo to the ravages of lung cancer five years ago.

For my eightieth birthday Moreno made me promise that I would go back to visit Marzabotto with Maria and all of his family. Perhaps it is time to take this last step for who knows how many years I have left.

I agreed, with a resolved hesitancy, to go back to the mountain on the day of my birthday and that I would join them in prayer at the ruins of the farmhouse and at my old home. I suppose it's a gesture that marks the occasion when I bend the knee at these places for if there is a God I believe he must be a monstrous creature who revels in the blood of the innocents. I will not be able to pray there for it is an art that has been lost by me through the events of time, but I promised myself that at least I will show respect for my dead family and will contain my oaths at the ones who took their lives.

Epilogue

April 18th 2011

Moreno has come in his estate car to take us up the mountain. Maria and I have been silent for much of the morning. I think she is trying to respect my quiet and thoughtful demeanour.

Moreno opened the door and came in with Monica and the children. 'Hi Papà, happy birthday. You two all set then?' We both smiled and nodded.

The journey was a little cramped in the car but I was glad of the children's singing and childish chatter. It seemed to fill us with just the right level of levity. Soon the mountain came into view and the car began the steep ascent up the winding road. I noticed that there had been no tarmac laid and it looked exactly the same as yesteryear.

We finally came to the small track leading up to my Aunt and Uncle's farmhouse and Moreno slowed down. We had to stop about fifty metres from the farmhouse as the track had, over the course of time, become quite overgrown. As we got out the car I heard the sound of the birds singing in the trees. It has always been so here. Perhaps it was the amount of trees and shrubbery lining the track that attracted them there.

The farmhouse came into view and my first reaction on seeing it was sadness at the ruin it had become.

As we walked into the courtyard the video in my head began playing the scene I often saw in my sleeping hours, whilst at the same time I was taking in the fact that there were three white crosses, each with a Star of David, arranged in a straight line in the ground. I slowly walked up to them and with Moreno's help I knelt beside them. I ran my fingers over the three names and the inscription on them which read, '*Murdered on the 29th September 1944 by the SS.*'

Tears ran down my face as I quietly sobbed at the memory of these three wonderful people. Moreno helped me to my feet as I slowly walked back to the car. I had seen enough there.

I could hear Maria's voice as if in the distance saying, 'Do you want to go on, Bruno, or have you had enough?'

I looked at her and said, 'Don't be concerned, I'm just a silly old man.'

We drove up the dirt road again to my old house and as I looked out the car window I thought I saw smoke drifting up from the valley floor. For a moment my heart jumped in fear. When I looked again I could see that it was just some clouds hanging low over the mountain.

When my old house came into view I could feel everyone's eyes focused on me in a caring way. I was resolved not to break down and to pay my respects in an orderly manner.

The old house was in pretty bad shape as the rafters had all rotted away. The only parts still standing were the outside stone walls and some of the internal ones.

Set in the ground were six white metal crosses with the Star of David on them. The names inscribed on them were still visible; Moreno, Carla, Gianpiero, Benito, Ricco and Lisa, with the inscription under their names being the same as I had read at the farmhouse.

I closed my eyes and could feel the warmth of the sun on my face and could hear my brother's calling me to play football as they ran ahead to the meadow. The aroma of Mamma's cooking wafting through the open window became intensely real, as was the sound of my father sharpening his knives on the circular stone he turned with a pedal. I could even see my little sister Lisa shouting out in glee and tottering around the courtyard as she chased the chickens we kept.

I was transported back over sixty-five years to a happy childhood playing on the mountain of the sun. I thought

I could hear my Mamma and Papà saying to me 'Bruno, don't be sad, let it go and live your life in the present.'

I don't know how long I stood there but Maria told me afterwards that she had seldom seen me look as happy. I had a smile on my face stretching from ear to ear.

When I opened my eyes and looked around the wreckage of my family home, it was with a new sense of realisation. For the first time ever I felt I had jettisoned the bitterness I had harboured for all these years, I was experiencing a calmness I had never felt before.

I didn't want to walk round the back of the house to the spot where the Germans had brutalised and killed my mother. She wasn't there now and it would not have done me any good to see it. I decided that I didn't want to go into the ruins and relive my horrific memories. Strangely, I did not have any thoughts of Kuller or his evil deeds. They had gone. I looked around at my own family gathered round me and smiled at them, 'I'm ok; it's been laid to rest. Let's go home.'

I've had plenty of time to think about my visit to the mountain and how it affected me. I can never, ever accept what happened but I have to move on. There will always be evil men in this life who will try to inflict evil on humanity, but I am convinced that at the same time there will also be good men who will stand up to them and their evil ways and defeat them because we will always be more in number.

My family were the victims of an evil creed that many men espoused at that time, and like all evil creeds, they will always find followers, but man is essentially moral and instinctively knows right from wrong and will eventually find the path to goodness.

I thought of Graziano who was so eaten up with hatred and the idea of revenge that he had killed thirty innocent people and had ended up being murdered himself. Even my own life had been filled with that same hatred for Kuller that it had motivated Italo and me to plan and execute a murder. I was fortunate that I was not found out by the authorities; however it is something I still have to live with.

The evil from the massacres seemed to continue consuming lives and taking lives long after the event.

Now I know that if I had remained in that place of darkness, then evil would have won the day and my family would have died for nothing. I realised late in life that evil can find a way to embitter the innocent and bind them to the past, but I lived and loved and raised a family and now have grandchildren. I also found a way to eventually come to terms with what happened without accepting it as being right. To let go of the hatred, fear and bitterness that had lived inside me for many years and to experience real peace for the first time. The one thing I am still convinced of is that the religious mind suffers from self-delusion if he thinks that his God will protect him from any harm. Many of the SS soldiers who took part in the massacres were from religious backgrounds; however their Christian beliefs did not deter them from carrying out their bloody mission. On the other hand, the majority of the villagers were very religious people, as were my own family, and I am sure they must have called out to their God for his mercy and protection to no avail, but how could a myth possibly have answered them.

So, this is my story. If it strikes a chord with you and helps you to perhaps come to terms with your own personal tragedy, then writing it has not been in vain. No matter the size or type of traumatic experience you have gone through, don't let the evil in it chew you up inside; believe me, it will ruin your life.

If you have read this story and think *this is not for me, my life is pretty ordered*, you can never be sure that in your lifetime you will not encounter something that has the potential to completely devastate your entire life. If that time should come remember, be strong and stand firm against it, and yes, try to understand it but never accept it, fight it all the way. Above all, don't let it eat you up inside, for if you do then it has won. Let it go, it is not a sign of weakness but of strength.

The Devil's Bridge

To Nonna Rina

Author's Note

The correspondence between Mussolini and Churchill mentioned in this book is factual, although the contents of the letters are purely speculative and rely heavily on the rumours of the time.

The Devil's Bridge is still in use today and sits over the river Serchio at Borgo a Mozzano in Northern Tuscany in the province of Lucca. It was built in the early 11th century and is a well-known landmark.

The Moschettieri Del Duce (The Duce's Musketeers) was an elite force of Blackshirts, mainly of officer rank, who were Mussolini's personal bodyguard. They were also used as the ceremonial guard on state occasions and during the fascist rallies. All the Moschettieri took a personal oath of allegiance to Mussolini unto death.

Chapter 1

Lieutenant Kurt Muller of the Waffen SS hurried along the long corridor of Palazzo Vittorio to the high wooden double doors at the end. He paused for a moment to look out of one of the many windows lining the corridor at the frenzied scene in the courtyard below. His was to be one of the last military convoys to leave Milan before the Allies arrived and his men were busy loading crates of documents, ammunition, and essential supplies onto a line of trucks parked outside the main Palazzo entrance. On the other side of the courtyard, some of his men were burning important papers: army codes, strategic military positions and operational plans that had to be destroyed, as they couldn't take the risk of them being captured. The black smoke from this rose in curling swirls into the clear blue sky above, adding to the atmosphere of feverish activity. He took all of this in before resuming his hurried approach to the wooden doors ahead. He knocked on the double doors and heard a loud voice in Italian telling him to enter.

Benito Mussolini stood with his hands clasped behind his back looking out of his office window at the activity below. Without looking round he said, 'Well Kurt, what bad news do you bring me today?'

Kurt Muller came to attention with a click of his heels, 'We will be ready to leave within the hour Duce, the Allies are very close and we can't hold them back for much longer.'

Mussolini bowed his head as if accepting the inevitable. No more the strutting dictator, but a war weary old man. 'Yes, I can hear the sound of their heavy artillery close by. The sound of battle has always made me aware that the lives of thousands of men are dependent on the right or wrong decisions by their commanders in the field. Who would have thought it would come to this, to a point of destiny, should I run or should I stay?' As Muller looked at the Duce of the Italian Empire, he seemed to have lost the will to live. Muller had been detailed by Hitler himself to make sure that Mussolini was protected from any attempt on his life, and he was determined to follow those orders to the letter.

As he looked around the room, he noticed there were some of Mussolini's fascist leaders sitting at a table. One of them, the party secretary Pavolini, stood up and said, 'Duce, we have a thousand loyal Blackshirts outside who will fight to the last man for you. We can make a last stand and die with honour instead of skulking away like rabbits as we try to escape.'

Mussolini turned to face him, 'And what of the thousand men we are asking to give up their lives for no other reason than our honour? What of their wives and sweethearts, and what of their children? Have not enough Italians died already for our pride and honour?' He paused for a moment before continuing, 'I've decided to leave here and try to reach Switzerland without endangering the lives of any more Italians.'

The room fell silent as the Duce turned back to face the window. After a few minutes, Mussolini said, 'Kurt, I want you to provide an armed escort for these comrades here and take them to the Swiss border. Make sure that the partisans don't capture them. After doing this, your men can head for home or rendezvous with you as you head north.'

'And what about you Duce, will you be leaving with my convoy?'

'Give me thirty minutes, I have some things I need to attend to first, then I will join you.'

Kurt Muller came once more to attention, gave Mussolini the fascist salute then left the room to supervise his men below.

Mussolini then turned to face his comrades and motioned for them to stand. 'Time is now short dear friends and this is the end of our association together and the end of the fascist era in Italy. Go now before the Allies, or even worse the partisans capture you. Don't waste any more time. Lieutenant Muller will detail an escort strong enough to deter any partisan attacks. I would put all of you in even more danger if we left together. Hopefully we will all make it to Switzerland.'

One by one, the Duce embraced his loyal supporters and thanked them for their friendship and service to the fascist state over the years. Some of them were visibly moved to tears as they left the room. Soon he was alone, still gazing out of the window, still in a reflective mood. How different things could have been, he thought, if I had not entered a pact with that maniac Hitler. If I had stayed out of the war like Franco did, how different it would all have been. With that thought still in his mind, he walked to his desk and pressed the intercom. A voice answered, 'Yes Duce.' He paused for a second before saying, 'Get me Sergio Rossi immediately, and tell him to come straight up here.' The answering voice said, 'Sì, Duce,' and hung up.

Sergio Rossi was eating his lunch in the small dining room used by the Palazzo staff when one of the Mussolini's bodyguards found him. 'Sergio, the Duce wants to see you straight away. He's in his day office.' Sergio thanked the bodyguard and immediately left the table. He had been one of Mussolini's personal aides since his promotion from the ranks of the Blackshirts in 1937 and he was well used to being summoned at short notice. As he walked along the corridor to Mussolini's office, he paused for a second at a window overlooking the courtyard. The Germans had finished loading the trucks and were lined up in three ranks being addressed by Lieutenant Muller. Sergio could see that they were ready to leave and he wondered what the Duce was planning to do. He gave an audible sigh and continued walking to the Duce's office.

The last time he had been called here, he thought, it was to deliver flowers to Mussolini's mistress, Clara Petacci. No job too small, he thought as he knocked on the office doors.

Mussolini was sitting at his desk as Sergio entered the room. He gave the fascist salute and approached his beloved leader. Mussolini stood to greet his aide and motioned for him to sit in a seat across from him. 'Sergio, I have a very important mission for you to carry out.' Sergio remained silent. 'Over the years I have been corresponding with the English Prime Minister Winston Churchill, and I have kept the letters safe in my keeping for just such a time as this. The letters show that I was a moderating influence on Hitler in this damn war, and that Churchill recognised this fact. If it weren't for me, Hitler would have invaded England in 1940 when Britain was on its knees. Instead, with my influence, he turned to the Soviet Union and invaded there instead. Churchill almost begged me to help stall the invasion of England.'

Sergio sat there, still in silence, but stunned at this revelation.

Mussolini continued, 'Sergio, you are my most trusted aide and I now pass these letters onto you. If I should be captured by the Allies as I try to escape, then I want you to make contact with them and threaten publication of the letters if they try to shoot me. Make a deal with them. The letters for my life. I would rather live in a prison than to be shot like a dog. If, for some reason I should be killed as I try to escape, then I order you to keep these letters safe until Italy is stable and safe from Communism. Do you understand all of this, Sergio?'

Sergio stood up. 'Duce, I understand; however, I wish to be at your side until the end, so I ask you to please send someone else for this mission.'

Mussolini smiled before answering. 'Sergio, you are my most trusted aide, who else could I send? I have enemies all around me ready to stab me in the back.' He took Sergio's hand in his. 'Listen to me now. You will do as I ask. Change into civilian clothes and take the letters away with you. Hide them safely until they are needed. Now go to Milan station and take a train home.' Mussolini then opened a drawer in his desk and took out a folder, 'I have had new identity papers prepared showing you have worked for the last ten years in the foreign ministry in Rome. So old friend remember your mission and remember me with fondness.'

Filled with emotion, Sergio walked around the desk to Mussolini and hugged him. 'I take this liberty Duce because

I have followed you from the beginning with complete loyalty and I will miss you as I would a brother.'

Mussolini took a few moments to recover his composure before saying. 'Thank you Sergio. Time is short, so take the briefcase and leave now.'

Sergio stood to attention and gave the fascist salute to his Duce, took the briefcase and left the room without looking back.

Mussolini sat for a few more minutes on his own thinking about what might have been. He reached out for a bottle of grappa sitting on a nearby table and poured a large measure into a crystal glass on his desk. He drank it quickly and then made his way down to the courtyard below.

Kurt Muller, standing at the head of the convoy watched as Mussolini slowly approached him. He took note of the resigned expression on his face, almost as if he had accepted the fact that this was the end of his time. Muller decided to keep his conversation with him to the minimum. 'Duce,' he said. 'In order to disguise your appearance in case we are stopped, I request you put on this Army greatcoat and helmet. I have ordered the men in the trucks not to mention to anyone that you are with us, and not to talk to you under any circumstance. Sit at the very end of the row nearest the cab and everything should be fine.' Mussolini entered the truck, made his way to the rear and sat down. He pulled the collar of his coat up round his neck and lowered the German helmet down over his eyes and pretended to fall asleep.

The convoy headed out of Milan towards Lake Como, which they hoped to reach before nightfall. Along the road near the village of Doongo, which was a few miles from Lake Como they came across a large tree lying in the roadway blocking their way. Muller, who was in the lead armoured car, stopped just short of the tree and immediately looked up at the surrounding hillside to see if there were partisans hiding there. What he saw there sent a chill through his heart. The top of the wooded slope that rose above them was filled with partisans with their weapons trained on them. He was about to give the order for his men to take up defensive positions when a partisan appeared at the roadblock and approached them with a white flag of truce.

When he was at Muller's vehicle he introduced himself,' I am Count Pierluigi Bellini Delle Stelle commander of the partisan forces in this area. I am under orders to ensure that all Italian citizens, military or civilian, are removed from all German convoys leaving this area.

Muller stepped down into the roadway and stood facing Bellini, 'we are German soldiers returning home and we have no wish to fight with Italian partisans. Stand aside and let us through.' Bellini laughed. 'Have you Italians citizens on board the trucks Lieutenant? If you have none then you can proceed, but first we have orders to check every convoy or vehicle travelling on this road.'

Muller thought for a moment, 'and if I refuse?'

'Then I will order my men to open fire with mortars and machine guns. In fifteen minutes you will all be dead.'

Muller took a moment before answering, he thought, 'if I fight, then I take the risk that Mussolini may be injured or, even worse killed. I cannot take the chance.'

Reluctantly Muller stood aside and let Bellini and his partisans begin their search of the vehicles. He signalled to his men not to resist and to sit where they were.

Bellini moved forward and ordered two men to search each truck whilst he concentrated on the armoured car.

After about ten minutes one of his section commanders, Bernardo Nicoletti came up to him, 'Commander, may I speak to you.' Bellini could see that he was excited about something, so he moved aside with him out of German earshot. 'I think they have hidden Mussolini on the fifth truck in line, he's dressed in a German army greatcoat and helmet. I thought I better tell you in case there's trouble getting him out.'

Bellini stared at the man as if he was mad. 'Are you sure it's him?'

Nicoletti nodded a few times, 'I am really sure commander, and he's sitting on the right side of the truck at the back beside the cab wearing Italian Generals trousers.

Bellini turned on his heels and called his second in command to him, a partisan called Franco. 'Franco, Nico thinks we have Mussolini on the fifth truck down. He's dressed in a German greatcoat and helmet. Don't make a big show of this, as we don't want a fight with the Germans unless it's really necessary. Take six men and go with Nico to check this out. If it's him, then arrest him and get him away from the Germans as quickly as you can.'

Franco went back to the hillside and selected six men, then returned to the convoy and went with Nico to the fifth truck. He dropped the tailgate of the truck and lifted himself up to the annoyance of the troops inside. They began muttering at him. Franco bellowed out 'Silezio!' and motioned for his men to cover the Germans with their weapons. He walked to the back of the truck and saw a figure in greatcoat and helmet slumped against the cab. What took his eye was the soldier was wearing Italian military red striped Generals trousers. If it wasn't a serious moment he would have laughed at the sight. 'Duce' he called out to the figure. The soldier beside him made a motion as if drinking from a bottle, 'my friend is drunk', he said.

Franco called out again 'Duce', but this time came closer to him and removed his helmet. He could now see quite clearly that it was indeed Mussolini.

Franco took his rifle from him and said, 'Benito Mussolini, I arrest you in the name of the Italian people, please come with me.' Mussolini looked up for the first time and nodded. He stood up to face the partisan. 'Do you have any other weapons,' Franco asked. Mussolini reached inside his greatcoat and handed over an automatic handgun and said, 'I'm glad this is all over.'

Outside the truck Franco searched Mussolini for other weapons, then when he was satisfied he was clean, he led him away without fuss to the other partisans up the hillside.

Bellini turned to Muller, who had been watching what had been happening to Mussolini, and said, 'Lieutenant Muller, you were only doing your duty; you are free to leave now.'

He signalled to the men on the roadblock to move the tree aside. '*Buona fortuna*,' he said as he saluted Muller, turned, and left to join the rest of his men. Muller thought, what do I tell Hitler about what just happened? He shook his head and signalled to the convoy to get moving.

Bellini and some other partisans drove Mussolini to the town of Dongo where they placed him in a room under heavy guard in the local town hall. Before long Clara Petacci, his mistress, who had been captured with her brother trying to escape to Spain with fake Spanish passports, joined Mussolini. Sometime later, his other loyal fascist ministers, including Pavolini, joined them in captivity. They had been taken prisoners at the same roadblock Mussolini had been captured at. Pavolini told him that Bellini had threatened to destroy them all if the Germans hadn't surrendered them, and his escort had willingly given them up without an argument.

Mussolini wondered what their fate would be.

A few hours later the door to their room opened and Bellini entered. 'I have new orders from the provisional authorities and I have to take you Signor Mussolini and Signora Petacci to a safe house where you will stay overnight.'

Mussolini noted that he was not addressed as Duce.

They were taken under armed guard to a car waiting outside and were then driven to a farmhouse in the country. The farmer and his wife, who were communists, showed them to a large attic bedroom, which though clean had little in the room but a double bed. Clara Petacci sat on the bed and wept as Mussolini stared out of the window through misty eyes. Presently the door opened and the farmer's wife came in with a tray of bread and cheese, two small plates of pasta and a small carafe of red wine, which they devoured hungrily without saying a word to each other.

When it came time to go to bed, they slept with their clothes on next to each other. Mussolini felt that he should try to console his mistress with some words of comfort, but he didn't know what to say, nor had he the energy to say it. Clara Petacci sobbed throughout the night, much to Mussolini's irritation.

There had been little sleep for both of them, when daylight suddenly burst through the thin curtains on the window. They could hear a lot of activity outside in the yard and when Mussolini looked out the window that overlooked the yard outside, he saw several cars parked there with about ten partisans round them having a heated discussion. From what he could make out, the argument was about who had jurisdiction over their prisoner. The newcomers were saying that they had orders to take Mussolini to Rome, whilst their captors were awaiting fresh orders from Milan. Eventually the newcomers left, saying that they would get the Rome provisional government to contact the Milan partisan authorities to get this sorted out. After they had gone, their captors huddled together in deep conversation for quite a while and frequently pointed up to Mussolini's room. Mussolini had a bad feeling about it all. Before long there was a knock on the door and when opened, two partisans with automatic machine guns entered the room. 'We have instructions to take you both with us now.' 'Where are we going,' said Mussolini. The partisans did not answer.

They were pushed into a Citroen car sitting in the courtyard with three partisans inside. Two others stood on the running board and held on as the car left the farm. After a few minutes, the car came to a stop beside a large field bordered on three sides by a dry stonewall. Mussolini and Petacci were taken out and stood against the wall side by side. The lead partisan said, 'we have orders on behalf of the Italian people to execute you both now.' Mussolini said, 'shoot me first but not in the face.' Clara Petacci screamed and threw herself in front of her lover in a vain attempt to protect him. Mussolini gently moved her aside and kissed her lovingly on the cheek, '*Cara mia*, this is our fate,' he said. 'Let's hold hands and meet the Gods.'

The partisan aimed his machine gun and shot them both in the chest. Mussolini and Petacci fell to the ground in a crumpled heap.

Not a sound greeted the end of Fascism, not even the small birds in the nearby trees made their usual tribute to the new day. The partisans stood in silence looking down at the dead body of the Duce: the leader, not knowing whether or not to cheer his demise, or to savour the moment as a historical footnote of a momentous day.

Eventually, they picked up the dead bodies and loaded them into a van before driving off to Milan.

Chapter 2

7th April 1945

Sergio Rossi stood looking at the military convoy coursing its way through the Milan streets. He felt no bitterness towards them. It was just a fact of life that they had won the war. When the Americans had eventually joined in with the other Allied Armies, the outcome for him had never been in doubt. From where he was standing, he could clearly see the American soldiers on the trucks chatting to each other with that easy air of familiarity born from the confidence of being victors. Sergio's hatred was reserved for the Italian communist partisans who seemed to be everywhere now that the war was almost finished. He saw them as traitors and could not forgive them. He watched with dismay at a column of partisans marching down the street, in front of him, singing their songs of victory as they waved to the cheering people lining the streets.

During a gap in the traffic, he crossed over to the railway station. Sergio gazed at the tall building with a feeling of sadness. Before the war, this had been a magnificent building now the roof was barely supported by the girders he could see peeking through some of the shattered glass covering. Milan was still suffering from the effects of the Allied bombing raids. Parts of the city had been severely damaged over the last few weeks and it was with a sense of relief that the Milanese were now trying to return to normality. The Allied Armies were entering the city and the Wehrmacht was in full retreat and heading back to Germany. With the arrival of the British and American forces the Milanese knew that their war was over.

Squads of local men had been conscripted to aid with the clearing of the rubble and other bomb damage from the streets and some of them had been tasked to help clear the main railway station of debris. They were busy working in the main concourse as Sergio entered the building.

He was surprised to see partisan squads moving easily amongst the travellers as they searched for escaping high ranking fascists. He walked over to a bench in a far corner of the Station and sat down, quietly taking in the disturbing scenes unfolding all around him.

The main prize they were all looking for was Mussolini. No one knew where he was. All people knew was that yesterday he had left his Milan headquarters and tried to escape the country. Sergio smiled to himself, what stupidity these communists were showing if they really thought that Mussolini would be travelling by train to Switzerland. He was one of the most recognised people in the world and he would never put himself in such danger.

He was brought back into the present by some partisans checking the identity of a family sitting on an adjacent bench. The partisans compared their papers against a checklist of known people they were looking for. Apparently satisfied, they moved onto Sergio. 'Papers please?' said the leader of the group. Sergio tried to hide his fear as he searched for his papers and handed them over to the partisan. He silently prayed that his name, Sergio Rossi, would not be recognised by the group or was on their checklist. The partisan checked the identity papers against his list before asking Sergio 'where are you heading for?' Sergio said 'I'm going to my home in Borgo a Mozzano.' The partisan looked at him searchingly for a while before saying 'why are you not in uniform or with the partisans?' Sergio replied 'I was injured in the bombing last month when I was staying with relatives in Milan and I have only recently been released from hospital.' 'What did you do before last month comrade?' Without hesitating Sergio answered, 'I worked in the Foreign Ministry in Rome for ten years, so I was excused military service.' One of the other partisans said, quite sarcastically,' so comrade you have also bled for Italy but are you a fascist?' At this, Sergio stood up and said 'comrades, my name Rossi means that I am as red as the armbands you all wear.' At this, the partisans laughed before moving onto the next bench and repeated their questioning there.

The man they spoke to appeared very nervous and stuttered out his answers. The lead partisan took some time in examining the man's identity documents before asking him, 'why are these papers so new looking comrade?' The man went white with fear and took a deep breath before answering him, 'my papers were lost when my home was destroyed in the bombing. These are new papers from the Allied Military Government in Rome.' With a shaking hand, the man pointed to his photograph on the ID card. The partisan looked at him suspiciously. 'Why leave Rome at this time to come into a conflict zone.' The man answered hesitantly, 'my family live in Lucca and I hope to find some work on one of the farms near there in the Garfagnana.' The partisan stared at him without speaking for some time, which had the effect of making the man even more nervous. The partisan noticed this, 'You appear to be very nervous friend, are you not feeling well?' The man stood up and furtively looking around him, made a dash for the station entrance. One of the partisans lifted his Lee Enfield rifle, took aim and fired. The shot hit the man in his back and he fell to the ground screaming in agony. In seconds, the blood from his wound had turned his shirt colour bright red. Two partisans walked up to him, kicked him a few times in his side before lifting him up and carrying him to a truck parked close by. They lowered the back down and without ceremony, threw the man in. No medical aid was offered to the man, but Sergio reasoned that he was as good as dead anyway.

His screaming and shouting for help could still be heard after the shooting, and continued for a while until two partisans left the group and jumped into the rear of the truck. A shot rang out and the screams stopped. Sergio wondered how many other bodies lay dead in the truck.

He watched all this without comment. He noted how the partisans appeared quite detached about the whole affair, and how they carried on their search for fascists as if nothing out of the ordinary had happened.

Sergio picked up his briefcase and carefully draped his overcoat over it to hide the fascist emblem. It would have caused problems with the communists if they caught sight of it. He crossed over to a platform near the centre of the station where he knew he could usually catch the train to Lucca. He wanted to move away as far as possible from the shooting. He felt anger at the way these communist bastards moved so openly and with such authority. How different it was under the Duce when they were put in their place. He reflected that Mussolini was never given the credit he deserved for saving Italy and much of Europe from the dangers of this vile creed.

It was only a few years ago, that The Italian Communist Party had made plans to invite the Red Army into Italy with the aim of setting up a Communist state, but Mussolini had soon put paid to that. When he came to power, he set in place a crackdown on all opposition to the fascist party. Yes, there were a few beatings and arrests but when you looked at the broader picture, was it not worth it? Even Churchill had praised Mussolini before the war calling him 'That Roman genius,' and 'that magnificent Roman law giver.' Men of vision and influence had come to Rome to meet him; he thought how different it was now. However, Sergio reckoned that with the correspondence he was carrying he now held the key to people realising once again how great a man the Duce really was.

Patiently he waited in line for the expected train. He knew that the Allies had ceased bombing the train tracks a few days earlier and that there had been lot of activity from the provisional authorities in attempting to repair them. The railways were now trying to run a limited service and with luck, there would be a train today.

He heard loud shouting from a group of partisans on the platform facing him. Sergio looked up in time to see them dragging a man out of a carriage. '*Fascista bastardo*' they cried out as they threw him to the ground. 'You must be mistaken' shouted the man, in a frightened voice to anyone who would listen. 'There is no mistake 'said their leader, 'You are Antonio Renaldi, Mayor of La Spezia and fascist secretary of that town. You are accused of ordering the deaths of up to forty partisans, and as such you will be tried for those crimes.' He gave a wave of dismissal with his hand and three partisans led a struggling, sobbing man away to certain death at the hands of a firing squad. The man, still protesting his innocence, fell to his knees and pleaded for mercy. 'I was only obeying orders comrades, I didn't want to do it.' he sobbed. 'If I hadn't obeyed orders I would have been imprisoned myself.'

The oldest of the partisans turned on him and hit him with his rifle butt two or three times in the head until the man was unconscious and collapsed to the ground. Sergio noticed a large dark bloodstain spreading from his head. The man lay there motionless as if dead. No one came to his aid or even to see if he was still alive. Around the station, people looked away or busied themselves elsewhere. No one wanted to interfere in case they also became the focus of attention from the communist militia.

The partisans picked him up by his arms and legs and carried him to the truck parked a few metres away and threw the body into the back of it as if they were handling a sack of corn. One of the partisans remained behind to stand guard over their grisly cargo, while the others joined their comrades in their continuing search. They laughed and joked together with no apparent thought to the murder they had just committed. Sergio noted that there were several more bloodstains on the station floor and wondered how they got there.

He realised that the same fate awaited him if the partisans found out who he was. All over the north of Italy, partisan squads were committing the most brutal acts of reprisal and murder against anyone even suspected of being a fascist or having fascist connections. It was not just the partisans who were involved in the killings, but also the local people were now taking up arms against them following the collapse of fascism.

Sergio had probably escaped their checklists because he was not a prominent figure in the fascist regime; he was just an aide, a non-important cog in a very large wheel. He consoled himself with this thought and turned his attention to the sound of an approaching train. A ticket collector standing close by shouted out, 'due to track repairs this will be the last train to Lucca for two days; please wait until all passengers have disembarked before boarding.' People moved closer to the rails to make sure they got a seat.

Slowly the train pulled into the platform and came to a shuddering halt at the buffers. Sergio waited until all the passengers had alighted and the people waiting on the platform had boarded and found seats. He wanted to see if there were any military types in the carriages and if there were, he wanted to avoid any contact with them. After satisfying himself there was none, he entered a carriage and sat opposite a young girl and her mother. He reckoned it would be safer to talk to them if he had to than some of the other passengers. He was surprised at how empty the carriage was. He reasoned that the uncertainty of the military situation had prevented people from travelling by train.

After what seemed like a long time, but was in fact only a few minutes, the train gave a jolt, and slowly began to move out of the station. Sergio visibly relaxed and smiled at the little girl. He put his head against the window, moved the briefcase under his legs and settling down in his seat he prepared for his journey. He knew it would take around four hours to reach Lucca. Apparently, the tracks in some places were only temporary and the trains could only move very slowly over them.

Some time past and he felt hungry. He reached inside his overcoat pocket and pulled out a salami. He cut off a few slices with a small pocketknife and ate some. He looked at the little girl and seeing her eye the salami hungrily, he offered a few slices to her. She looked at her mother for some sign whether or not to accept. When she was sure it was all right, she put her open hand forward and said '*Grazie, signore.*' Sergio smiled at her and cut off a few more pieces for himself. He said 'what's your name?' She answered 'Carla.' She took the Salami and shoved it all into her mouth in one go. Sergio watched her eat it and realised how hungry this little girl was. He offered her mother the remainder of the Salami, saying 'please, take it, I'm not very hungry'. She accepted it with an embarrassed smile. After a while she said, 'Are you travelling far, *signore?*' He paused for a moment before answering her. 'Not too far, I'm travelling home to my family outside Lucca.' She nodded to him as if in agreement, 'So am I, *signore*. My family lives in Galliano. We have been travelling for two days to get this far.' She paused to cut off a slice of Salami and hungrily ate it. 'The Germans took my husband before they retreated from Firenze. They shot him for suspected partisan activities and we had to leave the city very quickly before they took us as well.' She had tears in her eyes as she continued. 'I couldn't even bury him; I left him lying in the street like a dog.' She dried her eyes roughly with the sleeve of her coat before continuing.

'The partisans came to our door one night looking for food. What could we do, they had guns and we were helpless. We allowed them into our home and we fed them what we had. One of our neighbours, a fascist, saw them and reported us to the Germans. The partisans had left by the time the soldiers arrived. They beat my husband with their rifle butts because he couldn't tell them where the partisans had gone. Then they took him outside. I hid with my daughter in the small field in front of our house and watched them push him to his knees and shoot him in the back of the head. I tried to stop my daughter seeing it, but failed. We saw his life's blood flow from his wound into the gutter. He did nothing wrong, he only wanted to get by and live in peace.' She dried her eyes again. 'Thank you for your kindness *signore*; it's the first we have eaten in two days. We escaped with nothing but our lives.' Sergio turned silently away and faced the window again, leaving the widow and her daughter alone to their grief and tears. Italy is dying, he thought, this is our season for tears.

Eventually he fell asleep and was only wakened by the train clattering over the tracks outside Lucca. He waited until all the passengers had left the train before he picked up the briefcase and stepped down onto the platform. Thankfully, he knew this station well. This was the main town of his region and he had often used it prior to the war. He made his way to the side entrance and exited onto one of the main streets. He walked along steadily for a few minutes trying hard to avoid eye contact with other people. He was concerned in case he met someone he knew. When he did eventually look up, he saw that others who passed him on the street were doing the same. The sense of fear from them was tangible. Sergio realised that people were scared in case they were labelled as being fascist. Changed days, he thought, as he remembered a time before the war when the whole of Lucca came to hear the Duce speak at a rally in the town.

He turned left and walked into the local bus station where he bought a ticket to his home town of Borgo a Mozzano. The clerk told him there was a bus about to leave from the stance outside, so he quickly boarded it and waited impatiently for it to leave. He tried hard not to look at any of the other passengers as he settled down lower in his seat.

Sergio had never told anyone, not even his family, of his involvement with Mussolini, that he was his personal aide. They thought he was merely a Blackshirt in the Rome Cohort and they had no idea how close he was to the Duce. They knew he believed in fascism, but then, before the war, most of Italy did. His family would question him why he had returned home at this time; however, he was prepared for that. He would tell them that like many other Italians, he had become disillusioned with Mussolini and now that the war was nearing its end, he had decided to come home to be with his family and to forget that he was ever fooled by fascism.

Some other people boarded the bus, shouting at the top of their voices, 'The partisans have just caught Mussolini. It was on the radio.' Sergio was stunned. How could this have happened, he thought. Mussolini a prisoner of the communists. His whole world had been swept away with the thought of the Duce being held a prisoner of the partisans.

'Let's all drink to the brave comrades who caught that murdering bastard' one of them said, as he pulled a bottle of grappa from a bag at his feet. Everyone on the bus took a drink from the bottle before passing it on. When it was handed to him, Sergio took the bottle and held it to his lips without drinking from it. He fixed a smile on his face and clapped his hands in time to the singing that had started. When the other passengers sang the partisan anthem *Bella Ciao*, he joined in with them even though his heart was breaking.

'He was dressed in a German Army overcoat;' said one of the new passengers to no one in particular. 'A partisan brigade under Count Bellini Delle Stelle stopped a German convoy near Lake Como heading for home; they searched it for escaping Italians. They saw one soldier wearing a German overcoat with Italian red striped Generals trousers hiding in the back of a truck, and when they checked him out, they found our beloved Duce. The Germans didn't want to give him up, but they were given the choice of surrendering him at once and being allowed free passage home, or fighting their way out and perhaps dying in the attempt. They soon saw sense.' They all laughed at this before giving out another chorus of *Bella Ciao*. Sergio sat out the remainder of the journey in a stunned silence. He just couldn't comprehend an Italy, or indeed a world, without Mussolini.

After about an hour, the bus reached Borgo a Mozzano, Sergio got off, holding the briefcase close to him. He walked along the familiar streets for a few minutes before he saw in front of him the curved outline of the Devil's Bridge.

His family had told him the story of how it was built. In the eleventh century, the townspeople had tried to build the bridge themselves, but were stopped by bad weather. The Devil volunteered to finish it for them if they would give him the soul of the first person to cross it. The townspeople agreed. The next morning they sent a pig out first to cross the bridge. The Devil was thwarted and the town had their bridge.

He walked onto the narrow bridge, stood in its centre, and gazed upwards to the wooded hillside beyond to get his bearings. Over many years, the steep hillside had grown denser with vegetation and trees. He had first come here as a little boy playing with his friends and he was familiar with the area. The sun was now at its highest in the sky and the glare from it filled the surrounding countryside bringing the colours of the leaves and shrubbery all around to life.

Shielding his eyes from it he eventually saw what he was looking for, a large oak tree standing on its own just set off to the right of the bridge on the crest of the hill. Still holding the briefcase, he made his way up the hillside in the general direction of the tree. He found the steep incline testing, especially as he now felt very tired and hungry. The branches from the trees whipped against him and the thick undergrowth impeded his progress. He stopped and watched a family of rabbits scurry away to his left. How lucky they are, he thought, they don't know the whole world has gone mad. He had always enjoyed listening to the birds up here singing in the trees, but today their songs went unnoticed.

After some twenty minutes of walking, he reached the tree and sat down on the grass resting his back against it. He spent some time looking around to make sure he was alone before he opened the briefcase and reverently took out one of the tightly packaged papers.

He read the first one, a letter from Winston Churchill, Prime Minister of Great Britain to his most Gracious Excellency Benito Mussolini, Duce of the Italian Fascist Party and First Duce of the Italian Empire.

Downing Street
1st June 1940

My Dear Duce,

In continuation of my last letter to you, and after consultation with others in power, I am now in the position to offer you new lands to add to the growing Italian Empire. These lands were former colonies of the French, however with France itself now an occupied territory their ownership can be easily transferred to Italy.

I have also spoken to His Majesty King George and have some agreement with him that he would be willing to resign, as reigning Monarch in favour of the Duke of Windsor, who as we all know would be more acceptable to Herr Hitler. His majesty feels that he would be willing to abdicate if it was the catalyst needed to placate him. The Duke, who is a man of right wing views, is well known to be open to the Nazi philosophy.

All that remains to be done is for you to mediate on our behalf with Herr Hitler and to persuade him that it would not be in the best interests of our two great nations to attempt to invade our sovereign domain. Influence him to understand that the cost in men, machinery and money would be too great a price for him to pay at this time and that he should delay invasion until Germany and her allies have consolidated their present gains. This will give us the breathing space we so desperately need at this time. I also urge you Duce not to enter this conflict, but to stay neutral, as General Franco has already done, and I can assure you that in the long term it will prove to be the best policy for Italy.

Please be assured of my undying friendship.
Yours faithfully,
Winston

Sergio was amazed at what he had read. Now he understood that if these letters fell into the hands of the Communists they would never see the light of day. The Communists would try to conceal the fact that Mussolini was not the mad Dictator they made him out to be, but a great political leader who had influenced world events and was a benign influence on Hitler.

He realised that these letters were invaluable to the right and the left wing parties and could, after the war, influence the result of local and national elections. He put the letter back in the briefcase and was about to close it when he noticed a smaller bundle tied separately. He took it out and opened it. It consisted of photographs of Mussolini taken in private with various people. He recognised some of the faces: one was of the Duke of Windsor sitting with Mussolini at a dinner table in Rome. The Duke had his right arm raised in the fascist salute and a glass of wine in the other. Another photo was of Churchill, also taken in Rome. Churchill was standing alone with both his hands around a bust of Mussolini, kissing it. Another photo showed Mussolini and Churchill standing together, cigars in their left hands and their right arms raised in the fascist salute. There were probably another twenty photos in the package.

He put the photos back into the briefcase, and pulled from his overcoat a large piece of oilcloth. Hoping that this would protect the letters from the effects of the elements, he wrapped the briefcase tightly in it. He looked around at a heavy boulder sitting on the ground about three feet from the tree, and moved over beside it. Placing his feet against it and shoving a little, he moved the boulder over to reveal a hole about two feet wide and about three feet deep. He placed the briefcase in the hole, and moving over to the other side of it, repeated the process with his feet until the boulder was pushed back in place.

As a young boy, he had dug the hole and used it, as a hiding place for the special things he wanted kept secret from prying eyes. It was the perfect hiding place for the briefcase. He had added the boulder in his late teens as an extra precaution. He was certain that no one would ever find the briefcase and its contents by accident, and he had never told a living soul of this place. Sergio was the type of man who would never divulge a secret or a confidence. He had a high moral code and was known as a man who never gossiped or spread stories about others.

He sat down again with his back against the oak tree and relaxed a little. He felt exhausted and hungry. He had not eaten a proper meal all day; this coupled with the drama of the last few hours had left him feeling drained. He thought about what he had heard about Mussolini's capture. Should it be true that he had fallen into the hands of the partisans and not the Allies then he would most certainly be shot. What should he then do with the briefcase? Sergio thought for a few moments more before coming to his decision. He would keep the briefcase hidden and tell no one of its existence until he felt the time was right, just as the Duce had requested. He wearily got up, walked slowly down the hillside onto the Devil's Bridge, and stood in the centre of it gazing down onto the swiftly flowing Serchio River. He thought of the many people over the centuries that had stood in this same spot, looking down at the river, wondering how they were going to survive their particular war. Nothing has changed, he thought, only the faces. We still have our senseless wars and senseless killings, nothing changes and never will.

The next day he heard that the partisans had shot Mussolini and hung his battered body from an Esso garage hoarding in Milan. The crowd that had gathered to see the dead Duce of the Italian Empire hanging upside down like a lump of meat erupted in fury. They beat his body with anything they could get their hands on and cursed his name. They tore the clothes from his back, leaving him with only his red striped trousers on. They spat on him and his mistress. A man wearing the feathered hat of the Bersalglieri Regiment lifted a little boy up high enough so that he could urinate on Mussolini's face. One woman, who had lost her husband and three sons in the war, fired a pistol four times into his corpse, shouting at him, 'you killed all my loved ones you bastard. Here's a bullet for each one.' The crown laughed at this empty gesture.

Mussolini's mistress, Clara Petacci, and six other men who had been his high-ranking officials in the fascist government shared the same fate as him. One partisan, for the sake of modesty, tied a rope around Clara Petacci's skirt to stop it from falling around her waist.

All around Milan fascist emblems, statues and busts of Mussolini were pulled down and destroyed. Fascist flags, identity cards and literature were burned in the streets fuelling large bonfires around the town. People joined hands and danced around the flames.

The prostitutes who had serviced the German army barracks in the city were rounded up by the partisans and abused by the local women. Most of them were shot by firing squads, although some of them escaped this fate. They were spared being shot only because they had prostituted themselves to feed their children and were not considered real professionals who did it for financial gain or voluntary collaboration. These women had their heads shaved as a sign of their collusion with the enemy. The locals would spit at them and call them *puttane* as they walked past. Some of the women felt they would have been better off being shot rather than being subjected to this abuse and being ostracised by the local population.

Reprisals against the fascists, or suspected fascists gained momentum in the North of Italy. By the time the madness had subsided, it was estimated that between twenty to thirty thousand people had been murdered. The Allies did not intervene to stop the slaughter.

The next day he learned that Hitler had killed himself and that the official surrender of the German Military in Italy would take place on 2nd May 1945, signalling that the end of the war in the rest of Europe was only a matter of a few days away.

In Borgo a Mozzano the news that the Germans had surrendered and that the war had officially ended was greeted with wild jubilation. Street parties took place all over the town and lasted until the small hours of the morning. The town council, who had been ardent fascists were taken into custody, imprisoned for a while and eventually released. They were advised to leave the town and to make their home elsewhere. A new communist town council was elected very quickly and Sergio watched without comment as the fascist emblems on the walls of the town hall were removed by stonemasons using hammer and chisel. He also didn't comment as the fascist street names were changed to more seemingly patriotic ones. Before long, there was no sign in the town that there had ever been a fascist state in Italy. As be observed the transformation, Sergio was amazed at the number of communist townspeople Borgo a Mozzano apparently always had.

After the war and the resulting witch hunt for fascists, Sergio was asked to attend a meeting of the Committee for Democracy, a group of prominent citizens set up with the intention of clearing out, in a peaceful manner, any last fascists from their midst. The leader of the group was the newly elected mayor of the town, Umberto Collini who was well known to Sergio from their school days together. The meeting took place in a small room at the rear of the town hall.

Sergio entered the room and was asked to sit in a chair in the middle of the floor facing a top table of committee members. The Mayor opened the meeting by asking Sergio to state his name. Sergio laughed out aloud before saying, 'If you have brought me here to ask stupid things like my name then you can all fuck off. I went to school with most of you here, so let's be real.'

As Sergio got up to leave the embarrassed Mayor said, 'Sergio, please sit down and co-operate. This is a serious business. We have to make sure that we don't have any fascists in our midst spreading their poisonous doctrine.' Sergio's face showed the anger he felt before he replied, 'So let's be serious then. You have brought me here to find out if I was a fascist during the war. Yes, I was for a time, but so were most of you in this room. I even remember going to a fascist rally in Lucca with you Umberto to hear Mussolini speak, and how taken you were with him. I remember that you joined the fascist party the next day.' The Mayor shifted in his seat uncomfortably. Sergio carried on speaking, 'I was an aide to Mussolini. Nothing more and nothing less. I was like a servant in a king's palace and was never part of his entourage or was ever taken into his confidence. What more can I say? You may as well interrogate every soldier who served in the army, or every police officer, or every civil servant. They were as complicit as I was.'

Silence greeted his remarks as the committee members looked at each other as if searching for inspiration. The Mayor cleared his throat before coming to his feet and saying, 'we thank you for your attendance here today Sergio, and I think you have satisfied us all as to your role in fascism. You may leave.' Sergio looked at the citizens committee with open disdain, 'If I come or go, I do so of my own free will, and not at your command. We fought a war to establish that right.'

Sergio got up and made for the door. He stopped before opening it, turned round and said, 'One more thing before I leave. I have heard the rumours about me going around the town and I want this to be very clear to all of you here. I know nothing about secret papers or briefcases. All I can tell you about is the colour of his shoe polish, or the type of shaving soap he used.' He turned once again and left the room.

He worked hard to avoid being tarnished by his fascist background. He appeared to everyone in the town as being apolitical, however in his deepest self he knew he would never change. The Police had interviewed him on a few occasions over the briefcase's disappearance, and once, even Churchill's staff had spoken to him. The great man was on a painting holiday in Lake Garda and had sent his staff out to try to find the letters. Sergio had always denied any knowledge of its whereabouts and eventually he was left in peace.

To Sergio the fascist ideology was deeply imbedded in his heart. It aggrieved him when he heard of Nazism and Fascism being compared as if they were identical ideologies. Yes, Hitler in the early days had been influenced by Italian fascism, but it was in Sergio's eyes a different creed. Nazism was a racist and anti-Semitic philosophy that had openly murdered millions of innocent people in pursuit of its aim. Fascism on the other hand was a return to the glory of the old Roman state and its grandeur. It had been used by Mussolini to bring unity to a disparate people. Sergio remembered that Mussolini had often said in private that Garibaldi had made a united Italy but that he had made a united people. The symbols and salute used by fascists were Roman and Mussolini's Blackshirts were fashioned in Cohorts, Centuries, and Legions, just like the armies of old. Jews were involved at the highest level in the party and even Mussolini's mistress was a Jewess, proving that the Duce, in Sergio's eyes, was not a racist or anti-Semitic.

Mussolini had come to power as prime minister at the invitation of the King of Italy who was still head of state in Italy. Not like Hitler who had assumed all power in Germany. Mussolini had also accepted the motion of the Fascist Council of Ministers in 1943 that had voted to take his powers way from him, forcing him the next day to see the King to discuss the way ahead. The King had imprisoned him, and he remained that way until Hitler had him rescued him in a daring raid on his mountain top prison. Hitler had then set up a Republican puppet state in the North of Italy at Lake Garda with Mussolini as its titular head. It became the rallying point for Italian fascists from all over Italy; however, it proved to be the end of independent action for Mussolini. He was guarded by SS guards at his villa and not Italians, and even his domestic staff at his home was German.

In discussions with others, Sergio always made the point that after the war there were no Italians convicted of war crimes, and that it was the Nazi's and not the fascists who built and ran the concentration camps that had led to the Holocaust. In Sergio's eyes, Mussolini's biggest mistake that led to his downfall was his involvement and later subservience to Hitler.

After the war, he never discussed his beliefs with anyone, not even his wife. He instead waited until the day Italy was not threatened by Communism and unfortunately, that day never came around during his lifetime.

Chapter 3

June 22nd 1965

Angelo Corti was a thankful man, his life was in his eyes very good. He had worked hard to build this life ever since arriving from Italy in 1948 to make Scotland his home and he was content. He was 53 years old and in good health. He was a big man with a temper to match and even in his middle age, it didn't do to cross him too often. He had a loving wife and a strong son who all worked alongside him in his Glasgow ice cream business and the future looked rosy. However, today he felt uneasy, a sense of caution overtook him as a voice from his past caught up with him.

Angelo walked across the room to a walnut cabinet in the corner and opening one of the doors took out a bottle of grappa. He poured himself a drink and walked back to his seat. He sat down with a heavy sigh and took a sip from his glass. Memories of his past life in Italy came flooding back to his mind, events that he had forgotten about, or if truth were told, he had tried hard to forget. He closed his eyes and once again heard the charismatic voice of Mussolini holding the adoring crowd gathered below him, in his hand. He heard their response as they cried out 'Duce, Duce, Duce' and Mussolini standing on a balcony with his hands on his hips and sporting a jutting jaw, basking in the adulation of the crowd. He also remembered the part he played in this theatre of dreams, and how it had all started.

★★★

Angelo was 25 years old in 1937 and had been a member of the Rome Cohort of the Blackshirts. He had travelled down from Tuscany to join them out of his devotion to the Duce himself, and he worked with great zeal to establish himself as a worthy follower of fascism. Eventually he was promoted to the Moschettieri Del Duce, Mussolini's personal bodyguard and it was there that he met Sergio Rossi. Initially they became friendly because their home villages were only a few miles apart. Sergio in Borgo a Mozzano and he in Coreglia, but through the hot summer of 1937 they became firm friends.

Sergio was eventually given the opportunity to be the personal aide to the Duce and understandably, his free time was at a premium; however, they still managed to meet on his day off for a glass of wine at one of the many Café's in the area and discuss the events of the day. All through the war, they had kept in touch with each other and when Sergio invited Angelo to his wedding as his best man, he gladly accepted.

When the war eventually finished they frequently met up with each other in Lucca and when Angelo immigrated to Scotland they kept in touch by letter, but regrettably, they never met again. Now, unexpectedly, Sergio's wife Maria had phoned to say that he was dying of cancer and he had expressed a wish to see his old comrade again. 'Come quickly Angelo' said Maria, 'He doesn't have long.'

He remembered Maria with fondness and thought back again to their wedding day in Rome and the arrival of Mussolini who had unexpectedly come to join the wedding celebration as an ordinary guest.

As a sign of respect for Sergio, the Duce had come with a wedding present, a cut glass decanter with the fascist emblem near the top inlaid with gold leaf. Underneath this, also inlaid in gold leaf was an outline bust of Il Duce himself.

Mussolini had been dressed in a white suit and spats and Angelo remembered him soaking up the adulation of the other wedding guests as they went wild with joy at the sight of him.

Angelo took another sip of his grappa and savoured the experience as the strong liqueur slipped easily down his throat.

He once again reflected on the life he had made for himself here in Scotland. No one knew, not even his son, that he had not only been a Blackshirt in the prestigious Rome Cohort, but had also been one of Mussolini's personal bodyguard, a member of the Moschettieri Del Duce, the Musketeers, the elite Cohort that had taken an oath of allegiance to the Duce and had sworn to protect him with their own lives if need be. Their cap badge was a silver skull with crossed swords and they had proudly carried Mussolini's personal standard as their own. They had distinctive black uniforms and specialised black weapons.

He reflected that the rifle used to kill the American President Kennedy two years ago was the special Moschettieri issue 6.5mm Carcano, one of only two hundred made exclusively for them. How Kennedy's assassin Lee Harvey Oswald's claim to have bought this rare valuable rifle through a mail order catalogue was always beyond his understanding. What a mail order company was doing with this rare rifle on their shelves was indeed another mystery.

If the history of his past life became general knowledge in Scotland then he was finished, his business would be ruined and his family disgraced. Memories of the war were still fresh in many people's minds and when he was asked what his role was, he had always passed off his war years to inquisitive questioning as a farmer in the Tuscan hills who watched from a distance the passage of hostilities.

He wondered if Sergio had ever told anyone of his own closeness to Mussolini. Angelo thought for a few minutes before deciding that even if Sergio had told his family about himself, which was unlikely, he was certain that he would never have told them anything about his closest friend without first asking his permission. Angelo also realised that Sergio was perhaps the most secretive man he had ever known and there was no one he trusted more with confidential information.. He visibly relaxed and finished off the rest of his grappa before reaching for the phone to make his arrangements to visit Italy.

★★★

The plane landed smoothly at Pisa airport and Angelo, with a smile on his face, thanked the flight staff before descending the metal stairway to the tarmac. He had never flown before and the experience was one that had felt both exhilarating and terrifying. He walked alongside the other passengers into the terminal building, towards passport control. He was thankful that he had the foresight to apply for a new passport the year before at the Italian consulate in Glasgow or he would not have been able to leave the U.K. He had thought about applying for British nationality, but he felt guilty enough at leaving Italy behind when he had immigrated without losing his Italian identity. Angelo was still in his deepest heart of hearts very Italian. He lived the lifestyle of an Italian, the food he ate was Italian, and the music he listened to was Italian.

Even his wife Elizabeth, who was a small redhead of Scottish Irish descent, preferred the Italian way of life and the Italian culture to her own Scottish background. He had met her in Lucca at the end of the war in a military hospital where she was working as a nurse. They had struck up an immediate friendship and had started dating. Eventually they decided to get married and move to Scotland to start a new life there. At first, he worked as a hospital porter in the Glasgow Infirmary until he was offered a job by a fellow Italian who was the manager of an ice cream company. Angelo worked hard and learned his trade well. Eventually he started his own Ice cream business in the city's east end not too far from Celtic Park football ground. The business was soon well established and Angelo took great pride in the fact that he supplied ice cream for the majority of Italian café's that were a common sight in the city. He was also very proud that Corti's ice cream was a byword for quality in the city.

His son, Marco was 18 and about to be called up for his Italian military service, as all young Italian males of that age were. Even though he was born in Scotland, Angelo had made sure that his son's birth had been registered in Italy. This had made him eligible for the eighteen-month military conscription all Italian males had to do.

He approached the customs control and held up his new passport for inspection. The customs official barely glanced at it and waved Angelo through the barrier without looking at him.

Angelo felt aggrieved that he was not given the courtesy of a welcome greeting. 'Ignorant man, he must be from the south,' thought Angelo as he headed for the Avis rental desk to pick up his hired car.

Once on the road and heading towards Lucca, Angelo thought again of his past life.

He remembered the first time he had been given the honour of guarding Mussolini at a state function in Rome. How nervously he had walked behind the great man as he escorted him to his table at the state banquet and stood to attention behind him during the proceedings. His eyes roaming over the room and the excitement he felt as he recognised amongst the assembled guests, Presidents, heads of state, dignitaries, film stars, and other famous faces. How privileged he had felt to be there and to witness all of these people assembled at the table of the Duce.

He approached Borgo a Mozzano from the south and drove along the banks of the river Serchio until he came to Via della Repubblica; he turned into the street and saw the house he was looking for, a small-whitewashed cottage sitting on its own just off the road end.

Maria and Sergio had lived here all their married life together. Sergio was a keen gardener and he reflected how run down and overgrown it now appeared to be. The first time Angelo had visited here was a lasting memory for him. He had arrived with the Duce one night when the Duce had been travelling south from Milan to Pisa by car and on a whim had made a detour to visit Sergio who had been on leave at the time. Mussolini had three bodyguards and a driver with him, and they had all been made very welcome.

Maria had prepared a meal of chicken and pasta with ragu for them all and Sergio made sure there was plenty of wine on the table. Mussolini was very relaxed in this company and contributed well to the conversation around the table. They sang the fascist songs of the time together and, to the delight of all,

Mussolini had given a solo rendition of *Giovinezza*, the official fascist state anthem. Eventually, in the small hours of the morning, his bodyguards, leaving behind a twittering Maria, still on a high, helped a slightly inebriated Mussolini to his car. Sergio and Maria never told anyone who their famous guest that night was.

He stopped outside the house and gently knocked on the front door. A white faced, tired looking woman with her hair tied back from her face answered the door. She gazed at Angelo with hesitant recognition before saying,' '*Dio bono*, it's Angelo. It's been such a long time, come inside' and at this she stood aside to let Angelo into the house. Angelo hugged Maria and kissed her on both cheeks, 'It's been such a long time Maria' he said as he hugged her again.

He was taken aback with how old Maria looked. Their ages were similar, however the strain of what had been happening to Sergio was certainly showing on her face. 'Maria, how is he?' Maria stood back a little and took her time to answer. 'The doctors say he could go at any moment. He is sedated quite heavily; perhaps you had better go up and see him.'

Angelo kissed her again on both cheeks, climbed the stairs and entered the bedroom where he was surprised to see about ten people gathered around Sergio's bedside reciting the Rosary. One woman was taking the lead role and praying aloud on her own: 'Hail Mary full of grace the Lord is with thee blessed art thou amongst women and blessed is the fruit of thy womb Jesus.' This was followed by the others in the room praying out in unison, 'Holy Mary mother of God pray for us sinners now and at the hour of our death Amen.' He stood at the back of the room listening to the prayers and looking at a barely conscious Sergio on the bed.

Angelo was a confirmed atheist; he now felt that what he was listening to was merely superstitious mumbling. He also knew that Sergio felt the same way, however if it helped the people praying in believing they were aiding Sergio's journey to heaven, then he accepted that no harm was being done.

He moved closer to the bed and took Sergio's hand in his. Sergio opened his eyes and after a few moments gave a nod of recognition to Angelo. He said something in a barely heard whisper, causing Angelo to move closer to the bed and lower his head to his.

Sergio gave a thin smile and whispered something conspiratorially into Angelo's ear before closing his eyes again and slipping back into a semi-conscious state.

Angelo returned to his place at the back of the room and watched as his old friend lay dying. Maria came into the room and sat by the bedside. The gathering did not have to wait very long before Sergio gave out a low rasping sound and breathed his last.

★★★

Three days later, Sergio's requiem mass was held in the local church of San Pietro. It had been a long time since Angelo had been to mass and he felt strangely out of place in the ornate surroundings of the church. He had no belief in a God, and if there was a God he reckoned that he was a vile creature and not worthy of all this adoration. What he had witnessed in the war had convinced him that this was all just superstition. If this God cares for every sparrow that falls, and has every hair on your head counted, why does he decide to allow such suffering to take place. He looked around at all the people praying out aloud and somehow felt pity for them.

His attention was now taken up by the priest sprinkling holy water on the coffin in the centre aisle near the alter rails and thought how futile all this was. The blessing with incense followed and filled the small church with a familiar smell that brought many memories back to Angelo.

He remembered his time as an altar boy in Coreglia, and the happy childhood he had shared with his family there. He made a mental note to visit their graves soon. As the mass ended, he rose to take his place with the other pallbearers and carry the coffin from the church to the cemetery behind.

Angelo was visibly moved to tears when he helped lower the coffin into the ground. The grave was the family lair, with Sergio's mother the first to be buried there some years before. The priest read something from a prayer book over the graveside and sprinkled holy water down onto the coffin. The sound of the women sobbing was lost in the reciting of the rosary prayers, and when they had finished, the gravediggers moved in to fill the grave with earth.

After the funeral, the small band of mourners walked along the road from the cemetery to the town centre in brilliant sunshine. Angelo reflected how different the culture was in Italy compared to Scotland that for weddings and funerals in the small towns and villages the Italians preferred to walk the short distances involved.

They arrived at one of the local restaurants where Maria had arranged a meal for her family and close friends. Their table was set outside, for about fifteen people, in the late morning sunshine. Waiters placed bottles of local wine on the table and took the orders for the meal. Angelo sat beside Maria, holding her hand and tried to offer her some words of comfort.

He remembered some of the faces around the table from his distant past and he spent some time talking to them about the old days. Inevitably, the subject of the war was brought up. They swapped stories and laughed at some of them. Sergio reflected that as with most stories the passage of time had brought a little embroidery to them. The sun had now moved on and they were now sitting in the shade. He could not believe that four hours had past since they had first sat down for the meal.

After the lunch and what he considered an appropriate length of time, he began to make some comments to Maria about leaving. He had been in Italy for longer than he had originally planned and now felt it was time to go home. He told Maria that he had a flight to catch in a few hours' time at Pisa Airport and he would now have to go.

He was about to say his farewells when she took him aside in private. 'Angelo, Sergio made me promise that after his funeral I would give you this.' She took from her pocket an envelope that had seen better days. 'He wrote this some years ago and during his illness he frequently made me promise that I would not forget to give it to you. I have no idea what it says, but I do know that it meant a lot to him. He told me to tell you that this was his greatest secret and that he could share it with no one but you.'

Maria paused as she handed Angelo the letter, 'Angelo, whatever is in this letter, promise me that you won't bring disgrace to Sergio's name.' Angelo hugged her and kissed her with real affection. 'Maria, I would never dishonour his name. You can trust me, I promise.'

Angelo took the envelope and put it in his pocket; he then said his farewells to Maria and the others before setting off in his car for Pisa Airport.

It was only during the flight that Angelo remembered the envelope. He pulled it out of his pocket and held it with some care. His mind went back to the moment when Sergio had whispered in his ear the old fascist motto '*Credere, Obbedire, Combattere*' (believe, obey, fight) and he wondered why, after all this time he had chosen these as his whispered last words. Perhaps the drugs had affected him, or maybe it was just a deathbed rant. Certainly in appeared that Sergio had remained a fascist to his dying day. He put these thoughts aside, opened the envelope and pulling out a letter, he read;

Caro Angelo,

By the time you read this letter I will have passed on. I am writing it to explain many things to you, things so fantastic that I have kept them to myself since the last time I saw the Duce in Milan. You once asked me why I didn't stay with the Duce until the end and I know that you weren't satisfied with my answer, however I wasn't able to tell you the truth as the Duce had made me promise to keep what I am about to reveal to you a secret until death.

The Duce gave me a briefcase filled with correspondence between himself and Churchill proving that Mussolini was being courted by Churchill not to enter the war on the German side but to be a moderating influence on Hitler. The Duce was promised new lands for the Italian empire and in his replies to Churchill showed that he was open to this approach.

Many people have wondered why Hitler delayed for two days at Dunkirk when he could have finished off the British Army in France and the letters show it was Mussolini who convinced him to delay. The same with the invasion of England when Hitler could have walked into London with little resistance. It was our Duce who was behind it and the letters are full of praise from Churchill who recognised this. In 1940 instead of the expected invasion of Britain Hitler turned his attention to Russia, and again the letters show that this was through Mussolini's intervention as he convinced Hitler that the real enemy was Communism.

After the war, Churchill spent three summers at villas in the Lake Garda area under the pretence of painting holidays; however, his staff was very active in the region searching for the briefcase. They spoke to many locals, including ex-partisans, however with no success. Churchill knew that Mussolini, in his final days, always had the briefcase with him, however when he was captured there was no sign of it. Churchill had come to the conclusion that Mussolini either had hidden the briefcase himself or had given it to an aide to hide for him.

Mussolini had frequently called the letters his insurance policy. If these letters were found, they would paint Churchill in a different light and could compromise him as an appeaser where the Duce was concerned. They would also show Mussolini as a moderating influence on Hitler. The Italian right and neo fascist parties would also welcome getting their hands on the correspondence, as would the socialists and the far left. I also suspect that the British government would be interested in ensuring they stayed secret.

So dear friend I now charge you with their safekeeping and ask you to renew your vow to the Duce as you once before did in Rome.. There is no one else alive that I would trust with this mission. You must make sure that they do not fall into the wrong hands and you must trust no one with the secret of their existence or of their hiding place.

I now ask you to remember how we worked together for the fascist cause and how proud we felt being part of the Duce's bodyguard.

Angelo stopped reading at that point and feeling a little numb from the shock of the letters contents, asked a passing flight attendant for a coffee and a small brandy. Fortified with these he read on.

The Duce had placed the letters in a black leather briefcase, which I took from him in Milan. I left Milan before he did at his insistence and travelled to Borgo a Mozzano. On the bus there, I heard that the Duce had been captured, so I knew that I had to find a safe hiding place for the letters. I remembered a place I used as a small boy when I wanted to hide special things and decided to use it again.

I went to the Devil's Bridge and stood in the centre of it, facing the wooded hillside. I used the right hand parapet as a marker and looked onto the ridge just to the right of it where I saw a tall oak tree standing on its own. I made my way up the hillside to it and saw a boulder near the foot of the tree.

When I moved the stone aside with my feet, quite a large hole came into view, so I wrapped the briefcase in a large oilcloth and placed it in the hole before replacing the stone. I checked on the condition of the briefcase every year and thankfully, there was little deterioration.

So now my dear friend Angelo, you are the keeper of this secret, and must decide on your own what is the best way ahead. Always keep in your mind the thoughts of the Duce in this matter and make sure the letters do not fall into the wrong hands. Be careful and trust no one.

Eia! Eia! Eia! Alalà!
Your friend,
Sergio

★★★

Angelo slowly closed the letter and put it back in the envelope. He sat stunned, staring at the back of the seat in front of him. He had been pulled back into a time in his past that he had wanted to forget and he saw no way of ignoring it. Names from the past flashed before his eyes. Mussolini: Moschettieri: Fascismo: Blackshirts. He felt as if he was in a whirlpool and was being sucked into the very centre of it. He asked the flight attendant for another brandy and closed his eyes as he slowly sipped it. What should he do next ? Should he return to Italy and check on the briefcase? on the other hand, should he wait until he had decided what the best way ahead was. One thing for sure, he could not ignore the mission that Sergio had given him, even if he had wanted to. The die was cast and he was not only part of the events surrounding the letters, but it appeared that he had the lead role.

Chapter 4

1 8th April 1987
It was Angelo's 75th birthday and his family had organised a celebration at his home. All of his friends and most of his relatives were there. He had taken great care today on his appearance. A smart navy blue suit and a new white shirt and a navy tie.

Angelo looked around the lounge at the host of people who were there. His older brother Vittorio, who was named after Mussolini's son and his wife Eia waved over to him. Eia's name was part of the fascist chant 'Eia! Eia! Eia! Alalà', which didn't mean anything as such, however it was always been used by the fascists at their rallies. Eia's father had been a committed fascist and, much to her embarrassment had named her after it.

He looked around for his son Marco and saw him talking to one of the guests. Angelo felt a surge of pride as he walked towards him. 'What a handsome man' he thought, with a father's pride. Marco was over six feet tall and built like a rugby player. His hair was jet black and he wore it longer than the current fashion. His smile was easy, showing off white gleaming teeth. Angelo reflected that he had his mothers' temperament, which was more easy and warm, than his own brusque personality.

He was proud when Marco had joined the Italian Army. He knew many Italian fathers who were disappointed that their sons had turned their back on the old country, but not his. He knew that Marco had found it tough at first to fit in. The other Italians had called him 'Inglese' and laughed at his accent, but Marco had stuck it out and eventually made many friends.

Thankfully, all his service was seen out around Rome and not overseas.

Not like his service in the British Army. Angelo had been against his volunteering for the Para Regiment, but Marco, being as strong headed as his father decided to go ahead. Even there, he had a tough time in being accepted until he dropped the 'O' from the end of his name and became plain Mark. When asked what the Italian connection was he would simply shrug his shoulders and say, 'Oh I think someone in my past was Italian, but I'm not sure.' This seemed to work quite well for him, that, and the service he saw in Northern Ireland with his regiment. The one thing guaranteed to forge friendships is when men see active service together.

'Marco, could I have a word with you.' 'Sure dad,' said Marco. Angelo led his son to a small room on the ground floor that he used as a study. He closed the door and sat in his favourite seat. 'Sit down son,' he said, pointing to an armchair facing his. Marco was surprised at his father's quite formal bearing rather than his usual friendly approach, however he put it down to him having a few drinks earlier on in the evening. 'What's on your mind dad,' Marco said as he made himself comfortable. Angelo got up and crossed the floor to his desk, opened a drawer and took out a bottle of Grouse whisky. He picked up two glasses from a cabinet close by, returned to his seat, and poured two large whiskies. 'Saluti' said Marco, as he took the glass from his father.

They sipped their whisky in silence until Angelo said 'son, I have something very important to tell you and I would like you to hear me out before commenting.' Would that be alright?' 'Sure dad, it sounds serious' said Marco as he put his glass down on the table near by. 'What I'm going to tell you Marco is a tale so incredible that I hope you believe it and not put it down to the ramblings of an old man.' He put his own glass down on the table, reached over and took Marco's hands in his. Marco could see that his father was deadly serious so he took his time before saying 'dad if this is important to you then it certainly is important to me. Go on, I'm ready to listen.'

Angelo smiled with affection, 'son, I've kept this secret from the world for 22 years and I have to pass it on now, as I don't know how much time I have left.'

He took another sip of his whisky before speaking again. 'Marco do you remember the stories I used to tell you of secret letters that passed between Churchill and Mussolini during the war, and how you dismissed them as storytelling?' 'Yes I do,' said Marco. 'Well they were all true and I am the guardian of their whereabouts.'

Angelo waited a moment to let this sink in before continuing, 'do you also remember my old friend Sergio Rossi who died in 1965 and I went to his funeral in Italy?' Marco nodded in agreement. He felt too stunned to speak. 'Well Sergio wrote me a letter before he died and his widow gave me it at the funeral. When I read it I felt pretty much as you do now, so perhaps the time has for you to read it as well.'

He reached inside his jacket pocket and pulled out the letter, still in its original envelope, and gave it to him. Marco took the envelope and removed the letter from it; he opened it and began to read.

After some ten minutes, he stopped and lifted his head. His face had a bewildered look on it. 'Dad, is this all true, the bodyguard bit, Mussolini and secret hiding places?' 'Yes son, all of it.' Marco got up from his chair, walked to the study window, and looked out. 'What's this got to do with me dad?' 'I've got nothing to do with fascists and Communists; I just run an ice cream business?'

Angelo got up and joined his son at the window. 'Marco, I brought you up to know the difference between right and wrong and I know you were never interested in politics, however this is different. 'This involves rewriting history; it involves a truth that needs to be declared about those times that no one else is aware of.' 'We are the guardians of that truth and now that I am too old to take the next step with it, I have to pass it on to you.' 'Dad this is just history, I know it's important to you but for the ordinary Joe it's just history, dead and boring.' 'I'm sorry dad, but it happened over 40 years ago.'

Angelo gave a sigh of frustration before answering. 'Marco, let me explain the relevance of these documents for today. Should the communists or socialist parties in Italy get a hold of them, then it would cause turmoil, as they would spin things to their advantage. They would make capital of the fact that Mussolini whilst saying one thing to the Italian people was secretly negotiating with the enemy. They would say that it shows you can never trust the right. That in itself could cause civil unrest in a country still divided between left and right and where the wounds of a civil war have still not healed.

Should the neo-fascists get them, then they would show that Mussolini was not the mad demagogue that the left make him out to be, but was a moderating influence on Hitler and a friend of Churchill. This would raise their profile in Italy as a force for good, much to the annoyance of the left.

There is also the spectre of the British Government not wishing to be embarrassed with their wartime leader negotiating with the enemy. It could be viewed as some sort of compromise being sought with Mussolini to help a beleaguered Britain and I am sure they would be anxious to keep these letters secret. I suspect that the British would go to any lengths to keep them so.

Finally, the Italian government would also be interested in keeping the status quo in Italy. If the publication of these letters could be the source of civil unrest, then the Italians would also want them kept secret.

Therefore, you see Marco, what on the surface appears to be irrelevant history could in effect be the catalyst for a very volatile situation developing. If Italy becomes unstable, then there is the possibility of other countries in Europe with a history of left and right conflict following suit. You should also remember that Italy has more members of the communist party than any other country, apart from the Soviet Union.

Marco sat down on a seat by the widow and looked out at the garden. He didn't answer for a while as he took in what his father had just said. Finally, he said, 'I don't even know what Fascism is or was dad, perhaps it would help if you could tell me a bit about it.'

Angelo took another sip of whisky before continuing,' At the turn of the 20th century Italy had only been united for 40 years and was still coming to terms with the new concept of nationhood. Italy was still an agricultural economy mostly run by landlords who rented out parcels of land to tenant farmers. As the tenant's families grew and the farms were sub-divide amongst them, there was not enough land to grow sufficient food to feed the growing families. When the land was again subdivided amongst the new generation it caused real hardship and in some cases hunger.

This caused unrest amongst the contadini: the tenant farmers, and hence the rise of communism. When the war ended in 1918 and the soldiers returned from the front, they wanted and expected a better life than before. Many Italians emigrated to the new world, to Australia, and other places to escape the poverty but many stayed to try to bring about change. This led to the riots and fighting between those who had and those who had not. These were bleak times indeed with many Italians on both sides being killed and the government of the day was powerless to stop the violence. Into this maelstrom stepped a leader who offered a way out, a way of compromise, a way of unity. This leader, or Duce, was Mussolini. His answer was Fascism. A movement of unity for all classes, a third way. He invited corporate Italy to join with the masses to provide employment and prosperity for all under a strong government led by him. He saved Italy, and perhaps Europe from falling into the hands of the communists. No Trade Unions, no communism, and no exploitation of the workers. A fair deal for all. The people saw him as their saviour, and corporate Italy saw him as providing the means of profit. He built the Autostradas: the new roads, he built the new hospitals and railways, he built the biggest naval fleet in Europe. Coupled with this he recruited into the Army and the Police, which gave the people a feeling of security. He crushed the Mafia in the south of the country and he built new prisons. Italy entered into the 20th century as the envy of the world, that's what fascism did in my estimation.

Marco took all of this in before saying, 'what would you have me do dad?' Angelo put his arm round his son's shoulders and said, 'son, over the years I've had plenty of time to consider all the angles in this, and I don't believe there is an easy answer.

We could destroy the documents and no one would ever know they existed, or we could deliver them into the hands of the Italian Security Services who in turn would ensure that no political party would be able to capitalise on them. They would guarantee that they are used by the Italian State in a responsible way. I personally feel that the latter choice is the most credible.'

Marco asked his father, 'what about giving the letters to the British government?' Angelo answered, 'that would just be like destroying the documents as I don't think they would ever see the light of day again. The British would more than likely destroy them or keep them secret for a very long time. They would look upon them as some sort of slur on Churchill's name. The very fact that Churchill was compromised in negotiating with Mussolini would not be acceptable to the British Government or the British people.

'What I ask you to do Marco is to make contact with someone in the Italian Security Service and probably take them to the site at the Devil's Bridge to recover the briefcase. It will involve a high degree of secrecy in case one of the political parties find out what you are doing, I would not trust the politicians in the government as they have a vested interest, and the newspapers and media are mainly owned by Berlusconi who would have his own agenda.

'How would I get in touch with the Security Services,' said Marco, 'I wouldn't know where to start?' Angelo took another sip of his whisky before answering, 'I have an old friend Carlo Togneri who used to be in the Italian equivalent of the Special Branch of the Carabinieri, I'm sure he would be able to help you. He kept in touch with me over the years and is now retired in Lucca.'

'Would I have to tell him why I want to contact them?' said Marco 'Only in a general sense that you have some information that you can only give to the Security Services in person, that should be enough of a cover to satisfy him. He's a clever man and quite sharp so he may suspect there's more to it, but as long as you stick to that story it should be ok.' 'When should I do this?' said Marco. 'Angelo looked at his son for a few moments, and then said, 'I think as soon as possible. I'll phone Carlo and tell him to expect you in the next few days.' Angelo hugged his son and kissed him on both cheeks before saying, 'Marco, be careful, be very careful, many people would do anything to get hold of those letters, anything: including murder.'

After a while when Angelo was alone he thought of Carlo and how they had worked together during the war.

They had first met at a fascist rally in Rome. Angelo had been with the Moschettieri for some time and was obviously a trusted member of this elite force. He was responsible for the Duce's safety at all of the fascist rallies and it was his job to liaise with the Special Branch of the Carabinieri over security matters. They would tell him the status of potentially dangerous characters in the area that could pose a threat to Mussolini and they would try to put them under lock and key for the duration of Mussolini's visit.

Over the years, a friendship had grown between them even though Carlo was not a fascist, anything but. They had discussed many times over a coffee or a glass of wine what it meant to be a fascist, or in Carlo's case, what it meant to be a communist and they had never agreed. Angelo accepted Carlo for his beliefs and had never seen him as a threat to the Duce, or a dangerous man in any form. Carlo was a cultured man. A man of reason and a man of peace. To Angelo such a man could never contemplate violence, except perhaps in the course of his duty as a police officer. Angelo admired the man and always felt challenged by him when they debated the politics or events of the day. He saw Carlo as an intellectual communist just as he was an intellectual Catholic, meaning that he believed in his mind but did nothing about it in reality. He was very pleased that they had become friends, and to Carlo the same feeling of friendship applied in equal measure. Carlo believed that one day, when the war was over, it would take Italians of all varying persuasions to build a unified Italy.

Now he wondered if Carlo would help him again.

Chapter 5

23rd April 1987

The taxi stopped outside the apartment block on the Via Romano in Lucca. Marco paid the driver and stepped out onto the pavement. He studied the apartment block for a moment before entering the foyer. He looked at the list of names on the board and pressed the buzzer against the name Togneri. 'Pronto' said a voice through the intercom. 'I am Marco Corti,' he said, still holding the buzzer. The door to the apartment hallway opened with a loud click.

He entered the lift, pressed the button for the third floor, and found apartment 3B. He took a deep breath before pressing the bell on the doorframe. He waited for a while before a tall grey haired man opened the door. 'Signor Togneri?' said Marco, holding out his hand. With a smile on his face, the tall man shook hands with him and stood aside to let Marco into the apartment. 'Call me Carlo,' he said, 'and you are obviously Marco?' His English was heavily accented but Marco was pleased he could understand him. Although Marco could speak fluent Italian, it seemed to him good manners in this situation to speak in the language that Carlo preferred to use.

'Come in and sit over here,' he said pointing to a chair near a large window overlooking a park. Marco sat down and let Carlo carry on speaking. His father had told him that Carlo was a charismatic man who loved to talk, and he was finding out how true this was. Carlo was explaining to Marco that the flowers in the park were still out of season and if he had visited next month when they were in bloom, he would have seen a beautiful display of colour. Marco smiled politely, and accepted the espresso coffee Carlo handed him.

When he eventually sat down, his approach changed to one of asking questions about Angelo and his wife Elizabeth, and their life in Scotland. 'Have you taken over the family business,' he asked. Marco grinned,' I don't think Italian fathers ever completely retire, but yes, on paper I'm now in charge.' Carlo laughed at this, showing off a mouthful of perfect teeth set below a 'Clark Gable' type moustache. After a few more minutes of idle chat Carlo became more serious saying 'well Marco, your father said that I may be able to help you with a small problem you have.' 'Tell me about it.'

Marco had rehearsed this on the flight over and he was ready with his answer. 'My father tells me that you may have contacts within the Italian Intelligence Services and that you may be able to introduce me to someone I could talk to about a situation I have.' Carlo showed no sign of surprise at this. He was silent for a moment before saying, 'Even if I am able to do this, could you tell me a little more of what this is all about?' Marco nodded a few times before saying, 'I have some information that I believe would be of great interest to the Security Services.' 'And what would that information be?' said Carlo.

Marco realised that this was not going to be as easy as he first thought. 'I can't tell you what this is all about. It's not that I don't trust you, it's just that it's too sensitive and the less people who know the better.'

Once again, Carlo was silent for a while before saying,' I know people I can contact within the intelligence community; however, at this moment in time I am not sure if I should. If I don't know something about this, then I can't possibly involve the Intelligence Services,' he said taking a sip of his coffee. 'You must understand that I have a certain reputation to uphold, a reputation that means that these people take me seriously and know that I won't waste their time. For all I know you may want to discuss the weather in Scotland with them. Do you understand what I'm saying?'

Marco realised that they had reached an impasse. Without some insight into the situation, Carlo was not willing to help and without his help, he couldn't take this forward. 'I can tell you this' said Marco, 'it involves something that was found in Italy and the importance of which I can only share with the security services of this country.'

'Well Marco,' Carlo said, 'Thank you for sharing what you can with me. Just one more thing, can you tell me how old this find is?' Marco thought for a second or two then said, 'It belongs to the first half of this century, and I really cannot say anymore about this. If you can help me then please do so, if not, I should go now.'

Carlo realised that he had pushed Marco as far as he could. He stood up at this point and thought for a few moments about what had just been said. 'Leave me the name of your hotel and room number and I'll call you later this evening, hopefully with good news. I believe I know who can help us. Your father and I go back a long way, and I will do what I can.'

The meeting was at an end, so Marco stood to go, shook Carlo's hand, and gave him the hotel information.

As he left, he wondered why his father was so friendly with this man. Yes, he was charismatic and charming, but underlying this Marco felt he could detect something else. What that was he didn't quite know, but he didn't like it.

When he was alone Carlo sat down again and thought over his conversation with Marco. He wondered about what he had found that could be so important to the state. Something from the first part of this century and apparently sensitive material.

He thought about Angelo and his past in the Blackshirts and his service in the Moschettieri with Mussolini. He remembered his friendship with Sergio Rossi and how he had even attended his funeral all those years ago. Could these be the lost papers that people had been searching for all these years?

Eventually he got up and made a phone call to someone he knew quite well. He also made a phone call to the Commandante of the local Carabinieri Station in Lucca, a man called Enzo

Capaldi. He knew that Enzo had a SISI agent – the Italian Intelligence Service - operating out of there as a liaison officer between the two organisations.

Later that evening he made another phone call, this time to Marco. 'I've made arrangements for someone to visit you tomorrow morning at eleven in your hotel room. The person will show you some ID, so you can rest assured of their validity. It was considered the best place to meet in secrecy.' Marco thanked him and hung up.

Carlo then put on his favourite blue anorak and left his apartment. He walked for a little while along the street before he stopped at a jewellers shop with a large mirror in the window that the owners used to reflect the items on display. He pretended to look interested.

He used the reflection in the mirror to see if anyone was across the street watching or following him. He stood for a little while longer noting the cars on the road and the people that were walking past. Once he was satisfied that he wasn't being followed, he turned round and headed back the way he had just come. He walked on a little further before going down one of the narrow alleys that were commonplace in Lucca and slipped into a small bar. Through the dim lighting, he saw a bearded man sitting at a table on his own. He walked over and sat down beside him.

They fell into a deep conversation for a few minutes, frequently looking round the crowded room, making sure they were not being overheard before Carlo, appearing satisfied with the outcome got up and left. After some ten minutes, the bearded man also left the bar accompanied by two companions.

Any casual onlooker would have thought nothing wrong with the encounter. Had they known that the bearded man, whose name was Lorenzo Storti, was an accomplished terrorist with many deaths attributed to his name, they would probably have found it hard to believe.

In the summer of 1980, Lorenzo Storti travelled from Pisa on Alitalia flight 375 to Sicily where he was met by a Libyan Arab named Yusef Ali Akhbar who was a member of Colonel

Ghaddafi's Intelligence Service, and who handled the transfer of contacts from Sicily to Libya. Some fifteen miles in distance, but a world apart in culture and political integrity. They met in the airport lounge at three- thirty as arranged and had a coffee sitting at a table at the back of the room.

Akhbar asked Storti for some identification and when he was satisfied as to his identity said,' I have arranged for a private boat to take you across the Med to my country. You could have taken a flight, however that would have been flagged up by the Italian Intelligence Services who monitor every flight to Libya from here. When you arrive at a small port near Tripoli, you will be taken by your contact to a desert camp where you will remain for six months. Your training will include everything you will need to know about become effective in terrorism on your return to Italy.

One more thing. You will meet many people at the desert camp from many different countries, and friendships may develop amongst you all, however when you leave the camp you must forget who you met or saw there, and never mention them again to anyone, ever. This is for your and the others security. Do you understand Lorenzo?'

Lorenzo nodded in agreement.

Akhbar continued, 'The site of your camp must also remain a secret. If we hear that you have broken these rules and have been slack in their observance, then we will hear about it and we will kill you wherever you are. Do you understand?'

Lorenzo looked at Akhbar with suppressed anger in his eyes, 'I understand what is required Akhbar. I have not come here to play games, and I can assure you that I will be discreet.' Akhbar, satisfied with this comment, said, 'We will leave now. Don't discuss anything with the boatman. He will take you to the landing port and introduce you to your next contact in Libya. Even in the camp, keep yourself to yourself if possible. Others in the camp will have been told the same, so it will not appear odd. I will wish you well here, and we will not speak to each other again. Walk a few metres behind me and when I stop at the boat I would ask you to carry on without looking at me again.'

Lorenzo did as he was told and eventually reached the desert camp. Six months later a tanned and fit looking Lorenzo, fully trained in all aspects of terrorism and killing returned to Lucca. It may have been a coincidence but round about the time of his return to Italy, a spate of bomb attacks and kidnappings happened in increasing frequency in the region of Tuscany.

Chapter 6

The alarm sounded shrill in the stillness of the room. Marco opened his eyes and reached to turn it off. He had slept later than normal and felt all the better for it. His first thought was to make coffee using the little sachets he found on a service tray beside the television. He filled the kettle and waited on it boiling.

Holding his freshly brewed cup of Nescafe, he opened the French windows leading onto a small balcony and he felt the freshness of the city below coming up to greet him. The morning sunshine crept into his room like a silent intruder. It felt good to be back in Lucca. He had loved this city from the first time he had come here as a small boy with his father. If he had time, he thought, he would love to visit the family he had here in Lucca and of course his fathers' birthplace of Coreglia. He reflected that he had more family in Italy than he had in Scotland. He always thought strange that his mother's side didn't really socialise together or keep in touch with each other, but he had put that down to them being dour Scots. He put the thought out of his mind; he was here on business and not for a family visit. Looking at his watch he realised that time was short before his meeting so he finished his coffee with haste and rushed off to the bathroom.

Marco examined his face in the shaving mirror before proclaiming his shave a success. He put on the shower and waited until the water was warm before showering with the scented hotel gel he found in the courtesy pack in the bathroom.

One of the only things in Italy that irritated him were the thin towels the Italian hotels always seemed to favour. He was used to thick fluffy British ones. It must be for the climate here, he thought. He reached for the aftershave he had brought with him. It was one of his weaknesses that he had nurtured since his youth that he put on after-shave three or four times a day. These days his favourite scent was Armani, and he made a mental note to buy some before he left Italy.

Marco wondered what the correct dress for meeting a spy was, or did people call them agents these days? Should he dress casually, or collar and tie? He decided that a suit with an open necked shirt was the best option.

He put on a red striped shirt and a navy blue two-button single-breasted suit jacket. He took the trousers out of the trouser press and admired the sharp crease before putting them on. As he finished dressing, he heard a loud knock on the door. Checking his watch, he saw that it was exactly eleven O'clock. Right on time he thought as he crossed the floor to the door and opened it.

Standing there was a tall, very attractive woman. Marco was taken aback. He had never expected to see such a beautiful woman at his door. With her long dark hair, piercing blue eyes and elegant dress, she would not have looked out of place on a Milan catwalk. 'Signor Corti?' she said in a voice that Marco thought sounded like a tinkling bell. She stretched out her hand. 'My name is Anna Bastiani.'

In her outstretched hand, she held an Identity Card. Marco smiled and took the card from her. After examining it, he handed it back. 'Come in Signora Bastiani,' he said as he stood aside to let her in. Anna entered the room and looked around before saying 'Are we alone Signor Corti?' 'Yes,' a surprised Marco answered, 'for some reason I never expected a woman, and one who speaks such fluent English.' He had almost commented on her looks but stopped himself at the last moment. Might appear too forward, he thought.

'People usually are surprised at a woman in this line of business,' she said as she opened the en suite bathroom door and looked inside. 'I learned my English at University in Pisa. I always thought it may come in useful.'

'You expecting someone in there? Marco said. 'You can never be too careful,' Anna replied. 'May I sit down,' she said, moving to a chair. 'Before we begin talking, may I see your passport? Just a precaution you understand.' She took Marco's passport and scrutinised it carefully. She checked the passport photograph against a quick glance at Marco. Eventually when she was satisfied to Marco's identity, she visibly relaxed. 'Before we begin our business together could you please tell me something about your background Signor Corti.' 'Call me Marco,' he said smiling again.

'Thank you Marco and you can call me Anna,' she confidently replied, smiling in return. Marco sat down opposite her. ' I was born in Scotland of an Italian father and a Scottish mother, so therefore I was raised bi-lingual. I was called up for Italian Army conscription and did eighteen months service stationed around Rome. Is there anything else you would like to know?' Anna thought for a moment before answering.

'Do you feel more Scottish than Italian Marco?' Marco was used to this question. Growing up in Scotland he was usually asked this from new friends or people he had just met. However, he was irked at being asked it just now. 'Why is that relevant to our meeting?' Anna calmly answered, 'It's relevant for me to know how you feel about your nationality and if I am speaking to someone who is involved or interested in Italian or British politics. You have to understand that I don't know a thing about you except your name and anything that you can tell me about yourself and your background is relevant.'

Marco pondered this for a moment before replying, 'It's difficult to choose between the land of your birth and the people of your birth, although at times the two seem to fuse together, however to keep the balance right I volunteered for a spell in the British Army after my Italian conscription and that seemed to satisfy my conscience. If pushed I would say that as my home is in Scotland, I would consider myself to be Scottish, but strangely not a Scot.

The race I belong to is the Italian race, and that is just a matter of fact and not choice. As for politics, I have no interest in this, either in Scotland or in Italy. I just want to run my family business and get on with my life.'

He was aware that Anna was studying him as he spoke. She appeared to be sizing him up. 'What is your relationship with Carlo Togneri?' She asked.

Marco paused for a second before answering her as this direct questioning was beginning to unsettle him. 'He was a friend of my father's during the war. My father knew him from Carlo's police service in Special Branch.

Anna thought for a moment before continuing,' what did your father do during the war?' Marco didn't really want to answer this as the Blackshirts in post war Italy were considered an unacceptable part of their past. 'I need to know,' said Anna. Marco thought long and hard on how to answer. She could probably know already what his father did during the war and was just testing how truthful he now was, or could she be really ignorant of his father's war record? He decided to be truthful. 'My father was a Blackshirt in the Rome Cohort, and was a Moschettieri Del Duce.'

Anna let out a little gasp of astonishment. 'I had no idea of his involvement with the Duce's bodyguard. She thought for a moment before saying, perhaps it's now time for you to tell me why you wanted to speak to us.'

Marco took his time, and starting with Sergio Rossi being the first guardian of the briefcase and its contents, he told Anna the whole story of how he had ended up as Sergio's successor to the letters. He told Anna that Sergio had hidden the briefcase in Tuscany where it had remained undiscovered for all these years. He told her of the circumstances of how the mantle was handed over to his father, and how he had no choice but to accept. He brought her right up to date, including his last conversation with his father before he left for Italy.

The only part he was sketchy on was where the briefcase was actually hidden. He wanted to be sure of the Italian Government's intentions before telling them. He was aware that even in the Italian government there was the possibility of enemies.

When he had finished, he looked across at Anna, who was sitting all this time still in her chair with an astonished look on her face. When she had sufficiently recovered her composure, she managed to say, 'So it's true then, there are letters.' Marco nodded in agreement, 'It's not just a story that's been re-told many times over the last forty years, but is a fact and I know where they are.' Anna said, 'When I was a young police officer I had heard of Sergio Rossi and how he could possibly be involved with the disappearance of the Duce's letters. I know the police had interviewed him in the early days after the war, and that he had always denied any knowledge of the letters.'

Marco explained, 'Sergio Rossi did not want the letters to fall into the wrong hands and cause division in Italy. He was adamant that neither the parties of the left nor the right should get them, only the government of the day, with certain assurances.'

She tried very hard to remain calm, 'Where are they now, and can you show me them?' Marco smiled at her impatience,' At this stage of our negotiations I won't say where they are, but when I am convinced what the Italian government are going to do with them, I will hand them over.'

'Do you want money? Marco felt his face redden with anger. 'I don't want anything from you or your paymasters, I only want assurances on what the Italian government's intentions would be concerning them.' He said in a frosty manner.

Anna felt sorry she had mentioned money. 'I'm sorry Marco; forgive me, I was wrong to say that.' Marco relaxed a little and gave her a smile. 'I shouldn't have reacted so strongly, let's start again,' he said. 'How do we move this forward? an embarrassed Anna asked 'Marco thought for a moment before saying,' I would like you to talk to your superiors and assure them that this is not a red herring, that I am serious about the briefcase, and ask them to give me an official letter outlining what they intend to do with the letters.' Anna frowned, 'what is a red herring? Marco laughed aloud, 'a red herring is an English way of saying that the letters are real and not a lie.'

What assurances would you require?' Anna asked.

'I would need to know that the letters would not disappear again, and that the Italian state would allow access to bona fide scholars. I would also ask them to display some of them in museums for the Italian people to view. Apart from these assurances, I have no further requests.'

Anna was impressed with Marco, she saw him as a confident and handsome man, a powerful combination in her eyes. She felt attracted to him. 'Marco, there is something you need to know. In Italy, every region has Carabinieri officers seconded to the Italian State Intelligence Service. This gives the SISI access to police resources and also gives the Carabinieri access to intelligence information on an ongoing basis. We find it helps us unite in fighting organised crime, terrorism, and the Red Brigades, in Italy. My role is as a Carabinieri officer seconded to the SISI. What I have to do now is go to my office in Lucca and contact SISI on a secure link and get instructions from them. I can meet you later on tonight and tell you what will happen next. Is that okay?'

Marco nodded agreement;' perhaps tonight we can have dinner together and discuss your proposals later in my room.'

Anna hoped that she did not appear too eager when she accepted the invitation.

On her way back to the Police Station, she pondered on her last meeting. She wondered why Angelo Corti hadn't come to Italy to oversee the retrieval of the documents himself. Perhaps he was not in good health, or was too old for this kind of activity. She came to the conclusion that perhaps Signor Corti thought the venture could just be a little too dangerous, or demanding for his time of life.

Her mind wandered to Marco Corti. She had to admit that she was quite impressed by his demeanour, and was looking forward to working with him. She thought, it has nothing to do with his tall dark handsome appearance, or his charming personality, it was purely business. She smiled to herself as she walked along.

Anna opened the door to the Lucca Police station and waved to the duty officer on the front desk. She knew that his eyes would be following her as she walked down the long corridor to the Commandante's office. The officer had made no secret of his attraction to Anna, and he appeared to enjoy looking at her whenever he could, especially from behind.

She barely noticed the secretary sitting at her desk beside the Commandante's door. She knocked and waited until she heard a gruff voice telling her to enter. Behind a cigarette-ash-strewn desk piled high with papers and coffee cartons her boss sat puffing away on the cigarette that seemed to hang eternally from his lips.

He was a small rotund man with thick grey hair who always seemed to be bulging out of a shirt with large sweat stains around the armpits. His teeth were yellowed with tobacco stains, as was the Mexican style moustache that grew untidily over his upper lip. His appearance was deceptive, as was his gruff manner. Enzo was one of the kindest, warmest men that Anna had ever known.

'What do you want Anna?' he growled over his desk. Anna always felt motherly towards Enzo Capaldi. He was a senior officer in the force when Anna had first joined and he had taken her under his wing. That was 12 years ago and she had retained a soft spot for him ever since. Enzo was due to retire next year, and the authorities had promoted him to Commandante of Station to sit behind a desk and see out his remaining time.

His was a well-known face in Lucca. He was born within the old city walls and had spent his whole working life in service to the community. As a young man, he had joined the Carabinieri and during the war had not let the politics of right or left interfere with his duty as a police officer in upholding the law. Due to this, he was viewed by the community at large as a fair and just man and had made many friends over the years.

Enzo had been happily married for forty years and had five children to prove it. His ruby wedding was in August and he dreaded to think of what the celebration was going to cost him.

'I've just come back from interviewing Marco Corti, the man who requested a meeting with SISI. I think we may have something here of interest.' Anna said, as she sat down in a chair facing his untidy desk.

Enzo took a long draw on his cigarette before stubbing it out in an ashtray. He reached for another one and let it dangle unlit from his lips. 'What do you think you have?'

Anna paused for effect. 'Mussolini's letters between him and Churchill.'

Enzo's eyes opened wide with surprise. 'Do you think he's for real?'

'Yes I do' she said without any hesitation, 'his father was a member of Mussolini's bodyguard during the war and was a close friend of Sergio Rossi.' Enzo knew who Sergio Rossi was. After the war there was a lot of speculation as to the whereabouts of the letters and the name of Sergio Rossi was frequently mentioned in connection with them. Enzo also knew that Sergio had consistently denied knowing anything about any letters.

He lit his cigarette with an old American Zippo lighter he had picked up years ago from a GI stationed in Lucca. 'What does he want from us? 'he growled.

'Nothing much,' Anna said, 'Just some assurances they won't disappear again and that scholars and museums would have access to them.'

'Is he on the level Anna, or is he publicity seeking? Anna thought for a moment, 'I believe him Enzo, and I think we should pass this onto SISI for authorisation. If they agree, we could wind this up quite quickly. I think a couple of plain clothes officers would be enough to provide back up as there appears to be no one else aware why Signor Corti is here.'

Enzo thought for a moment. 'What about Carlo Togneri, where does he stand in all this?'

Anna was expecting this question. 'Carlo is a confirmed communist. Although never militant, he was nevertheless intellectually in tune with their ideology. He always was and always will be, but he is also retired Special Branch and knows what is expected of him. Although I think a quiet word in his ear from you would be appropriate just to remind him of what that is. He has not been told about the letters, although he may have guessed by now.'

Enzo mulled this over before replying, 'Make contact with your superior in SISI and ask for authorisation, tell them to supply the back up as we don't want any leaks from this end. Also tell them what Corti has asked for in assurances and I will deal with Togneri.' Anna nodded in agreement and left the office.

Once again she did not pay any attention to the secretary outside, although this time she had been waiting until Anna had turned her back to her and walked away. The secretary then got up from her seat, reached for her jacket and walked to the Commandante's door. She knocked twice and entered. 'Yes, what is it?' the gruff voice asked her. 'If it's all right with you I would like to go to lunch now,' she meekly requested. The Commandant, still preoccupied with his last conversation, brusquely waved his hand in agreement and the secretary left.

Enzo looked at his watch and thought it was time for his medication. He reached into his desk drawer and took out tablets for Cholesterol, blood pressure, and for a prostate problem. He had been to the doctor two days ago for his annual check-up, and had been reprimanded for being overweight. Jesus, he thought, why can't they give me a tablet for that?

★★★

The Secretary walked along the narrow cobbled streets until she reached the Via Santa Anna and turned down it. She continued until she came to a small bar on the left and went inside. She saw the person she was looking for, a bearded man, sitting with two companions at a corner table drinking espresso coffee. She went up to him and sitting down beside him, they entered into an animated conversation. She told the bearded man that she had put the Commandante's phone on open line before his meeting and had heard everything he and Anna had said to each other through her own phone. The Commandante's desk was so untidy that he had never even noticed the small red light on it was switched on.

When she had finished her conversation, she got up, left and returned back up the Via Santa Anna where she bought a panino and ate it sitting on some church steps.

★★★

Anna finished her phone call, on a secure line, to SISI. She felt quite pleased with herself that everything was falling into place. Marco had proved to be, not only a positive asset, but also a very handsome and charming one at that. Her SISI superior had given the expected authority for a retrieval mission for the letters, and had agreed to the assurances that Marco had asked for.

They had also told her that a complete veil of secrecy had to be placed on the operation and that no other person, officer or civilian could be involved, or have knowledge of it, with the exception of the Commandante. They stressed that SISI would send two of their own operatives tomorrow to work alongside her, leaving Anna in overall control of the operation. She felt that this was a feather in her cap, and she was determined that it would all go well.

She walked along the long corridor again to Enzo's smoke filled office and knocked on the door, this time she felt she was being watched. She turned in time to see the secretary's cold eyes looking at her with open disdain before looking away. Anna was taken aback by the look. She was puzzled by it but there were other things on her mind at that moment, so she committed it to memory for another time.

She opened the door to the Commandante's office and she sat down again in the same seat as before. She repeated what SISI had told her and about the expected arrival of the two SISI officers.

As she was talking, she happened to glance through the cigarette smoke around Enzo's desk and noticed a small red light on the desk phone. She motioned to Enzo to be silent, as she walked quietly to the door. As she opened it, her suspicions were confirmed. The secretary was sitting with her back to office door listening through her own phone to their conversation.

Anna strode up to the desk and took hold of the secretary's arms. As she struggled, Anna took her handcuffs from her belt and managed to put them on the secretary's wrists. The secretary began shouting at the top of her voice, 'you have no right to do this, let me go at once.' Enzo came rushing out of his office and taking in the scene before him, he immediately understood the situation. He called some of the station officers over and told them to arrest the secretary and put her in a cell on her own.

A startled Anna and Enzo went back inside his office and closed the door. After making sure that the phone was back to normal, Enzo said, 'Anna we don't know what she may have heard, or who she may have told. I don't even know how long I can hold her on some trumped up charges, so move very quickly on this operation, okay.

Anna agreed. 'Do you think there's a chance she was just being nosy?' Enzo gave a weary smile, 'I don't think so Anna, she's worked here for over 20 years and she knows more about this place than I do. Besides, she's not the nosy or gossiping type. I really think there's more to it, and I think I may know why.

Some years ago, she got involved with the communist party here in Lucca, and was considering joining them until I pointed out that it was not a good idea to become too involved with political parties in that way. I said that it could also affect her position in this office. She reconsidered, and never joined them; although office rumour has it that she still holds sympathetic views, and extreme ones at that.'

'Do you think she may have been a mole working for the communists in this office?'

Enzo put another cigarette between his lips, and casually flicked the Zippo alight.

'I think that is a strong possibility, and if I'm right then she will already have told others of the letters. If she has told the communists then you may have trouble on your hands.

I again suggest you move quickly and be very careful. She may even have passed information onto the Red Brigades, and that would really spell trouble.'

Anna stood for a few moments taking in what Enzo had said. 'I'll move on this right now Enzo.' She said, moving towards the door. Enzo let out another puff of smoke before saying,' Anna, it might be an idea to draw a sidearm from the armoury. Just a precaution you understand.'

When Anna left the office, Enzo sat for a while and stared at the ceiling as if looking for some inspiration there. The business with the secretary had shaken him. If the Communists or the Red Brigades had people working on the inside of the Police then they were in serious trouble. How long this been going on for he didn't even want to speculate, however many important meetings involving issues of national security had taken place in his office and he wondered how many had been overheard. He decided he would interview the secretary sometime tomorrow when she had time to reflect overnight on the seriousness of her position.

He pulled out another cigarette and watched the smoke rise to meet the dark yellow ceiling. He reached for his intercom and called for his second in command to come to his office. Before long, there was a knock on the door. 'Enter' said Enzo.

Mario Pisani came into the room. 'Ah Mario, we may have a problem.' Enzo quickly explained what had happened and gave Mario a brief run down on the letters.

'I feel we should beef up our security in the station until this is all finished Mario. Don't tell the men the real reason why, however tell them that all stations in the region have been put on alert from possible attacks from the Red Brigades. Any questions?'

Mario just took it all in his stride and told Enzo he would make sure the secretary was kept isolated until the following day, and that station security would be increased. He got up, straightened his uniform jacket and left the office.

Chapter 6

It was around 7pm when Anna eventually left the Police Station. She had spoken again to SISI with the latest update on the secretary and it had taken some time to sort out how to move on. SISI eventually agreed to hold the secretary under anti-terrorism legislation for 14 days without charge. The down side was it had meant a lot of extra paperwork for her and that was something she hated. With the secretary under lock and key, there was a good chance that they could recover the letters with the minimum of interference from outside sources. She was also comforted by the extra weight of the 9mm Beretta pistol in her shoulder bag although she hoped she wouldn't have to use it.

She walked briskly along the road to Marco's hotel, turning up the collar of her overcoat against the chill night air. Although it was April, the nights were still quite cold, and she reflected that by the end of May the evenings would be too warm to even wear a coat.

She was familiar with this side of Lucca. As a young girl, she had gone to school at the nearby Santa Croce primary. Those were unhappy years she thought. The memories came flooding back of her mothers' fatal accident in a car crash in Pisa. Her father had been driving the car that night and had been unable to come to terms with her death. She remembered the night he killed himself by drinking a mixture of painkillers and whisky. That was just three months after her mothers' funeral.

She was just eleven years old when she found him in the morning still sitting by the window where she had last spoken to him. Some nights the memory of his cold body sitting in that chair with his eyes closed as if in prayer still haunted her. It had taken a long time for the pain to ease from her broken heart, only to be replaced by a cold numbness.

Her Aunt Rina, a kindly old woman, had taken her in and brought her up as her own daughter until she had left home at eighteen for Pisa University. The effect of her parents' death had left her with an inability to form lasting relationships with most people, especially men. Her counsellor had told her it was just an irrational fear that something may happen to them. She shivered slightly at these memories and consciously made an effort to focus on the job in hand.

She had phoned Marco to say that she would meet him just as soon as she was finished at the Station, and she felt slightly annoyed that she had no time to freshen up from the afternoon and change into something more appropriate for dinner.

It was only five minutes to the hotel but as she walked along, she felt an unease creep over her. She had been a police officer long enough to know it was not just her imagination. Was she being followed? She began to walk a little faster and reached the hotel within a few minutes. Instead of going straight inside, she opened the door and stood just inside the porch looking through the glass door onto the street.

The only person walking past was a tall bearded man who didn't seem to be interested in the hotel and who kept on walking past. Anna relaxed a little, and stood looking out onto the street for a few more minutes until the night porter came up and asked her if everything was all right. 'Yes, perfectly fine.' Said Anna. 'I'm just a little early for a dinner engagement.' The night porter saluted stiffly and walked away mumbling to himself. Anna put her experience down to a case of the jitters, and moved to the house phone to contact Marco's room.

There was a strange tension between Marco and Anna over dinner. Almost as if they were aware of the attraction between them, but not wanting to acknowledge it. Anna was decidedly quiet for much of the meal, and it wasn't until Marco ordered another bottle of Chianti that she began to relax, Marco had felt the awkwardness between them all night and now wanted to find out why. 'Are you feeling alright Anna, or have I done something wrong? Anna looked up from her plate and scanned the near deserted dining room before reaching across the table for Marco's hand. 'Marco, I'm sorry for being less than amiable. We may have a problem with our plans. The operation may have been compromised. The Commandante's secretary was listening into his office conversations and we believe she may have been passing the information onto others.'

'What others?'

'We suspect she was a communist informer and that we could be in danger from them, or from more extreme elements of the left. I was going to tell you later on after dinner. I also think I was followed to the hotel tonight.'

Marco sat upright in his chair, 'Why should anyone follow you here? It's not a secret that I'm staying at this hotel, or that you have visited me here.'

Anna lowered her voice to a whisper, 'Perhaps because they are trying to find out what we are up to, or planning to follow us to the letters.' Anna looked around the dining room one more time, making sure no one was within earshot before continuing,' I said we could be in danger and I don't think that's putting it too strongly. We have to be very careful and alert. The secretary has been arrested on some made up charge on anti-terrorism and is now in close custody, however she may have passed the information on before she was caught.'

Marco, who was still holding Anna's hand, smiled reassuringly at her, 'don't be alarmed Anna, we may be seeing danger where there is no danger, anyway, I'm not a novice to danger. I told you I spent some time in the British Army, well I was with the Parachute Regiment, and spent some time on the strects of Northern Ireland, which wasn't exactly a picnic.'

'You were a Paratrooper?'

'Yes, I was in for 6 years, then left to join the family ice-cream business.'

'Anna thought for a while before saying, 'You seem quite relaxed about this Marco? Do you have an idea of what you would like to do?

Marco nodded in agreement. 'We need to leave early tomorrow morning, probably around 4am. If we leave by the back door to the hotel, we should be able to avoid being seen by anyone watching out for us. They won't know were onto them at this stage, so we should get clear without being seen.'

Anna innocently asked, 'What's our destination Marco.' Marco gave a low laugh and took Anna's other hand in his before saying,'Anna, I can't tell you just now, but I promise you it will be worth the wait.' He looked at her earnestly in the eye, then said,'to save time and avoid suspicion I suggest you spend the night here.' Anna was surprised at his suggestion and felt herself blushing.

'It might be better if we just shared the one room,' Marco said. 'Of course, only in case some ones watching the front desk.' Anna smiled knowingly at him. 'Of course,' she replied. 'However I think it best if I go home, change clothes, and get a few hours sleep. I can pick you up at four outside the back door and we can go straight to the letters. I also have to meet two SISI agents tonight and brief them on our plans. They will also ensure were not followed to the letters tomorrow by any interested party' Marco sighed and gestured as if helpless, 'a man can only try,' he said, 'perhaps next time Anna.' She gave him a rye smile and said 'perhaps.' As she stood up, she leaned over the table and kissed him lightly on the cheek. 'See you in the morning Marco 'and she left. Marco, feeling quite pleased with himself, finished his glass of wine then asked for the bill.

The bearded man sitting at a back corner table put down the newspaper that had hidden his face, rose to his feet and approached Marco. 'Signor Corti?' he said in a heavily accented voice.'My name is Lorenzo, and I believe we both have a similar interest in something close to our hearts.' Marco took in the man's appearance. He noticed how tall he was, the expensive suit he was wearing, and the gold Omega Constellation watch on his outstretched arm. Whoever this man was he certainly gave off the appearance of wealth.

'How do you know my name? 'He asked as he shook hands with Lorenzo. Reaching for a chair, Lorenzo said, 'may I sit down *signore* and I will explain.' Marco motioned to the chair. Lorenzo sat down and joined his hands together on the table as if in prayer. 'I understand that you may have access to some correspondence that would be of interest to many people in this country and your own.' Marco remained silent. He decided to hear him out before saying anything.

'We feel it would be wrong if the interests of the people I represent are ignored. These people are at present in Glasgow and would not take kindly to the correspondence being given to the Italian government. Am I making myself clear *signore*?' Marco felt a rush of anger and had to work hard at restraining himself from pulling Lorenzo across the table. 'Are you threatening my family you piece of shit?'

'There are no threats necessary Signor Corti, just the realisation that as we speak my associates are in a top floor flat in Queens Park Drive in Glasgow and will remain there until the letters in question are handed to me. There is nothing left to say here, so if you wish to phone your family please feel free. I will expect the letters to be handed over to me tomorrow evening at seven pm outside this hotel, and if I am apprehended by the authorities, or followed by anyone, then my Glasgow associates will not be happy. If I am allowed to go on my way unhindered then I will contact my friends and they will leave Queens Park Drive without further incident. Is this clear to you?

Marco by this time had his head in his hands, and when Lorenzo had finished speaking, Marco angrily said, 'I will give you the letters tomorrow night, however If you touch a hair on their heads I will promise you I will hunt you down and I will castrate you before killing you. I am more than capable of doing this' 'Is that clear to you?

Lorenzo smiled nervously at Marco. 'I'm glad we understand each other. Once we have the correspondence we will have no further interest in your parents. Until tomorrow then.' Lorenzo got up and left without waiting for an answer.

Outside the Hotel, Lorenzo reflected on his conversation with Marco. Lorenzo's training in the Libyan Desert with Gaddafis' terror squads had been of the highest standard and he had recognised in Marco a toughness that didn't just come from bluff. Part of that training was done alongside some of the hardest and toughest individuals he had ever met. Some of them belonged to groups like Bader Mienhoff, PIRA, ETA and of course the Red Brigades. I would not be surprised if young Marco is ex military, he thought. Maybe he's one to watch.

Marco sat stunned. He felt fear grip his stomach, like a giant knot, spreading through his body until he was almost paralysed with it. His mind raced. What would happen to his parents? What should he do now? The more he thought on his conversation with Lorenzo the more bizarre it seemed. He remembered his father's words to him before he left for Italy: *people would do anything to get hold of those letters including murder:* and really, for the first time the reality of those words hit him full force. He realised that underneath the civilised façade of a very cultured people, lay open wounds, left over from the war that would perhaps never be healed.

Wounds that spoke of memories, passed down through generations, of brutality, murder, and other shameful deeds committed by both sides in a bitter civil war, of which even today are seldom spoken about. For the first time since he was a child, he felt tears well up in his eyes. He forced them back and tried to pull himself together. He thought of his military training, the mental and physical toughness required for Para selection and he pulled to the fore all his reserves of strength.

He gradually felt more composed, and his breathing returned to normal. Slowly a cold resolve took over his mental processes. He was once again back in the ranks of the airborne. He was once again a disciplined fighting force. He was once again in control.

He got up from the table, made for the phone booth in the reception area, and dialled Anna's home number. After a few rings, she answered. He briefly explained the situation to her and asked her to contact her superiors and tell them that they had until seven pm tomorrow night to come up with a credible action plan to rescue his parents. He also told her that any plan would have to be approved by himself before any course of action was decided on, as he didn't want any unnecessary risks taken with their lives. Anna agreed. She also added that there was no need to leave at four am now that the terrorists, as she called them, knew of their intentions. She suggested they left later, and have the two SISI agents follow close behind as back-up. They then set a time to meet and ended their conversation. Marco steeled himself to now phone his parents in Glasgow.

The phone rang out in the family home a few times before Angelo answered it. 'Dad, it's me. Are you both ok?' Angelo took some time to answer him. 'Marco, we are both ok and not harmed. The two men here say that they will not harm us so long as you do as you are told. They have left us alone in our bedroom and have promised not to hurt us.'

Marco was amazed that even though his father was under severe stress as a hostage, he had still been able to think clearly enough to tell him there were only the two terrorists holding them and that they were being left alone in their bedroom. 'Tell them it's all in hand for seven pm tomorrow night, so look after mum and stay cool Dad. It'll soon be over.' 'Look after yourself Marco and don't do anything foolish,' said a nervous Angelo, before hanging up.

Marco went to the bar and ordered a large brandy. The barman asked him what type of Brandy and pointed to the gantry. Marco pointed at a bottle and said, 'give me a large Napoleon.' Finding a comfortable seat, he sat down and thought about events as they had unfolded. He also wondered why Anna had called them terrorists and not kidnappers or criminals. He knew that he would never sleep that night, so he may as well try his hardest to relax as best he could.

His mind roamed back to his time in Northern Ireland with his unit.

★★★

It was 1970 in Crossmaglen, sometimes called bandit country by the army, and Marco was on night operations with his section.

They were staking out a barn in the middle of nowhere land that Army Intelligence suspected was going active that night. An informer had told them it was being used as a weapons dump by the PIRA, (Provisional IRA) and for the last four hours he had been lying in the pouring rain in a wet ditch that was gradually becoming swamp like, keeping a keen eye on the barn and the surrounding countryside with five other Paras from his unit. Their information was that the PIRA would be arriving that night to pick up weaponry for a planned op the next day, so they were all keyed up.

The NCO in charge had spotted through his night sight some movement to their left. Three shapes carrying rifles were seen moving in on the barn. They were difficult to pick out in the bad weather and the darkness of the night. The Paras waited until the terrorists had slowly moved in on the barn until they were about to pick up the hidden cache of weapons, before four of the Paras moved cautiously in on them. Marco was detailed with his best mate 'Dusty' Miller to cover their rear and to stop any terrorists from escaping.

The NCO shouted out, 'Security forces – lay down your weapons or we fire.' The PIRA squad turned, fell to the ground and immediately opened fire on them. In the dark, the noise of the firefight and the flash of the weapons, combined with everyone shouting at once, caused utter confusion for everyone involved. Marco tensed his finger on the trigger as he saw a shape moving away to the left. Was it a terrorist or one of the Paras? He reasoned that his unit wouldn't be moving in that direction, so he opened fire. The dark shape stopped moving. When it was all finished, the three terrorists were lying dead on the ground. The Paras had come through the fight unscathed. Thankfully, surprise had been on their side. Marco had remained quite calm throughout, and had been given the credit for killing the terrorists who had tried to slip away from the rest. He had never taken a life before and it had proved to be a traumatic experience for him. He walked over to the dead terrorist and stood over him. At first, he had felt quite cold inside, almost numb. Afterwards, in his room back at the barracks, he was sickened at what he had done. The feeling of revulsion he felt that night was almost physical, however he knew that if he had to, he could kill again without hesitation.

He took a sip of his brandy and thought, I did it once before out of a sense of duty, but if those bastards hurt my parents, it will be a joy to kill them.

Chapter 7

Lorenzo held a meeting in his home with a colleague, a left wing radical activist, who was used to working covertly on his own and who was also used from time to time as a hired assassin by the Red Brigade. Up to now, the police were unaware of his existence and Lorenzo used him for any jobs that needed a sensitive hand.

They sat in his kitchen enjoying an espresso and a cigarette. Lorenzo was clearly agitated over recent events. He took a draw of his cigarette and said, 'we have to get our little secretary silenced before she spills the beans on our whole operation. The other man nodded agreement. 'Do you really think she'll talk?' he asked. Lorenzo thought for a moment, 'I don't know for sure. We need to get access to the station to make sure she doesn't get the chance to tell the Carabinieri what she knows.'

The man was silent. He knew where this conversation was heading, and why he was called to the house. Lorenzo gave him a weary look, 'I think the preferred option would be to silence our little canary in her little cage before she gives away our plans, and probably as soon as possible.'

The other man said, 'do we use a gun or something cleverer to finish her off?' Lorenzo stood up and walked to a box on the kitchen table. Opening it, he took out an old German Army Luger and a silencer. 'This may look like a museum piece my friend, but it is a smooth working weapon. It also has the advantage of being completely unmarked and untraceable in case it has to be left behind.' He placed it back into the box and handed it to his companion.

His companion took it out and examined it. 'Has it been used before on any jobs?' Lorenzo shook his head, 'it was last used in the war, but it has been well looked after since then. It belonged to my friend's father who was a partisan with the Stella Rossa Brigade on Monte Sole. He was executed by the SS in September 1944, and the Luger was found by my friend after the massacre.'

'Why has your friend agreed to letting us use this? It obviously has sentimental value.'

'My friend died for the cause some while ago, and I don't think he would mind what we are doing.'

Stalin took the weapon and placed it in the shoulder holster he had brought along in expectancy of another job from Lorenzo. 'It will be a pleasure to use a weapon with such history as this.'

Lorenzo then reached for an envelope sitting on the table that contained the address of a printer in the city that was sympathetic to their cause. He gave it to the assassin, saying 'I want you to go to this address when you leave here. You will find a printer there who will provide you with a photo ID that will be identical to the one used by the SISI. This will give you access to the police station, and of course access to our canary. The printer is expecting you anytime now my friend, so I will ask you to leave and go to him. When you meet him, tell him that you are 'Stalin' and he should tell you that he is 'Rasputin'

Lorenzo shook hands with the man, and wished him good luck. He walked him to the door and watched him walk down the street. Stalin seemed to have the gift of merging into the background wherever he was. The original grey man.

★★★

The man Lorenzo had called 'Stalin' preferred to remain in the shadows. The less people knew what his speciality was, the better for him. The Spetznatz, the Russian Special Forces, had trained him in the Libyan Desert. They had taught him all there was to know about covert entry, surveillance and assassination methods. He felt confident he could enter the police station, kill his mark and leave again without leaving a trail for the Carabinieri to follow.

He had been used recently on a similar case involving a council official who had forgotten where his loyalties lay, and who had been speaking to the police about things he shouldn't have.

The council official, who was a communist, had developed cold feet and had to be 'eliminated.' Lorenzo knew the official's house was under twenty four hour surveillance as the police had been expecting an attempt on his life there, so Stalin decided to take him out at the council offices. He just walked in, walked up to his office door, opened it and shot him in the head with a silenced gun. He calmly walked out again without leaving any trace of his presence. No one in the building even noticed him enter or leave.

He approached the station on foot rather than driving. First rule of assassination: be like a ghost, and keep it simple. Cars can leave a trail and should be avoided if possible. Second rule: always be prepared. They had drummed into him the maxim – prior planning prevents poor performance. Many times over the last few years this maxim had saved his life. He had his Luger in his shoulder holster, ready, with the safety catch off. Lorenzo had told him that the Commandante and Bastiani had left the station for the night, so now was the ideal time to act. He put on a pair of fine black cotton gloves to prevent his prints being picked up anywhere in the station, and climbed the steps.

Third rule of assassination: act normal and confidently. This was perhaps the most difficult to achieve. He always found his heart rate increased on a job and he hoped it didn't show.

He opened the Station door and approached the officer on duty at the front desk. Giving his best impression of bon ami, he said 'Buon Giorno, I am Agent Giovanni Ciccero of SISI.' He handed the officer his ID. 'I am here to interview the prisoner Laura Moscardini.' The officer replied 'Buon Giorno, and examined his ID before saying 'We weren't expecting anyone from SISI today, agent Ciccero.'

Stalin smiled and said, 'perhaps you would care to verify this with agent Bastiani, who is expecting me.' The officer was still reticent to allow him access. He looked up at Stalin and said, 'agent Bastiani left a few hours ago and didn't leave us any instructions on this case.' Stalin still kept his cool, and said. 'Officer, please clear this with Commandante Capaldi at once. I've come from Rome on the orders of SISI and I have some urgent questions for this prisoner.'

The officer shook his head at Stalin, 'Commandante Capaldi is off station and will not be back until tomorrow morning, except for emergencies. I feel awkward agent Ciccero, this is an embarrassing situation.'

Stalin feigned an angry appearance. 'This is impossible officer, but we can sort this out. If you let me ask her two or three questions now so that I can report the answers to SISI, I will wait until the Commandante returns tomorrow before doing the main questioning. Is this acceptable? The officer, seeing a way out of this, readily agreed. Stalin even went further in his appearance of compromise. 'As I won't take long Officer, I can ask her two or three questions here in her cell. You don't have to prepare an interview room. The Officer readily agreed and led Stalin to the confinement area.

He opened the cell door and stood aside to allow Stalin access, then returned to the front desk.

Laura Moscardini looked at the smiling man in front of her, and stood up. Stalin put out his hand towards her, 'I am a solicitor hired by our mutual friend, Signora Moscardini. You have nothing to be afraid of; I am working to set you free. Laura accepted his handshake and said, 'I knew he wouldn't desert me.' Stalin kept on smiling, and said, 'tell me what you have told them so far Laura?'

Laura relaxed at this and said, 'Nothing *signore*, nothing at all.'

It was the last thing that she ever did. Stalin, still smiling, pushed his Luger into her mouth and fired. The heavy calibre bullet tore off the back of her head and splattered the cell wall with red gore. As a precaution, Stalin wiped the gun handle clean of prints, even though he was certain there were none, and pressed the gun into Laura's right hand. He wasn't concerned if the police thought she had committed suicide or not. Just another twist, another bend, to put them off the real scent.

Stalin straightened up and smoothed his clothes. He noticed blood on his shoes, so he used the corner of Laura's skirt to clean them. He left the cell and made for the reception desk. 'Thank you officer, you were most helpful. I'll come back later tomorrow when Commandante Capaldi is here.' Handing over the cell keys, he said, 'She's securely locked up again officer.' The officer took the keys back with a relaxed wave of the hand. 'Grazie, agent Ciccero, would you mind signing out now?' Stalin still smiling signed the out log with an artistic flourish, after all, he thought, this is going to be examined by experts.

★★★

Two hours later, Officer Dezzini was doing his routine check on the prisoner Moscardini. He pulled back the viewing flap on the door and looked in. He couldn't believe the scene before him. A dead Secretary lay stretched out on the concrete floor with blood spattered everywhere. He pressed the emergency alarm and ran for the phone.

Enzo was sitting at the dinner table with his wife, his three sons and two daughters. Their respective spouses were also there, plus his three grandchildren. He had just finished his meal and was sitting with two of his grandchildren on his knee when the phone rang. His wife sighed and watched a weary Enzo go to the kitchen to answer the call. She could hear him shout something about, procedures, before he came back into the room.

'I'm sorry,' he said with a sad expression on his face. 'There seems to be an emergency back at the Station. I need to go.' Enzo's wife gave a resigned shrug of her shoulders. After forty years, she was used to these calls at home.

'Call me if you are going to be late, you know I worry about you.' Enzo laughed, 'for forty years you've been saying the same thing every time there's a call out. Don't worry. I won't be long.'

★★★

When Enzo returned to the station, a very embarrassed Duty Officer, Franco Dezzini told him about the SISI visit. Enzo listened to him for a while, then said, 'did he have written orders?' The Duty Officer's face grew red with embarrassment, 'I didn't think to ask for orders Commandante. He had official ID.' Enzo took a cigarette out of his pack and placed it between his lips. 'Did you phone SISI HQ to check him out?' Officer Dezzini shook his head, 'no Commandante, I didn't see a need to.'

Enzo reached behind the desk for the cell keys and moved briskly down the corridor to the Cell area, followed by the Duty Officer. He put the key in Laura Moscardini's door and opened it. He was met by a gruesome sight. Laura was lying on her back, dead, on the concrete floor with blood all around her head. The back wall of the whitewashed cell was covered by blood and brain matter.

He shouted out instructions to other officers, 'Lock down the station, and look everywhere for anyone or anything unusual. He stood looking at the dead body from the cell door: not wanting to enter in case he contaminated the crime scene. He noticed the Luger in her hand and shook his head. A clumsy attempt to fool us, he thought.

One thing struck him as odd however. Most of the blood was to the head area and around the rear wall and floor. There was one small area on the hem of her skirt that was unusual. How did that get there, he thought. He knelt down to get a closer look at it. My God, he thought, the killer wiped his shoes on the hem of her skirt. That's black shoe polish mixed in with the blood. Enzo straightened up and reached for a cigarette, this is one cool guy, he thought, he even took time to clean his shoes.

He made for the nearest phone and alerted his immediate superior to the killing. After this call he told Officer Dezzini, who seemed to be in a daze, to bring the CCTV film of the reception and cell areas to his office, and to set up his video player.

He then put out a call for a forensics team and the duty doctor, who he knew had to confirm the death, to attend the scene.

He called out for a yellow tape barrier to be erected around the area to stop casual entry to the cell. Once he was satisfied that he could do no more, he went to his office and waited on the CCTV film.

He thought who would have the training and professionalism to carry out a hit like this. The killer was obviously someone who was used to this kind of work. The Red Brigades were more into bombings and kidnaps, and he was unsure if they would have the expertise to do something as subtle as this. He sat in silence trying to work it out.

Before long, the Station was buzzing with people all trying to out shout the next, as they went about their business. There was a knock on the Commandante's door. 'Come in,' Enzo said with his usual gruff voice. Officer Dezzini entered with the CCTV tapes in his hand. 'Set it up Franco and play it please.

Enzo lit up again and settled down to watch the tape. He slowed down the frames showing the killer at the reception, and said to Franco Dezzini, 'do you recognise him from the photos we have in the Red Brigade file?' Franco Dezzini looked more carefully at the stills and replied, 'No, apart from today, this guy is a stranger to me. Must be a pro though, the way he is so cool when talking to me is a practised art.'

Enzo looked at Officer Dezzini with surprise. 'Perhaps if you had thought of that before you let him in to see the prisoner we wouldn't be having this conversation now.' Officer Dezzini's face grew red again. Enzo continued, 'you better go along to the Senior Investigating Officer and give him your statement now.' As Officer Dezzini stood up to go, Enzo relented a little and softened his approach. 'Franco, I would probably have done the same as you, so don't feel so bad about it.'

Franco Dezzini left the Commandante's office with a smile on his face.

Chapter 8

The next day, Anna joined Marco at the hotel for breakfast at eight am. When he saw her, he immediately invited her to sit down and join him. 'Did you sleep well?' He asked. Without waiting for an answer, he called the waiter over and asked for another coffee. As they sat drinking it, Marco said,' Is there something Anna that I should know. Last night, why did you call them terrorists instead of kidnappers, or criminals?'

Anna was silent for a moment before saying, 'The two hostage takers are Mario Gilardi and Francesco Bari. They flew out of Pisa Airport yesterday afternoon for Glasgow. They are known to us as either members or supporters of the Red Brigades and are extremely dangerous. They are suspected of carrying out the bombing of a café in Sienna last year.'

'I've heard of the Red brigades.' Said Marco, 'but what would they want with us?'

'They are Marxist-Leninist terrorists who believe in extreme action to bring about a Socialist revolution, not just in Italy, but throughout Europe. In 1978, they were the group who kidnapped the former Prime Minister Aldo Moro and killed him. They will do anything to promote their cause. We pose a danger to them because of Mussolini's involvement with Churchill during the war as exposed by the letters. Anything that shows Neo-Fascism in a good light must be eliminated, hence their interest.'

'What do you mean by extreme action Anna?'

She quietly said, 'They bomb, maim and kill anyone who they think is a danger to them or who dare to stand in their way. They are usually organised into small cells of four or five members, with a cell leader who is the only one who knows the identity of all the other members.

'How did you find out about the involvement of Gilardi and Bari?'

'The Secretary we arrested yesterday, whose name was, Laura Moscardini, told us about her involvement with the Red Brigades as an informer. She also told us she didn't join the Communist party before when Enzo had spoken to her about it; because our bearded friend told her that she would be more useful working under cover in Police headquarters. She had a close relationship with Lorenzo Storti who is known to be a Red Brigade member, and we suspect she was his lover. Yesterday, someone posing as a SISI agent got access to her cell in the police station and killed her with a WW2 Luger. He tried to make it look like a suicide, however he placed the gun in the wrong hand as Laura was left handed. Also, how would she have gotten access to a gun?' 'CCTV images and forensics have drawn a blank as to the killer's identity. He could be a ghost for all we know.'

He shook his head in disbelief at the turn of events.

'Why have this lot not been arrested before now? 'said an increasingly tetchy Marco.

'Knowing something to be true and proving it is two different things Marco. It's one of the penalties of living in a democracy. Fortunately, we have her confession before she was killed which has given us some leads.

He reached for the coffee pot and poured himself another cup. 'What kind of plan did your superiors come up with to rescue my parents?' he asked, keeping his eyes firmly on her face. Anna shifted uncomfortably in her seat and said, 'they are still talking it out, it all takes time.'

'Time is something we don't have Anna. We have until seven pm tonight and that's it.' Marco said in an angry voice. 'I don't feel inclined to retrieve the documents and hand them over to you and let my parents get shot by some Red Brigade baddies.'

'I understand how you feel Marco, but we have to be patient and trust the powers that be to come up with some answers.'

'I saw how the powers that be handled things when I served in both the British and Italian Armies and I have to say it usually involved covering up their mistakes. I need something more concrete, a plan of action, or Lorenzo gets his letters. These people are killers and I don't want their next victims to be my parents.'

Anna understood the anger and concern Marco was feeling and probably if she was in the same situation, she would react in the same way. 'Let me go and check if SISI have come up with anything more concrete. If not, I will let them know what you said and try to push them on.'

'I have no confidence Anna in your SISI or State police, I only have confidence in my own ability to take these kidnappers, or terrorists as you call them, out myself. I still have time to catch a flight to Glasgow, and tackle these killers on my own, and I am prepared to do it if necessary.'

Anna was shocked at the aggression and confidence coming from this man. She really did believe he would carry out his threat to do it his way, and it scared her. 'Please Marco, please, don't react in this way. I know it's hard to believe in others, but I ask you now to believe in me.'

Marco sat smouldering with anger at the table, but at Anna's emotion filled plea, he appeared to calm down, and with softer eyes looked at her and said, 'We don't have much time left to save my parents Anna, do what you can to push them on. I'll sit back and wait for a while.'

Chapter 9

In a Roman office sitting in front of the Operational Director of SISI was Gianpiero Marchi, known as Pippo to his friends and family. Pippo had been recruited into SISI through the Intelligence branch of the Italian Army in the early sixties, and had risen through the ranks of SISI until he had been promoted to head up the intelligence analysis and risk assessment section. Generally known as Operational Intelligence, he had placed his unit on full alert to handle this emergency.

His manner was brisk and efficient and when he had worked in the field, he had built up an enviable reputation for dedication to duty. He had asked to see the Director this morning regarding the Corti family and the hostage situation. He waited patiently as the Director finished reading the file he had prepared for him last night. Eventually he put it down. 'Is this the same Francesco Bari that was involved some time ago with the Cosa Nostra in Palermo before he came up north?'

'Yes it is. We still don't know the reason why he has resurfaced in Lucca as a Red Brigade member, but we're working on it.' The Director tapped the desk with his pen, 'has there been any intelligence of The Mafia and the Red Brigades working together in the past?'

'No, Pippo said, we don't know if they are, or if this is just a disaffected Cosa Nostra member who has put his politics before his oath to the Mafia.'

'What's your assessment of the situation Pippo?'

Pippo cleared his throat before answering. He knew that the Director only wanted the headlines and not an operational briefing. 'I feel the situation is deteriorating Sir. We have gone from a simple retrieval of documents to a hostage situation in another country by the Red brigades, and a killing in a police station. There is also the added complication that one of the hostages in Glasgow is an Italian national. We have two other players on the loose, whom we suspect are active with the Red Brigades; however we don't know what their plans are yet.'

The Director sat back in his chair and stared at the ceiling, as if looking for inspiration there. Eventually he said, 'Is your take on this to alert the British through our Intelligence contacts over there, or do we go political and do it through our ambassador in London?' Pippo was ready for this question. Again, he cleared his throat. 'Going down the diplomatic route, although preferable, will take too long and we have only ten hours left to the terrorist's deadline. If we shortcut and use our intelligence channels, it may ruffle a few feathers but we can live with that. The SIS Director over there knows how to play the game and I'm sure, once briefed, will set up an op with British Special Forces. We don't have time to get to know their domestic MI5 personnel.'

He cleared his throat again before continuing. 'There is another option sir' although it may prove to be risky.' 'Go ahead,' said the Director. 'We could send a combat team in from our own Special Forces. My information is that they could be in position in five hours. I have them standing by at present.' My feeling is we have to keep this as low key as we can until we know what's in the briefcase. For all we know it may be full of wartime ration coupons and we could be made to look silly.'

The Director slowly nodded his head in agreement before saying, 'Veto any op involving our people on foreign soil. The fallout from that would be too heavy for us to survive. I'll phone Jack Bradshaw, The British Secret Service Director, on the secure line right now and advise him of the situation. He will have to get authority from his Home Secretary, so we had better get on to this right away. The protocol should be to contact MI5 for domestic operations and not the SIS, however

I know Jack of old and I know he'll understand the need for haste.'

'This is good work Pippo; thank your Agent in the field for me. 'The Director got up from behind his desk, crossed to his wall safe and removed a key. He opened a desk drawer with it and took out a red, secure line telephone. He looked up the number of the British Director of the Secret Intelligence Service, or MI6 as the public called it, from a red book he took from the safe, and dialled.

The phone rang three times before a voice answered, 'Jack Bradshaw'. 'Hello Jack, It's Remo Notrangelo, We have a problem.'

★★★

Jack Bradshaw sat in his office at 85 Albert Embankment off Vauxhall Bridge in London, with his Personal Operational Staff around him. He was one of the new breed of M16 Directors.' His background was state school and Durham University and not the Eton educated Oxbridge graduates who had run the service in the past. He was a small, fit looking dapper man, who spent his lunch hour practising Kata in his private office in the building.

Ever since his Army days in Hong Kong, he had practised Goju Ryu Karate for his mental and physical health. He enjoyed the feeling of confidence it gave him and the knowledge that if it got rough, he could give a good account of himself. He was known as a fair man to deal with and was well liked by his staff. This was one of the situations he felt he should take a sounding from them.

He had explained the situation as he had received it from the SISI Director and the permission for the Op he had received from the Home Secretary. He missed out the bad tempered reaction from the minister regarding the unorthodox channel the Italians had used this time. Jack had kept his frustration with the protocol brigade hidden. He was used to politicians sounding off about procedures. He usually just shrugged it off: he was more of an operations type. The Home Secretary had erupted about the Italians, and how he would have preferred it if they had contacted MI5. His reaction to this was to stick up his two fingers at the phone whilst saying 'yes sir.'

'How do we take this forward, and who do we use? 'Bradshaw asked the assembled group. His Deputy Director stood up and with a world-weary kind of voice said, 'Sir, with the time factor we have and the distance involved to Glasgow I don't think we have a lot of choice. I've made some enquiries and have perhaps found an answer. We have a reserve squadron of SAS – 23 SAS - based in Glasgow. It just takes the authority of the Director Special Forces to activate the on duty CTT {Counter Terrorism Team} and we could resolve this in a few hours. We have eight hours left and I think this is our best and perhaps only credible play.'

The Director turned to a staff member sitting near the back of the room. Frank, you're Special Forces, what's your take on this? Frank stood up to answer. He was conscious that every eye in the room was on him. Frank had been one of the SAS involved in the Iranian Embassy siege in 1980 and had since left the active side of the business through an injury to his leg sustained during a night jump in Columbia. It was a drug-busting op against the Mendellin Cartel and he had landed quite awkwardly causing his tibia to break and poke through his skin. Ever since then he had walked with a limp.

His knowledge of this type of operation was invaluable, as it came with the insight of practical experience learned on the job and was not just theoretical.

'Sir, the reserve squadrons are trained to the same standard as the regular SAS squadrons. I think with the time we have we would be wise to activate their CTT as soon as possible. They have men right now on standby, trained for this type of emergency and only stationed about two miles from the hostage scene. Even so, it will still take a few hours for them to sort out their kit and weapons and for their team leader to come up with a reasonable plan. I don't believe we have any other viable options.

The Director looked round the room, 'any other suggestions? He asked. He was met by silence from his team.

The Director thought for a few moments before reaching for the phone on his desk. 'Get me the Director Special Forces and buzz me when he's on line.'

Eventually his phone buzzed three times.

'Hello Tony, Jack Bradshaw here.'

'Seems we have a job for your boys in Glasgow. Here's the down.'

Chapter 10

Sergeant Tommy (Jock) Wilson was a forty-year-old red haired Glaswegian. He was born and bred in Cumberland Street in the Gorbals and had joined the Army as a raw eighteen year old recruit rather than face unemployment. If truth be told, it had probably saved him from Jail. He had been a member of a street gang called 'the young Cumbies' who, in his youth, had ruled the area around the Gorbals. Their main occupation was fighting other gangs in Glasgow using weapons like knives, hatchets, chains, and iron bars. Growing up in the Gorbals had toughened him to the point that he acquired a reputation as being a bit of a hard man, so the obvious choice for him was a military career. After his service experiences in Aden, Borneo and Malaya with the Argyll and Sutherland Highlanders he volunteered for SAS selection and was badged in 1970 as an SAS trooper at their Hereford base.

His SAS service had seen him involved in many operations overseas and at home and now at his age and rank he had asked to be stationed with the Glasgow reserve squadron to assist in their training. Even so, he had never expected the duty CTT of a reserve Squadron to be activated at such short notice, and by no less a person than the Director Special Forces himself. He was full of anticipation at the chance once again of seeing some action. He realised that something very important must be going down. He looked around the duty room at the other three troopers there:

Mike Fraser a thirty five-year-old ex Para Sergeant was an Aberdonian married to a Glasgow girl, and currently working as a Postman in Scotstoun, a district of Glasgow. He had left the Paras six months previously and applied for an SAS Reserve selection course on demob. He was the most experienced of the CTT troopers and had served 20 years with the Parachute Regiment in all theatres including The Trucial Oman Scouts and the Gurkhas. By the Regiments strict rules he had lost his Sergeants rank when he was badged SAS. Jock considered him his right hand man and felt lucky to have such an experienced soldier by his side.

The other two troopers, Craig and Brian, were both 25 years old and had been in the SAS Reserve for three years. This was the first time they had been activated. They had joined the Regiment about the same time and had gone through selection together, now they sat nervously waiting on what was to unfold. Jock knew they were steady types and would come through this with no problem.

Captain Peter Bradley, the Duty Officer, came striding in with a stern look on his face. Jock could sense the tension in the air. Peter was ex regular SAS as well and knew Jock from past operations. He knew that Jock was the man to turn to in a tight spot.

The DO looked around the room to catch their attention. 'Right lads, we've got a little problem to sort out, and we don't have a lot of time to prepare. Hence our CTT being activated. Seems like some Italian Red Brigade terrorists have taken two pensioners hostage in a nearby tenement and we have been tasked to enter the top story flat, take the players out and free them. We have just received some Polaroid snaps of the outside of the building, and we have a rough diagram of the lay out of the flat, faxed through to us a few minutes ago from the hostage's son.' He passed the snaps around the room. He then walked across to a blackboard and pinned up the diagram for all to see. 'As you can see the flat has one lounge, two bedrooms, one kitchen and one bathroom. The bedrooms and bathroom are at the back of the building, and the three public rooms are at the front.' He stopped and looked across at Jock. You've been on similar ops before Jock. What do you think?'

Jock stood up, and walked up to the diagram. 'How many players in there Peter?'

'As far as we know only two, although some local boys may have joined the party. We also have intel that the two hostages are being held in their bedroom at the back here.' He pointed at the diagram with his finger. 'They may be on their own in there so be careful on entry.'

Jock thought for a moment before saying, 'why would Red brigades be interested in two pensioners in a Glasgow tenement?' 'There's some business going down in Italy,' Peter said, 'and the two pensioners are the insurance end to make sure it comes off.'

Jock nodded in understanding before saying,' What's the time scale with this op?' 'We need to be clear by six pm, which gives us a four hour time scale to plan, prepare, and perform.' 'Shit Peter, we don't often get the opportunity for this type of operation, but when we do we don't have enough time to do it properly.' Peter agreed with Jock and once again looked around the assembled group. 'This is what you've trained for, I know it's sudden but that's the nature of these things. Jock's done this a few times before, so with his experience and your training it should be a walk in the park.'

Jock turned to the group, 'We won't waste any more time lads. We'll go down to the Armoury and draw our personal weapons and a few odd bits and pieces we may need.' Turning to one of the troopers he said,' Mike, you make sure we have enough PE (plastic explosive) det cord, and stun Grenades.' Mike nodded in agreement. Jock then turned to the other two troopers and gave them their instructions about getting rope, harnesses, and other equipment that may be needed for a forced entry.

Jock looked at his watch and synchronised all the CTT watch's together. 'It's now two pm, so we should get kitted up and do our weapons check, including live firing, by three thirty, then meet back here for a final briefing.' Peter, will you have any more info for us by then?' Peter gave a shrug of his shoulders, 'I don't know for sure Jock. I'm trying to get you a chopper from HMS Gannet at Prestwick to land you on the roof, rather than you going up the main staircase and frightening all the neighbours. So Jock I should know by then.' 'Right lads, get your arses in gear,' said a beaming Jock.

At three thirty pm, the CTT assembled again in the briefing room. This time they were all dressed in the black SAS operations kit, ready for the off. Peter stood up and addressed the room. 'We have a chopper waiting in the field outside. It will hover over the building, allowing time for you all to drop down onto the roof with your kit, before moving off again. Once you clear the house of bandits, MI5 will take the freed hostages to a safe house. Make the house safe before leaving, then head onto the roof again and await pickup from the chopper. Any questions? The room went quiet. Peter turned to Jock. 'Right Jock, over to you now.' Jock stood up and looked round the room. 'Mike, you and Brian go through the bedrooms at the back. Remember that the hostages may be on their own and frightened. We can't be sure, but be aware. I'll go with Craig through the front lounge and kitchen. We'll check our communications before entry. We'll use the Alpha call signs. 'Peter back at HQ is Alpha Tango, I'll be Alpha one, Mike you're Alpha two. Craig and Brian you're three and four. Once we all have the PE in place on the windows, we'll detonate together. The blasts should confuse the bandits. At that point, use the stun grenades and wait for the order to enter before going in.

I want a co-ordinated entry for maximum effect. Take the bandits down on sight. Remember they may be wearing body armour so two taps to the head to make sure they're neutralised. One last thing lads, remember your training. We're going in from opposite ends of the house, so we don't want to fire on each other. Keep a cool head and don't use the coms unless you have something to say. Any questions?'

No one answered.

'Right, said Peter, you'll leave now. It's three forty five pm, so you should be in position for around four pm. Remember my call sign here is Alpha Tango. Good luck and we'll debrief here on your return.

★★★

They loaded their kit into the chopper and then boarded. They knew the journey would only take minutes, so they immediately prepared the ropes and harness for their exit drop. They pulled on their balaclava headgear and goggles and waited. The chopper hovered over the building's roof for only a few minutes as the team quickly dropped down the ropes onto the roof, followed by their kit. Eventually when the chopper took off again, the unmistakable thud, thud of its blades went virtually unnoticed in the Corti house. If anyone outside on the street had noticed the activity on the roof, then they certainly gave no sign of it.

The team quickly split into two groups then lowered themselves down the building side to their appointed positions at the front and rear beside their designated windows. They set their PE with detonators on the window frames and then moved as far away as their ropes allowed, waiting on the order to detonate. Jock checked their status and when he was sure they were all ready and in position he gave the order.

Angelo and Elizabeth were sitting together in their bedroom with the door closed watching a programme on a small portable television, without really taking it in. They were holding hands and smiling reassuringly at each other, but were very concerned for Marco's safety and of course their own. The whole ordeal had proved to be very traumatic for them. Angelo had opened the door to the two men thinking they were new neighbours and when he was roughly brushed aside by them he had tried to defend his home. However, the sight of drawn weapons had convinced him to co-operate. Elizabeth, who was made of sterner stuff, had kicked Bari a few times in the leg before the sight of a gun held to Angelo's head caused her to give in.

★★★

The two terrorists, Gilardi and Bari were in the lounge watching an American War Movie on the main television set. Although their grasp of English was very poor, they were, nevertheless, engrossed in the re-enactment of the D Day landings portrayed there. They were relaxed as they could be in a hostage situation. The outside door and bedroom windows were locked, and the only telephone was in with them. The old couple were now giving them no trouble so nothing could go wrong. They only had to wait it out until Lorenzo phoned.

The sound of the blasts was deafening in the small lounge. Gilardi, who was closest to the windows, was showered with shards of broken glass and debris and was catapulted by the force of the blast from his armchair onto the floor. Bari, who was totally disorientated by the confusion surrounding him, managed to draw his weapon and make an unsteady dash for the lounge door.

The wall of sound and light that followed as the stun grenades went off threw him to the ground. Through the pain in his eyes, Bari could just make out the dim shape of figures coming in through the windows and raised his weapon to fire. It was his last act as Craig shot him twice in the head.

Gilardi, who had missed the worst of the grenades effects as he was already on the floor when they exploded, raised himself up on one knee and was about to fire at Craig when Jock dropped him with two shots in quick succession to the head.

Mike and Brian had stayed in the bedroom with the Corti's on the Team Leaders orders. They were both focused and in the crouch position now, with their weapons raised and pointing at the door. They would remain that way until they got the all clear from the team leader to stand down. When the team had confirmed the couple had been on their own, Jock had communicated with them that their role was now to protect the old couple by remaining with them in the bedroom.

The Corti's were totally confused at the fast acting drama they had been part of and were huddled together on the floor behind a settee where Mike had put them.

The first thing Jock did as he came in through the bedroom door with Craig was to check out the old couple for injuries. Apart from being deafened by all the explosions, they were both fine and in good spirits. He relaxed and smiled at the other three CTT members.

'Well done lads, I'm proud of you all. You performed like real professionals.' He then spoke into his throat mike. 'Alpha Tango this is Alpha one, over.' Through the static, he heard Peter answer straight away. 'Alpha one, go ahead, over.'

'House secure, two bandits down and hostages released unharmed. No team casualties. Over and out.'

Two Ambulances came to take the Cortis' and the two terrorists' bodies away. The Cortis' to an Army base Medical Reception Station, to be given the once over by an Army Medic before release into the safe hands of M15. The two terrorists' bodies were removed in the other Ambulance by MI5 and were never seen again.

The National and local papers reported the incident the next day as: 'A gas explosion in a top floor flat in Queens Park drive in Glasgow has left substantial damage to the windows and to some of the internal fabric of the flat. There is no indication as to what caused it at this stage, and there were no reported casualties. The police and gas board are investigating.'

The CTT were taken off by chopper and arrived back at base for a debriefing just after five pm. Peter greeted the team with a beaming smile. Hostages released unharmed, two terrorists dead, and no team casualties. This, and no evidence of an operation ever having taken place was just the type of result the SAS liked. It had taken the team just over three hours from briefing to successful return. The Prime Minister, Margaret Thatcher, personally phoned the Duty Officer to express her gratitude for a job well done, and had asked to speak to the team leader. Jock was delighted to speak to speak to the PM, and took the opportunity to praise his team.

By five thirty pm, Marco received a welcome phone call from his Dad explaining in an excitable voice the day's events.

Chapter 11

Lorenzo got the news of the events in Glasgow shortly after six pm. His contact there didn't know all of the details, but it was evident that things had gone very wrong. He had telephoned the flat in Glasgow, from a public phone box to verify for himself what the situation was and when a gruff Scots accent answered, he hung up very quickly. Lorenzo was a very resourceful man and in his mind he very quickly ran through the options he had left. Obviously, there had to be a change in plans, as Marco wouldn't now be handing the briefcase over to him at the agreed time. He made another phone call, this time to his accomplice Stalin, and arranged to meet him at six thirty pm that night in the bar he always used.

★★★

Anna and Marco lifted their celebratory glasses of wine and toasted the day's events. Marco was so relieved that his parents had been rescued. He felt so physically and emotionally drained he had promised himself that after this glass of wine he would soak in the bath, and have an early night. Anna emptied her glass and set it down on the table. 'I suggest we postpone the retrieval until tomorrow morning. We're both very tired tonight, and it's starting to get dark. What do you think?'

Marco looked at her with a steady gaze before saying, 'yes, that makes good sense. Perhaps you would like to stay for a while and have some more wine?'

Before Anna could answer there was a loud knock at the door.

'Who is it' Marco said in a loud voice, slightly annoyed at the interruption.

'Laundry service,' said an Italian voice.

'That's strange at this time of the day.' said Anna. The staff must be behind their work.'

Marco walked warily to the door, and as he turned the handle to open it, the door was kicked very hard in his face, sending him sprawling to the floor. A man, of medium height and weight entered the room. He closed the door behind him and motioned with the gun in his hand for Marco to get up. Anna rushed over to help him to his feet and with blood pouring from his nose he staggered to the bed. 'Who the fuck are you?' he managed to say, although still dazed from the blow.

'Never mind who I am, it's not important. What is important is the little journey we're going to make. Please be assured Mr Corti that unless you do exactly as I say, I will not hesitate to kill your little friend here.'

'Where are we going' said Marco. The stranger, with a look of contempt on his face, said 'that's up to you Mr Corti. My interests lie in the documents hidden somewhere nearby, and your going to show me where.' He turned to Anna and pointed his gun at her head. 'If you try to get funny and stall for time, I will not hesitate to shoot her in the head. She is of no interest to me Mr Corti, but I suspect she is of interest to you. I have had some target practice lately using talkative women in police cells, so you know I'm serious.'

Marco's mind was working overtime. Who was this man? Was he a communist or Red Brigade? Could he think of some way of overcoming him? How could he buy some time?

The man pointed to Marco's jacket lying on the bed. 'Pick up your jacket please and sit down again.

'Did you really kill Laura Moscardini? 'Said Marco.

'You sound surprised Mr Corti. Yes, I did, it was really quite an easy operation to accomplish. The Carabinieri were quite easily fooled.

'What about Anna?' Marco said anxiously. The man looked back at Marco and answered, My friend downstairs is coming up to look after her until we return with the letters, and if we don't return with them, then there will be a nasty accident tonight. Someone may fall from your balcony, or perhaps could be the subject of a robbery, and killed in the process. I have not worked out the details yet.' Marco picked up his jacket and sat on the edge of the bed. He put the jacket over his knees and appeared occupied in trying to stem the flow of blood from his nose. His shirt was turning bright red from the flow. 'What's your friend downstairs doing?' he said. The man gave a short laugh. 'He's getting rid of some rats that may cause us a problem later on.'

★★★

Lorenzo walked along the road parallel to the hotel for a while before turning left. His intention was to walk back down the street facing the hotel to check if anyone was sitting there in a car watching the entrance in case he turned up. The secretary had told him that two SISI agents were on their way to Lucca and he suspected they would be ordered to watch Corti's and Bastiani's back. He had given his accomplice orders to keep the couple in the room under the threat of a gun until he arrived. He would then stay with the woman in the hotel while Stalin would recover the briefcase with Corti.

As he walked up the street, he saw a parked Fiat with two men sitting in the front seats facing the hotel. He stopped to take this in and plan his next move. He opened his Anorak jacket, removed a hunting knife from its sheath in his belt, and deftly slashed a large hole in the left hand pocket of the jacket. He replaced the knife back in its sheath, then took out his Beretta semi-automatic and attached a silencer to it. He took off the safety catch and put the gun inside his jacket with the silencer sticking out through the hole. He again walked down the street and approached the Fiat car from the passenger's side. As he was level with it he slowed down, took aim, and fired at the passengers head. He heard the soft phut of the gun, and saw the targets head disintegrate. Slowly a red stain spread on what was left of the window glass. The driver turned his head round to look at what had happened and Lorenzo fired again. This time the driver's body lurched forward and draped itself over the steering wheel, blood oozing from the head wound.

He continued walking up the street to the hotel and entered through the main doors without anyone noticing anything suspicious. His gun was out of sight, but his finger was still on the trigger.

★★★

Anna knew that she had to do something quickly before Lorenzo appeared. She looked at Marco's bloody nose and an idea crept into her mind. 'I'll get you a tissue from my make-up bag,' she said and stood up from the bed. She motioned to the man that she was moving to the unit by the window where her bag was. He nodded in agreement. Marco saw his chance to distract the killer. He tightened his grip on his jacket and threw it in the killers face. Stalin was distracted for a moment, which was all the time Anna needed. She picked up her bag with her left hand and with her other hand pulled out her Beretta, turned, and coolly shot the man between the eyes. He somehow looked comical as he dropped to the floor with a kind of quizzical look on his face. Anna picked up her coat and shouted at Marco with an urgent voice, 'quick, out the door, Lorenzo's probably on his way up here now.' Marco was staring at the dead body on the floor, still unsure of what had just happened. Anna grabbed his hand and helped him to his feet. 'Marco, pull yourself together, we need to get out of here now.' They opened the room door and carefully looked out. Once they were sure the coast was clear they ran along the corridor. 'Use the stairs, not the lift,' cried Marco as they ran to the red door marked 'Scale.'

★★★

Lorenzo pressed the lift button for the third floor and watched as the red light above the door changed numbers. At number three the doors opened and he walked to the left towards Marco's room. Before reaching it he sensed that something was wrong. The room door was lying open. He carefully came alongside it, drew his gun and looked inside. He didn't need to go inside the room to find out what was wrong. His associate, Stalin, was lying on his back in the middle of the floor with a bullet hole between his eyes. He rested his head against the wall for a moment and tried to pull his thoughts together. It must have just happened, so they can't be far away. He made for the lift, pressed the button and hesitated. They probably took the stairs he thought, to be safe, in case they met me on the way up. He frantically made a dash for them.

Lorenzo was on the second level when he heard the sound of a door slamming shut on the bottom floor. The fire door, he thought. He reckoned it must be Corti and Bastiani trying to escape. He ran faster down the stairs and slipped on one of the metal treads and fell on his back. He cursed his luck and picked himself up. He felt the niggle in his back pull as he started running down the stairs again. It wasn't anything serious so he put it out of his mind and soon reached the exit door. He opened it carefully. When he was sure no one was there, he ran up the street as fast as he could towards the sound of running footfall.

★★★

'Keep up Anna' Marco shouted, your agents must be in that car just ahead.' He pointed towards the Fiat car parked by the side of the road about fifty metres in front of them. As they both kept running for the car Anna wondered why her backup didn't show themselves to find out why they were running.

Marco reached it first and recoiled in horror when he saw the scene inside. The two agents had exit holes in their heads as big as a fist. Their brains and blood were spread all over the inside of the car. Without further thought he opened the car door and reached inside the dead driver's jacket for his handgun. Taking it out he spun round just as Anna arrived on the scene. 'What's happened? Why are they just sitting there?' Marco pulled her away before she could take in the slaughter and led her behind the car for safety. He saw Lorenzo, running with a limp, towards the car with his gun visible in his hand.

'Are they dead?' Anna asked pointing towards the agents. Marco looked at her, solemnly nodded his head, then said, 'focus in Anna, this bastard wants to kill us as well.'

Lorenzo couldn't see his prey anywhere, but he knew they must be just ahead. The evening gloom was beginning to fall, and he found it difficult to see ahead clearly. The briefcase and the letters were not his focus now, only revenge. So far, he had lost four members of his cell and his blood was up. He could feel the pain in his back becoming more intense, so he slowed down to a brisk trot. He heard a male voice shouting from what appeared to be the SISI agents car ahead, 'Police, put down your weapon or we will shoot.' He stopped in his tracks and stared into the gathering gloom. The voice seemed to come from where the SISI agent's were but Lorenzo knew that was not possible. Perhaps, he thought, he had only wounded one of the agents and he was still able to function. He raised his pistol and began firing at the cars windscreen three, four, five times, more in hope than certainty. He saw the windscreen completely shatter, sending glass everywhere. The answering fusillade from Marco and Anna ripped into him and his lifeless body fell to the ground in an untidy heap.

Slowly, Marco and Anna left the shelter of the car and approached Lorenzo from different angles, all the time keeping their weapons trained on him. Marco reached him first and removed his pistol from his hand. He knelt beside him and felt for a pulse. Anna kept her gaze averted from the dark pool of blood spreading from underneath Lorenzo. Marco lowered his weapon, and turned to a tearful Anna. He held her close to him and gently kissed her cheek. 'It's all over Anna, it's finished,' he said. 'I'm not crying for him, 'she replied, 'I'm crying with relief.' She looked up into Marco's face and closed her eyes as he gently kissed her on the lips.

Their moment together was ended abruptly with the sound of sirens and flashing lights as two police cars arrived on the scene.

Uniformed officers with weapons drawn approached them. 'Throw down your weapons and raise your hands,' someone called out to them. Marco and Anna placed their pistols on the ground and did as they were told. Anna repeatedly shouted out, 'police officer, on duty.'

The senior police officer approached with his weapon aimed at them. 'Where is your ID Signora?' Anna turned her head and answered him 'inside my bag on the ground there.' She motioned with her head behind her. A police officer took her ID from the bag and showed it to the senior officer. After satisfying himself to Anna's identity, he asked her, 'what happened here?' Anna lowered her hands and answered, 'the man on the ground is a member of the Red Brigades and we have been following him for sometime. He came up behind the two officers in the car, who are SISI agents, and shot them. There is another dead terrorist in a room in the hotel Imperiali He attempted to kill us as well, but we were able to down him first.'

The police officer took in all of this information in an incredulous manner before saying, four people have been killed tonight, is that correct?' 'Yes,' Anna replied. He then turned towards Marco 'And who are you *signore*?' My name is Marco Corti, and I am helping the police with their enquiries.'

'What enquiries would that be sir? 'He said, looking Marco directly in the eye. Anna interrupted him. 'I'm sorry Officer, but for any further information you will have to contact Commandante Capaldi who is in charge of this operation. All I can say is that SISI have jurisdiction in this matter.'

The police officer, who had many years experience in the Carabinieri knew if the SISI were conducting this operation and with two of their agents murdered in the street in cold blood, then he should not ask any further questions of the two people in front of him. This looked like it was going all the way to the top and there was no way he wanted to get involved. He turned to his waiting officers and issued orders to set up a crime scene and to call for an ambulance. He turned to Anna again saying,' I will have to verify what you have just told me Officer, and I will contact SISI personally. In the meantime I would request you go back to the Station House and await instructions.' At that point, Anna and Marco left the scene of the carnage. Anna looked at Marco, who still had blood flowing from his nose and said, 'why don't you get your nose sorted out at the hospital. You've probably damaged something inside.' I have to report to my superiors about what's happened tonight. I'm sure the Officer here will be on to SISI before long and I want to alert them first.' Marco agreed. 'I'll catch up with you later' he said.

Chapter 12

Anna was finishing off her report for Enzo Capaldi when Marco appeared at her side. 'What a surprise to see you so soon,' she said. 'How's the nose?' secretly pleased that he'd come to the police station. 'A lot better,' he said. 'I thought we might have a chat Anna. I feel there are still some loose ends in this case.' Anna looked directly at him, 'what loose ends? Tomorrow morning we go for the letters and the case is closed. What's worrying you?' Marco was obviously unsettled about something. 'I don't know Anna. It's just the feeling that we're missing something important.'

Anna gave him a quick kiss on the cheek, 'don't worry, what can go wrong now?'

Marco gave her a nervous grin and said 'you're probably right, I'm just being silly.'

Being a little more positive, he said to her, 'fancy a glass of wine before turning in?

Anna smiled at him, 'that's my boy, give me five minutes to bring Enzo up to date and I'll be right with you.'

They went to a small wine bar along from San Michele church in the centre of the old town, called Bar Re. Marco liked this bar as it was usually quiet, and the sort of place you could have an intimate conversation without being overheard. They sat at the back of the bar in one of the booths and ordered a bottle of Chianti.

Anna had been thinking that as the retrieval operation would be completed tomorrow there was a good chance that Marco would be going home in the next few days, and she felt that they still didn't know each other that well.

She decided to seize the opportunity now. 'When do you think you'll be going home Marco?' Marco shrugged his shoulders. 'I really haven't given it much thought. I'll probably see how it pans out over the next few days.'

'Do you have anyone special waiting for you?' Anna asked.

'No one special at this time.' Marco replied. I was in a relationship for a number of years, but that ended some time ago.' 'What happened?'

'A dream job in America happened, and it just lost energy from there.'

Marco had never really shared this with anyone before and he was surprised how easy it felt to do it. He had feelings for Anna, but he wasn't quite sure what these feelings were. Their relationship had hardly been typical so far, with six deaths, a hostage situation, and a shootout with a terrorist being the norm. Perhaps eventually the future would look brighter for them , or did they have a future together?

'What about you Anna? Do you have anyone special in your life?'

'No one that I could call really special. I lost my parents when I was very young, and I was raised by an aunt who was very kind to me. I have had a few boyfriends however; things just never seemed to work out.'

Anna smiled at him; her record with relationships was poor to date. Every time it got serious she seemed to want to run, but this time it could be different. She continued, 'the hours with this job are a real drawback.' He decided to push the boundaries a little further on 'Do you think Anna we could see each other after all this is over?' Anna looked him directly in the eyes, reached out for his hand, and said, 'I really would like to see you again. I don't know how it would work out, with you in Scotland and me in Italy, but I'm willing to give it a try if you are.' Once this is over we can work something out,' said Marco. He asked for the bill, and once paid, they left together, hand in hand, both revelling in their newfound relationship. Marco stopped a passing taxi, and opened the door for Anna. They kissed goodnight, and parted. What was

I missing, he thought. It's staring me in the face but I can't see it.

The next morning as Marco was dressing; he reflected on the coincidence of the date. It was exactly forty-two years to the day that Sergio Rossi had first hidden the briefcase with the letters. What a morning to retrieve them, he thought.

He had arranged for Anna to pick him up outside the hotel at ten am, and they would drive straight to the hide. He pushed these thoughts from his mind and finished getting ready. He had decided that after today he would start making plans to head for home. He was concerned about his parents and how they were faring after their traumatic ordeal with the terrorists. They were getting on in age, and living in some temporary accommodation would only be adding to their stress.

He put on his jacket and turned to leave. He stopped at the door and turned back to his dresser for the handgun sitting on top. He had kept the SISI agent's pistol from last nights adventure and today he felt he had need of a little more insurance.

He stood outside on the hotel steps breathing in the fresh morning air. He loved Lucca, with its neat squares, many fine restaurants, and medieval streets and churches.

The Luchese also boasted of having the finest jewellers' shops of any Italian city in Tuscany. Perhaps I'll take a look in some of them before I leave, he thought.

The sound of a car drawing up to the pavement brought him out of his day dreaming. Anna lowered her window and shouted, 'buon giorno bello, you ready to go?'

Marco waved at her, walked to the passenger side and got in. Both of them failed to notice the car parked in the side street beside the hotel. The driver was pretending to read a magazine, but his eyes were firmly fixed on the couple.

Anna asked, 'is it in order to ask where we're headed for, or is it still a state secret?' Marco laughed and tapped the side of his nose. 'Just head out to Borgo a Mozzano and we'll park the car there.'

As they drove, the spring sunshine flooded the interior of the car, adding to the jovial atmosphere of the couple. They sat closer together than was necessary. Marco could feel the heat of where their bodies touched and restrained the desire rising up within him to reach out for her. They smiled a lot, laughed a lot and joked with each other. They could not be any happier. Isolated in their own private world, each wishing that their journey would last forever and never end.

★★★

The Black Alfa Romeo behind was in no hurry to keep up with them. The tracking device the driver had placed underneath the wheel arch of Anna's car last night gave out a constant reading of their position. He kept his distance to about four cars behind them. His focus was now on the couple ahead, and on revenge. After getting hold of the letters, he would take great delight in killing these two upstarts. They had proved to be a big stone in his shoe, and it was time to end this farce.

He thought back to the start of his mission to become part of the Red Brigades. He smiled to himself. Even though his politics were in truth left wing, he had a higher allegiance than mere politics. His cell knew nothing of his oath taken over forty years ago to an ideal that surpassed political parties. This ideal was guided by the ancient code of control and domination by stealth. Outside of the membership, the mere thought of such a power would have been laughed at, a joke, a delusion. He knew better. Lorenzo and his team were little more than puppets, as was much of the Italian state apparatus. He would build another cell of fanatics and forge them to be obedient to his will. They were not important. What was important is that the organisation he represented met their aim of control and domination of every facet of Italian life by stealth. Church, Financial, Political ,Military, Corporate and State. All subservient to the Organisation that he was part of. Even that fool Aldo Moro eventually understood the reach they had in Italian society.

He felt elated, refreshed. How could anyone stop the Organisation now.

★★★

Anna slowed down and stopped the car off the road onto a farm track, a few miles from their destination. Marco looked at her with suspicion, 'is this a scheduled stop, or have we broken down? Anna looked at him mischievously, 'I thought we could stop for a while and take in the view.'

'I thought I was already doing that Anna looking at you.'

Anna leaned over and gently kissed him on the lips. He could feel her closeness and he welcomed it. He pulled her closer to him and kissed her hair. 'Marco, where do we go from here? I mean, what are we doing?' Marco looked down into her eyes and said, 'what we are doing Anna is getting to know each other a little better. If it changes and develops into a romance, then I for one will be very happy. If it doesn't then we will have enjoyed each others company, and hopefully we will remain friends.' Anna was silent for a while before answering him, 'I want to be your friend Marco for the rest of my life, and I think I already am. Now I want to be more. I want to share my life with you in anyway I can.' Marco was taken aback by her openness and he held her close again.

'Would you remain in the Police or would you consider a more mundane role with me in Scotland?' She kissed him gently again, 'Yes Marco, as long as were together.'

They smiled at each other, and kissed again. Eventually Anna started the car and drove once more onto the road.

As they approached the outskirts of Borgo a Mozzano, Marco guided her to the small car park just off the Via della Republica. They parked the car there and headed for the Devil's Bridge.

As a precaution, Marco stopped short of the bridge and faced the way he had just come. Even though there was no sign of anyone following them, he stood for a while just to make sure. Eventually, when he was satisfied, he walked onto the bridge, and stood in its centre. He had memorised everything his father had told him about the location of the briefcase and now he felt the emotion of the moment. He was conscious of Anna looking at him, obviously wondering what he was about to do next. He faced the wooded hillside and looked for a large

Oak tree growing on the ridge, slightly offset to the bridge. He soon saw what he was looking for and taking Anna's hand, they crossed the bridge and set off up the hillside.

After some twenty minutes of walking through the rough undergrowth Marco saw the massive Oak tree standing directly ahead of him. He felt a surge of excitement coursing through him, so he put on a spurt, much to the annoyance of Anna who was being left behind. He stood before the tree and looked for the boulder sitting a little off from it. 'Quickly Anna, I've found it. It's here.' Anna, slightly out of breath, joined him. 'Where is it, I can't see anything,' she said, looking around frantically. 'It's under the boulder; give me a hand to move it.' They both got on their knees and pushed with their shoulders against the rock. It had not been moved for a few years and grass and weeds had sprung up around it making it difficult to shift. Eventually, they were rewarded with the sound of movement, and the boulder began to slide over just enough for them to see the hole it revealed.

Marco leaned over the hole and gently put his hand inside. 'I can feel it Anna, it's there,' he said, as he steadily pulled out the briefcase. With almost a feeling of reverence, as if viewing some religious relic, they just sat and stared at it. The oilcloth had all but disintegrated, although the briefcase itself appeared in reasonable condition. The fascist emblem of the bound rods and axe was clearly visible near the handle. Marco traced the outline of it with his finger. He noticed that Mussolini's gold initials on the side of the case were quite badly tarnished and he hoped that the contents would be better preserved.

Anna's voice interrupted his thoughts. 'Are you going to open it or just look at it? She said impatiently. Marco took a deep breath and turned the catch to open the briefcase. He pulled out a thick sheaf of papers and laid them on his lap. 'There must be about a hundred letters here' he said in an unbelieving voice. 'The outside letters seem to be damp affected, but not too badly. The main body of correspondence, thankfully, seem well preserved.'

'Can I read one,' Anna said stretching out her hand to take one, 'please.' Marco took one out from the centre of the bundle and gave it to her. 'Take great care with it Anna; your hands are holding a piece of world history.'

She saw that the letter was addressed from Mussolini to Hitler and was dated 1940.

My Dearest Fuehrer,

Once again, I write to you in the warmth of our friendship and of the certainty of our victory. Your Armies are poised for the invasion of England and at this moment I am concerned at the thought that as you shed German blood on the soil of Europe for the eventual victory over England, the Bolshevik hordes are gathering to the East for a traitorous thrust to your rear. We have often discussed that England is not the real enemy, that they only entered the war out of honour for Poland and that the Bolsheviks are our real historical and eternal enemies. There are many in England who identify with your aims, and your philosophy, from the average person to Royalty, and perhaps if given time to think about events, they may even decide to join in our crusade to crush the eastern threat together. What a crusade that would become and what a united force it would make to see the West unified against Bolshevism, with you at its head.

I know you to be a man who will do what is right for the glory of your people, and for you to take your place in history as the one who defeated Communism and united the West under your outstretched arm. Perhaps we should turn and face the threat all together instead of invading England at this time. It may well be that the forces of progress and reason in Britain will come to realise who the true enemy is and turn away from this futile conflict with fascism and join us in our victory.

I salute you Fuehrer and your vision
Benito Mussolini
Duce of Fascism

★★★

They dipped into the bundle of letters and avidly read more revelations of what actually happened behind the scenes to influence world events. They avidly looked at the photographs of world leaders with Mussolini, and were amazed at the scenes. After about an hour, Marco began to tidy the letters up and place them back in the briefcase. They both realised that what they had just read was political dynamite in the wrong hands. 'Do you realise that we have been reading private letters written by Churchill, Mussolini, and Hitler and been privy to their thoughts,' an excited Anna proclaimed. Marco looked at Anna with complete adoration. Her eyes were shining with emotion and as she dramatically waved her arms about as she spoke, she had never looked as beautiful or as desirable. He moved over beside her and gently took her face in his hands and passionately kissed her. At first, Anna was taken by surprise, but she soon recovered and kissed him back. He lowered her to the grass and began to unbutton her blouse. She responded warmly and passionately. They then entered a world of pleasure and joy. They explored each other's bodies with soft kisses, and revelled in the delight of touching each other, until eventually, unable to wait any longer; they joined together and were consumed by the intensity of their love.

When they were both spent, they lay quietly in each other's arms, softly caressing and enjoying the moment. They lay together in love, laughing, singing, enjoying the suns gentle rays caress them with its warm embrace.

Eventually, they dressed and just as they were preparing to leave, the sound of a rifle shot rang out, shattering the silence and changing their mood to one of fear. The round had penetrated the Oak tree beside Anna just as she had bent down for her shoe. They dived for the ground and sought cover.

Chapter 13

The black Alfa Romeo pulled into the small car park in Borgo a Mozzano a few minutes after Anna's Fiat. The driver got out carrying a small holdall and headed at a brisk pace for the couple ahead who were steadily disappearing into the distance. He watched them cross the Devil's Bridge and then followed them over. He waited at the foot of the hillside until he saw which direction they were headed and took a parallel route, taking great care to keep out of sight. He slowly climbed higher than his prey until he reached a vantage point looking down on them.

When the couple stopped at the big Oak tree, he positioned himself so that he could see what they were doing and have a clear line of fire. He quickly removed an M16 Carbine from his holdall and assembled it. The magazine was checked for rounds and fitted with a soft metallic click into the rifle. The same with the telescopic sight.

He watched intently as they opened a briefcase to read some of the contents. He was patient. He didn't want to make his move until he was convinced that they had retrieved everything that was hidden. He saw them make love through the telescopic lens and convinced himself it was his professionalism that kept his focus on them.

When he eventually saw them prepare to leave with the briefcase he took careful aim and slowly squeezed the trigger. Just at that moment, Anna had bent down and the shot that was intended for her head missed.

He quickly aimed again and fired once more.

'He's high up over to your left,' Marco called out from his position. As soon as the first shot was fired, they hit the ground and pulled out their weapons. He quickly realised that the shooter had the advantage of a higher position so ground cover was essential. Marco's old infantry training in the Paras kicked in, and he was pleased to see that Anna was lying off to his right, hidden in the undergrowth, with her weapon pointing in the direction of their assailant. 'Don't fire unless you have something to shoot at Anna. We need to conserve our ammunition.'

More shots rang out and the ground near Marco was disturbed by what seemed like angry wasps as the rounds hit the ground near him. He realised that the shooter couldn't see them now, and was probably being guided by the sound of their voices. He attracted Anna's attention with a thrown pebble, and motioned for her to be quiet. He made a circling motion with his hand, and Anna understood that he was going to try to circle around the shooter and surprise him from the side.

He slowly crawled stealthily through the undergrowth until he came to a large tree. He used the width of the tree as a shield to hide himself from the shooter and slowly raised himself to his feet. He let off a few rounds in the shooters direction and was pleased to hear him curse out aloud in Italian. The shooter moved out slowly to higher ground until he had a better view of Marco's position. He smiled as he partially saw Marco behind the tree loading his weapon. He took careful aim and fired at the restricted target.

A burst of automatic fire, like dancing Bees, hit the surrounding area around Marco and he fell to the ground, clutching his left arm. As he lay there, he felt a searing pain fill his body. Blood spewed from the wound onto the ground. One of the rounds had hit him in his upper arm and gone straight through the flesh. He reached for his handkerchief and tried to stem the heavy flow of blood.

Anna had seen him fall and was now trying to reach him. 'Stay where you are, you're safer there,' he weakly called out. As if to emphasise the point, the shooter fired another burst of automatic fire at Marco. Marco kept his head down and wondered if they would get out of this alive. His arm was losing a lot of blood and he was starting to feel dizzy. He was still alert enough to hear a change to the sound of the gunfire before he lapsed into unconsciousness.

Chapter 14

Angelo Corti sat staring out of the window of his temporary home. He reflected on the turn of events that had led him to this point. The hostage situation had awakened a hidden strength in him that was almost like turning on a tap. He should not have involved his son in this mess. He felt that he should have seen it through as originally planned. Now his son could be in grave danger from these Red Brigade animals that would not hesitate to kill him, and were probably at this moment on his trail. He was unsettled at the prospect of his son facing the Red Brigade on his own.

He went to his bedroom and took out a metal box, which he opened with a small key. Inside was a handgun, his service revolver, which had been presented to him by Mussolini himself when he had joined the Mosquatieri. He took it out and disassembled it into its component parts. He remembered a time when he could take it to bits blindfolded. He knew that if he spread the parts throughout his suitcase they wouldn't be picked up by x-ray machines at the airport. The rounds he would keep in his possession as he had a metal pin in his left knee that always set off the alarm when he walked through the metal detector. He also had a letter from a medical specialist explaining this in more detail in case he was picked up. The letter hadn't failed him yet.

He went back downstairs and once more sat in his chair. He looked at his wife, 'I'll need to go to Italy and help him,' he said aloud. Elizabeth stirred in her chair and replied, 'is that wise Angelo? You're not a young man anymore.'

'Young man or not, my son needs help, and I can't sit back knowing he's in danger.'

He rose from his chair and reached for the phone to book his flight.

★★★

The light rain smirred the windscreen of Angelo's hired Fiat as he drove away from Pisa Airport on the road to Lucca. He was heading for Marco's hotel and he reckoned he should be there for mid-day. He hoped he was in time to accompany him to the site. Apart from wanting to help Marco, he was impatient to see the briefcase again. This damn briefcase, he thought, if only Mussolini had burned the letters instead of ordering Sergio to hide them.

He had tried to phone Marco's room at his hotel, but the receptionist had said he had gone out. I'll try the hotel first, he thought, and if he isn't there, I'll go to the *Carabinieri* Station. He knew that Marco had been dealing with a SISI Agent from the Station, and he might be in time to catch him before he leaves.

The road was familiar to him. Many times over the last twenty years, he had made this journey to inspect the briefcase, and each time he had thought the same: So many Italians had died for the ideals of fascism and communism, and today they are consigned to the fringes of the political arena. Not considered relevant by the majority of Italians and probably considered the last refuge of the fanatic and the zealot.

He pulled the car up in front of the hotel entrance, and entered the hotel. He saw the reception desk in front of him and walked up to the desk.

'*Buon giorno, signore,*' said the young female receptionist. 'May I help you.'

'I would like to speak to Signor Corti in room 306 please.'

The receptionist gave him a gleaming smile that made Angelo wish he were forty years younger. 'I'm sorry *signore*, but Signor Corti left the hotel after breakfast this morning.'

'Did he say where he was going,' Angelo asked her.

'Once again I'm sorry *signore*, he didn't say where he was going.'

Angelo thanked the receptionist, and left the hotel. He drove through Lucca to the Police Station and parked the car in the Parcheggio – the car park – behind the station. He entered the station and asked the duty officer if Signor Corti was in the station. 'I'm sorry *signore*, I wouldn't know.

Angelo sighed, 'would it be possible to tell Commandante Capaldi that Marco Corti's father, Angelo Corti ,would like to see him.'

The Duty Officer recognised the name of 'Corti,' and knew he should notify the Commandante of his presence.

'Take a seat *signore* and I'll see if the Commandante can see you.'

After some five minutes, Angelo Corti was asked into the Commandante's office. Enzo Capaldi was certainly surprised to see him there. He shook his hand and invited him to take a seat. How can I help you *signore*?' said Enzo, over a cloud a smoke. Angelo explained, 'With all the events of the last few days I thought I would come over myself to see the briefcase being recovered.' Enzo blew out a cloud of smoke before saying, 'Your son and Anna left Lucca about ten minutes ago and from the information I have been given from their radio, they should be at the site by now.' 'Then I'll try and meet them there Commandante, I really want to try and witness the briefcase being recovered. After all this time I just feel I would like to witness history being made.'

Enzo looked at him with a strange sad look in his eyes. 'History was made here a long time ago Angelo when our people killed each other without mercy.' Angelo nodded his head in agreement. 'Were you involved Commandante?'

'Not at first. I was a police officer doing my duty for the whole community. It was after the war when I was asked to help collect the evidence of massacres carried out by the Germans that I felt the full force of the atrocities committed by them. I was involved in the investigation of war crimes at

Monte Sole where the 16th Waffen SS under Major Walter Reder committed one of the biggest mass murders of civilians in the Italian war. Whole communities were wiped out as the SS searched for partisans in the hills. They rounded up women, children and infants, herded them into a walled cemetery, and machine-gunned them. They blew up barns full of people with hand grenades without mercy. He stopped for a moment, and gave a deep sigh. 'Over eighteen hundred Italians were killed over three days. Thankfully most of the SS involved were brought to justice.'

Angelo could feel the sadness of the moment, 'there were things witnessed during the war that it's best not to talk about. Some of my comrades in the Black Brigades were captured near Trieste by the Yugoslav partisans, the Titoists. They were tied with a long rope around their necks to other suspected fascists and their families, including women and children. They were then marched through the snow and ice, up in the mountains, until they came to some deep ravines. The partisans shot the first person, who fell down the ravine and the rest, screaming in fear, were pulled after him to their death. There was no need for this sort of barbaric action. They could have killed them, if they had to, by bullet. I understand that some two hundred Italians were killed. It's now up to our generation to make sure that this doesn't happen again.'

Enzo pursed his lips, 'these letters have already been the catalyst for death. It has even stretched its hand into my police cells.'

He got up from his seat and approached Angelo. 'I hope that these letters don't act as the catalyst for further violence in Italy.' Angelo agreed, 'that's why it's important that they don't fall into the wrong hands.' Together they walked to the door, two old men, full of memories and respect for each other.

During the car journey, they again discussed their respective roles in the war and Angelo was pleasantly surprised to find out that Enzo, although not a fascist then, had strong sympathies for their cause. 'I have moderated my views a little now to encompass the modern era, but I am still right wing at heart,' said a talkative Enzo, blowing clouds of smoke from the ever present cigarette dangling from his mouth.

Eventually they reached the small car park at Borgo a Mozzano, where they left their car. As they were crossing the bridge, they heard gunfire coming from the woods ahead. 'That's not the sound of a hunter's weapon,' said Enzo, it definitely sounds like an M16 Carbine.' 'Let's get up there and find out what's happening,' an agitated Angelo said. They moved as fast as they could up the wooded slope until they were close to the source of the gunfire. The climb had taken its toll on the two older men and they rested for a moment to recover their breath. Angelo looked over at Enzo's ashen coloured face and heavy breathing with some concern, 'maybe it's time to stop the cigarettes before they stop you.' Enzo looked at him with disdain, pulled a cigarette from a pack and placed it between his lips.' I'll light it later,' he said in short gasps.

They continued up the slope with caution until they could see someone in a prime position firing down on two figures lying down flat in the undergrowth. Enzo drew his weapon and moved stealthily forward towards the shooter. 'Stay here Angelo, you don't have a weapon.' Angelo smiled and pulled out of his anorak pocket the old Beretta, 'this is my service revolver and I've kept it in good condition.' 'You can charge me later for not having a licence for it, but right now I'm going to help my boy.' Enzo saw there was no way he was going to stop him helping, so he merely said, 'Take my lead Angelo, okay?'

They moved forward in an open formation towards the shooter so that they were converging in on each side of him and when Enzo thought they were in a good position and close enough, he called out, 'police, cease firing and throw down your weapon.' The shooter seemed to freeze when he heard Enzo's voice. Enzo repeated, 'if you don't put down your weapon we will open fire.'

The shooter knew he was cornered., trapped. All his careful planning had come to this moment. Was that the voice of Enzo Capaldi shouting on him from behind? What irony, he thought, the fat man himself. Realising the impossible position he was in he knew he had no choice but to surrender to the police. He also decided to drop his veneer of urban charm and good manners that had served him well, and be the man he knew he was.

The shooter laid his rifle on the ground, and waited on his next instructions. 'Stand up slowly and raise your hands above your head now.' The shooter stood up slowly and did as he was told. 'Now, turn and face me,' said Enzo, keeping his gun trained on him. The shooter hesitated at first, and then slowly turned to face the two men. Angelo let out a gasp of astonishment as he recognised the man in front of him; Carlo Togneri.

Enzo also recognised Carlo. At first they were too taken aback to speak, until eventually Angelo said, 'Why Carlo? You of all people, you were my old friend.' Carlo spat at the ground. His eyes were ablaze with a fanatical zeal that was far removed from his usual calm appearance. 'What do you know of friendship, you and your fascist ways of old? Friendship to you is leaving your country when it desperately needed your help in rebuilding it from the ruins of your fascist war. You thought of your own needs over those of your country. Even you Enzo, after the war you scorned the call of the people for a more just society, and became an American lackey in their police state, so don't speak to me of friendship.' An astonished Angelo and Enzo listened to the deranged tirade in silence. Carlo was obviously extremely unbalanced and very dangerous.

Carlo continued, 'and what of the friendship displayed by the German and Fascist forces in the north of Italy with over seven hundred separate massacres of Italians to their name. You seem to forget as the Allies fought the Germans that we had a bloody civil war here at the same time with countless thousands killed or starved to death.'

Angelo shook his head in desperation; He saw that there was no reasoning with this man, who was very clearly deranged. 'There was brutality on both sides Carlo, there are only victims in war and today Italy needs healing from those memories if we are to be a united nation.'

Enzo, having recovered from his shock of seeing Carlo, moved forward to handcuff him and just at that moment his foot caught in a tree stump in the undergrowth. He lost his balance for a second, but this was all the time Carlo needed. For such a big man he moved forward with tremendous speed and agility. He threw himself at Enzo and grabbed his gun arm. Enzo tried to fight back but he still wasn't recovered from his climb up the hillside. They wrestled for a few moments until Carlo seized Enzo's pistol and pulled him in front of him as a shield. 'Drop your weapon Angelo;' he shouted, holding the pistol to Enzo's head. 'I will have no hesitation in shooting Enzo if I have to.' Angelo, who all this time had been trying to line up a shot, quickly weighed up the situation. If he dropped his weapon, Carlo would probably kill them both. If he didn't, then Carlo would kill Enzo. He dropped his weapon on the ground and raised his arms above his head, hoping for an opportunity to overpower him.

Carlo knew that if he wanted to escape without any pursuit he would have to kill the two men in front of him. He aimed his pistol at Angelo. 'Sorry Angelo' he said with mock sadness, 'I wish it could be otherwise.' He cocked the pistol and his finger put pressure on the trigger.

A shot rang out and Carlo dropped to the ground with a large hole appearing to grow in his chest and a surprised look on his face. Angelo looked down at Carlo, marvelling at the bloodstain spreading slowly across his body. 'What happened, who shot him?' He said in amazement.

Anna appeared from the woods, still aiming her pistol at Carlo's body as she bent down to take his weapon. She felt his pulse before looking up and saying to the still stunned men, 'he's dead, and it's all over now.' She ran to Enzo, hugged him with relief, and kissed him. She was still shaking with emotion as she said, 'I heard loud voices coming from over here so I crawled over to investigate. I moved slowly through the undergrowth hoping that the shooter wouldn't see or hear me and when I saw Carlo holding Enzo I positioned myself behind him, stood up and fired.' She turned to face Angelo, 'Marco's been shot and he's lying on the ground back there.' She pointed behind her. 'I think he's unconscious.'

Enzo thought for a moment, 'go down and radio in for assistance Anna, you're the fittest one here. We'll go and see what we can do for Marco.'

At that, the two men, rushed over to where Marco was and did their best to stem the flow of blood from his arm. Angelo used his trouser belt as a tourniquet on the injured arm. At the same time Enzo, using his pocketknife, began to cut some wood for a makeshift stretcher. The two men used their shoelaces to tie some cross bars to the frame, and after ten minutes or so, they were finished. They gently lifted Marco, who was still unconscious, onto the stretcher. Angelo then lifted the briefcase and placed it at Marco's feet. They then lifted the stretcher, and slowly carried him down the hillside, with Angelo leading the way. Their progress was quite slow as they were careful to avoid tripping over anything in their path.

Just as they reached the road, they heard the sound of sirens. An ambulance and two police cars were speeding towards them. They lowered the stretcher and waited on the vehicles reaching them. Instinctively, Angelo took the briefcase from the stretcher.

The ambulance pulled up beside them and they were both surprised when they saw Anna getting out of the front. 'I met them at the car park below and jumped in to show them where you were. How is he?'

No one answered her. They lifted Marco gently into the ambulance. Angelo then climbed inside, still clutching the briefcase. With the siren blaring they were about to move off when there was a loud banging noise on the back doors. When the attendant opened them, Anna was standing there with tears streaming down her face. 'Please let me come with you in the ambulance Signor Corti, I love your son and I don't want to leave him like this.'

Angelo was visibly moved. He gave Anna his hand and helped her climb in. He looked at her tear-stained face and reddened eyes and felt unexplainably close to her. He hugged her and said 'You love my son?' She stopped crying and said to him, 'yes, I really do.' Angelo nodded and turned to the driver saying, 'Ok, let's get my son to the hospital.'

Enzo, who had stayed behind to direct the removal of the dead terrorist's body, pulled another cigarette from a packet and put it between his lips. With a practised flip of his Zippo, he lit it and revelled in the private cloud of smoke billowing from his nose. He drew deeply on the cigarette until the lit end glowed deep red.

How had it come to this? He thought. Eight people killed over some letters from people who are long dead. He thought of the hours of report writing he had in front of him, and the endless meetings with SISI and his own superiors because of these damn letters. He drew deeply on his cigarette and cursed. He was retiring next year and his only thought was for a quiet time, and now this. He wondered if it would have been any different if he had managed to have that talk with Carlo before all this started. Perhaps it may have changed things, who knows. With an exaggerated sigh, he pulled out another cigarette.

Through the cloud of smoke, he reflected on Togneri's role in recent events. Who was he representing? Was he Red Brigade or not? He remembered a story a Mafioso he arrested some years ago had told him. The Mafioso had said there was someone high placed in the Lucca Carabinieri who was a Made Man in the Cosa Nostra, and who had infiltrated the Red Brigades posing as an activist. The allegation was that he, under orders from his Don, had been using the Red Brigades as the Mafia's private assassination squad whenever they required someone done away with. The police investigation that would then follow focused on the Red Brigades, and the Mafia, as usual, stayed silent in the shadows.

Enzo wondered if the story was true. Internal Affairs had investigated the allegation, but had found no evidence to support it. He laughed at this. He well knew that there was nothing, simply nothing that happened in Italy without the knowledge or consent of the Cosa Nostra, or Our Thing. The organisation without a name.

Enzo pulled out another cigarette, and wondered what truth was. His father used to say that in an argument the truth had three sides to it. Both parties presented their interpretation of it, and then there was the true truth.

He threw down his cigarette and again thought of the report writing and endless meetings in front of him. What he didn't need was another can of worms opened up regarding some speculation, without evidence, of Cosa Nostra involvement. He drew another cigarette from his pack and decided to let sleeping dogs lie. He wasn't about to take on the Organisation himself.

Chapter 15

Spring had turned into summer and Marco stood at the window watching with delight the antics of the birds playing in the trees. It felt good to be alive, and especially today. Anna was coming to the hospital to pick him up for the ceremony taking place at the town hall in Lucca,

He was being decorated with the Order of the Cavaliere Della Merita by no less a person than the President of the Italian Republic. This was the closest to a British Knighthood that the Italian State could bestow on one of their citizens and Marco was thrilled to be considered for this award.

After the shooting, he had been taken to the intensive care ward at Lucca hospital, where he had remained unconscious for three days. During that time the doctors had fought hard to save his life. He had lost a lot of blood and his wound had become infected. The Doctors thought they would have to amputate his arm, and had told his parents and Anna to be prepared for the worst. Slowly he had responded to the treatment, and the arm was saved. That had been six weeks ago and now he felt ready to carry on with his life. The wound in his arm was healing well. He knew that he had lost part of the muscle and that it would never be the same again, however, he was alive and in love. He adjusted the sling around his neck slightly.

Anna had been to visit him every day, and they had spent many hours alone in the ward talking about the future. He had made up his mind that this was the day he would ask her to marry him. They were deeply in love and couldn't bear to be apart from each other. He planned to ask her after the ceremony and he wanted it to be a big surprise to her. He loved her with all his being. He was sure of this, not for the joy he felt when they were together, but for the ache in his heart when they were apart. He knew for sure that this was true love and he was sure that she felt the same towards him. He had been planning the surprise for a few days now, and had even asked a jeweller to visit him in the hospital to show him some engagement rings. He had finally made his choice. A single diamond solitaire on a gold shank.

★★★

Anna looked even more stunning than usual. She was wearing a light blue two-piece suit, with a matching hat. The skirt, almost reaching her knees, showed off her long slim legs and the overall impression was one of beauty and elegance. She was also wearing diamond earrings with a matching pendant that had belonged to her mother.

The events of the last few weeks had disturbed Anna more than anyone realised. Being involved in the recovery of the letters and in the deaths of so may people had led her to question her role in the Carabinieri. A few days ago, she had come to the decision that she needed to resign from the force and take some time off to consider her future. However, all that was for another time. Today was a celebration.

She knocked on the ward door and went in.

Marco's face lit up when he saw her. 'You look so beautiful I could cry,' said Marco as he held her close to him. 'Just be careful of my makeup,' she said, pulling back slightly. 'Let me look at you Cavaliere Corti.'

Marco stood back and bowed for effect. 'I've never seen anyone close up in tails before', said Anna smiling. 'You just look so handsome. Let me see you with the top hat on.' Marco put on the top hat self-consciously and posed a little more.

'I think we should leave now,' said Anna, 'before I voice my wicked thoughts.' They both laughed and made for the door.

The band was playing the Italian National Anthem and the watching public were standing out of respect for it. When they finished playing and the people sat down, the Italian President walked onto the podium. He took out his notes and began to speak: 'Dear friends, honoured guests, ladies and gentlemen. We have come to this place, in the beautiful city of Lucca, to pay homage to a very brave man who by his actions has enriched the Italian nation. By these actions, with disregard for his own life when he was wounded, he recovered valuable documents that shed light on a period of history when the world went mad. These documents are now being examined by academics from around the world and once their studies have been completed they will, on rotation, be displayed in museums throughout Italy. Today, I am pleased to announce that the Italian State is honouring this brave man with the Cavaliere Della Merita and I ask him to come forward to receive it.'

Marco stepped onto the platform to the sound of thunderous applause. He walked up to the President and stood to attention before him. The President opened the decoration's clasp and pinned it on Marco's jacket lapel, to yet more applause. The President kissed Marco on both cheeks, shook his hand and led him to the microphone.

Marco looked out at the crowd, paused for a moment, looked directly at the TV cameras then said. 'Your Excellency, honoured guests, ladies and gentlemen and last but not least, my parents. I am honoured and delighted to be awarded this prestigious decoration, for myself and for my parents Elizabeth and Angelo. I thank you all for coming here to join me in this celebration and I thank the President for taking time out from his busy schedule to present me with it. Thank you all.'

The audience applauded and cried out bravo, bravo. He signalled for them to stop and sombrely said into the microphone. 'One last thing before I go. I would like to ask my girlfriend Anna Bastiani, the most beautiful girl in the world, in front of the TV cameras, to do me the honour of being my wife. I love you very much and I want to marry you very very soon. Please say yes.'

The crowd went wild, as only an Italian crowd could do. Even the President was applauding. They began to chant Anna, Anna, Anna. Anna, who was sitting near the front with Marco's parents, was stunned. Eventually she came out of her daze and stood up, smoothed her suit and ran towards the platform She couldn't get up beside Marco as her skirt, was too tight until Enzo and Angelo came to her rescue and lifted her up between them. She stood facing Marco with her eyes sparkling with joy and kissed him fully on the lips. After what seemed an eternity, she tore herself away from him, reached for the microphone and shouted 'yes, yes, yes,' into it. They embraced and kissed again, then waved to the applauding crowd. Marco then went down on one knee and opened the ring box he held in his hand. He took the ring out and put it on Anna's finger. Anna cried with delight, and with unrestrained joy danced a little jig on the platform.

Chapter 16

The wedding ceremony took place in Lucca at the church of San Michele in Foro in the main square with all Marco's and Anna's friends and family present. Anna had asked Enzo to give her away and her Aunt Rina was delighted to be her Matron of Honour. Anna wondered if Enzo could last the whole mass without a cigarette.

Marco had been in contact with his old army friend, Dusty Miller and he was over the moon to be asked to be his best man. Dusty was now a car salesman in Manchester, still single, and looking forward to catching up with his old buddy again.

The reception after the nuptial mass was held in Il Bugno, a restaurant in Fornaci di Barga, a village not far from Angelo's birthplace of Coreglia. Il Bugno, which means beehive, was a large restaurant set in the Tuscan hills of la Garfagnana, (the great woodland) with lots of room for dancing. Just perfect for a wedding celebration.

Angelo stood up after the meal to say a few words,' it is with great joy in our hearts that Elizabeth and I welcome Anna into our family. She is a special girl and we love her as a daughter. I hope that she and Marco will be as happy in their life together as Elizabeth and I have been in ours. So raise your glasses in the time honoured way and say together *Cent Anni, Cent Anni.*'

The guests responded by tapping their wine glasses with a spoon, along with the cry of *a Hundred years a hundred years*, echoing round the room.

After the toast, a small rotund figure slipped out of the restaurant and stood in the restaurant car park with an unlit cigarette dangling from his lips. The metallic click of a Zippo lighter could be clearly heard as a small flame lit up his moustached face.

Chapter 17

4th September 1998

It was Angelo's tenth birthday and he was enjoying the moment as all small boys do. His mother and father had taken him on holiday to Italy and they were now standing in front of a glass display case in the Lucca museum. 'Is that one of the letters you saved from the Red Brigades dad?' the small boy asked, with the direct innocence that most children have. Marco answered him, 'yes there were quite a few letters son. The rest are being shown in museums throughout Italy.' Angelo looked at his dad with doubt written on his face, 'did you and mum really fight them before I was born dad?' Marco looked at his son and ruffled his hair as he said, 'Yes Angelo, we did. And I don't know anyone who could fight with your mum and win.'

'Can we go for ice cream now mum?' Anna answered, 'Ok, but I'm sure it won't be as good as the ice cream we make at home in Scotland.'

'When are we going home mum?' Asked Angelo.

'Tomorrow son, tomorrow we fly home to Scotland.'